M000099139

VAMPIRIC RED

THE ROGUE OF VAMPIRES

MORIAH JANE

Vampiric Red:
The Rogue of Vampires by Moriah Jane
Copyright © Moriah Jane

Cover Design by germancreative
Interior Design by Kevin G. Summers

All rights reserved. No portion of this story may be reproduced in any form
or by any electronic means including information storage and retrieval sys-
tems without written permission from the author except in the case of brief
quotations embodied in critical articles and reviews.

All stories, incidents, and characters mentioned in this story are entirely
fictional.

ISBN: 9781087817026

To those who love vampire stories
without romance

CHAPTER
ONE

"ALRIGHT, HERE is your order!" the waitress at Rodeo Grill House announces. "One plate of smoked ribs for you, sir." She slides the oval plate of tender meat in front of Willow's dad. "And one Mighty Round Up Steak for you, little lady!" She slides a plate in front of her, the slab of juicy meat as big as Willow's head.

"Steak!" Willow squeals in delight. She breathes in the mouth-watering mix of seasonings garnishing her perfectly browned dinner. "Let's eat, let's eat!"

Willow's dad, Mr. Hunter, smiles. But Willow can still see the sadness hidden behind his contented facade. "Alright. Go ahead. But make sure you cut them into small pieces and chew well."

Willow nods and snatches up her knife and fork. She saws exuberantly and quickly stuffs a chunk of thick meat between her lips. She slows down only after the seasonings grace her tongue and the meat squishes between her teeth.

Mr. Hunter chuckles genuinely as he pulls a rib clean from his meat. Willow doesn't miss it. She knows he cries at night over the loss of Mrs. Hunter, but he tries to hide his pain during the day. She resolves to bring another genuine chuckle from him before dinner is over.

The lights in the restaurant flicker and Mr. Hunter's smile is lost. He glances up.

Fwoom! A distant explosion makes the lights flicker again then black out.

BroooOOOOOOOOOOOoooo! Sirens wail outside.

The staff of Rodeo Grill House call to their guests to hide in the kitchens. The emergency generator flicks on as families are ushered from their tables.

Willow's heart pounds. "Daddy…?"

Mr. Hunter jumps up. "Wills, Daddy needs to go to work. Go with the waitress and stay with her, okay?"

Their waitress hurries over and kneels by Willow's seat. Her expression is calm but her voice reveals panic. "Sweetheart, I'm going to take you to the kitchen, okay? We have some little chocolates back there! Would you like one?"

Willow shakes her head. "I'm going with Daddy!"

Mr. Hunter circles to her side and hugs her. "Go with the nice waitress, okay? Daddy will be right back. I promise!"

A sour memory pops into Willow's mind. Her lip protrudes. "That's what Mommy said, too."

Mr. Hunter clamps his mouth shut. Tears form at the corners of his eyes, but he blinks them away. "I'll always be here for you, Wills. I promise you that. Now go with the nice waitress and make sure to save some chocolate for me."

Willow bites her lip and nods. "Come back. You have to."

He smiles sadly. "I will."

Mr. Hunter runs from the building, pulling a concealed Glock from under his shirt. Willow watches him go before taking the waitress' hand. She follows her behind the bar and crawls under a counter with another child who is nibbling on a little chocolate square.

The thought of food suddenly makes Willow's stomach churn. She looks away, focusing instead on the pale expressions cast in the shadows of the low lighting.

The waitress crouches beside her and hands her some chocolates with a faux smile. "Make sure to save some for your dad, okay?"

Willow takes them with shaky hands and nods.

Another explosion, this one closer, makes the restaurant tremble. Moments later, gunfire explodes outside the restaurant. Something slams against the walls, the windows in the sitting area shatter. Growls and screams and shouts flood into the kitchen. The waitress moves closer to Willow, eyes switching between the kitchen's only two entry points to the seating area.

Some of the guests whimper whenever a new explosion rattles the utensils above. Some cover their ears or eyes as though they can hide from reality. A spare few grip carving knives and other sharp or long tools, prepared to protect themselves and others if the need arises.

Willow watches the entry points with wide eyes, waiting for the noise to stop flooding her senses and for her dad to return with open arms. But the longer it takes, the more she thinks about her mom—the puncture wounds, her still form.

CRASH!

Everyone jumps as something barrels through the seating area. Willow's heart slams against her chest as spoons clang into view and glasses shatter. A figure steps into the entryway, red eyes bright and lips pulling into a thirsty grin.

"Jackpot…" he hisses.

Several guests rush the vampire, stabbing and beating him with their tools. He breaks their arms and gores them with their tools. The staff throw pots, pans, and dishes to ward the vampire off. But every hit makes him grow angrier.

The vampire lunges at the nearest staff member and rips at his neck. He snatches a fleeing waitress and sucks up some blood before throwing her aside in disgust and moving to the next.

Guests scream and run in a tangle of legs before Willow's eyes. The vampire catches a few and bites into their shoulders or neck or whatever appendages he can clamp down on.

Willow watches with wide eyes. She scans for an escape. When her eyes alight on a small hole between fleeing adults, she darts. A chef slams to the floor in front of her and she scrambles over him. Several guests knee her face and arms in their wild attempts at fleeing. She runs for the hole but gets shoved into the vampire. He topples over and she dives madly for the exit, not stopping until she reaches the seating area.

Tables are turned and smashed, chairs are in pieces, the floor is littered with warm meats and sticky sauces, shards pepper the floor, and culinary implements of all kinds are scattered about. Willow's head snaps around, looking out all the windows for her dad. Every uniformed man catches her attention, but none are Mr. Hunter.

The flash of MP40s lights up the dark streets, its blackness accented with hungry red eyes and shouts for back-up. Familiar faces pass but Willow doesn't want just anyone, she wants—no she *needs*—Mr. Hunter. Her breath is raspy as she trips toward a shattered window and climbs out. Something stings her hand and she looks down at her palms. Her heart misses a beat.

Red.

A hungry growl snaps her attention around. She screams as a vampire flies at her.

A trashcan cracks against his skull and the vampire skids across the asphalt. A Region Commander named Ashe pours ammo into the downed vampire with a victorious cry. "I'll teach you to attack children!" she roars.

"Willow!" Mr. Hunter races over and scoops her up. "I told you to stay with the waitress!" he scolds.

Tears streak her cheeks as she buries her face into his shoulder. He sighs and softens his tone. "Hold on tight, Wills."

Willow jostles back and forth as he carves through a path of corpses and war cries. When Willow looks up again, they approach a friend cleaning off a Karambit in an alley as his team takes a moment to reload.

"Dube!" Mr. Hunter yells over the onslaught of grenade explosions and the crunch of metal from thrown cars. "I need someone I can trust. Take Willow back to Foxhound for me."

The large man's expression hardens in determination. "She will be safe. I promise," he says in a deep Zulu accent.

"No!" Willow objects, tightening her arms around Mr. Hunter's neck.

"Willow," Mr. Hunter says sternly. "Hidden Hill is very dangerous right now. I need you safe so I can focus on work."

"You have to come with me then!" she cries.

Dube puts a hand on Willow's back. "Your father is a strong man. Trust him. He can slay an entire army of vampires just for you."

"But... I don't want him to."

"I know, Wills," Mr. Hunter says sympathetically. "But there isn't time to argue. Go with Dube." He hands her off to him then gives her a kiss on the forehead. "I don't want to lose you, Wills. You stay safe and I will stay safe. Sound like a deal?"

Willow's lip protrudes. "Promise?"

"Promise."

She hugs Dube, and they set off at a run. Over his shoulder, she watches Mr. Hunter exit the alley and mix with the blood-thirsty chaos.

CHAPTER
TWO

WILLOW'S BREATH comes in steady pants. Her hands work quickly. She slides out her Glock's old magazine and slaps in a new one. She exhales and whirls around the tree trunk, gun aimed directly at the black clothed target.

PABAM!

A perfect hit, but the target turns and charges in a bellowing mass of muscle.

Willow grips her Glock tighter.

PABAM! PABAM! PABAM!

All three shots nail him where a vampire's vital artery would be. The target trudges to a halt four paces from Willow. He chuckles and removes his armored mask.

"You are a perfect marksman, Pre-Initiate Hunter," Region Commander Dube compliments. "Just like your father."

Willow allows herself a small smile and lowers her Glock. She's aced her Hunt and Pursuit practice, again. "Thank you, Sir. But I'm not striving for the perfection of a marksman. All I want is to hit my target."

"A wise choice, Pre-Initiate. Perfection is an important part of our field, but it sometimes causes intense stress. And that," he gestures to Willow with his mask, "can be anyone's downfall."

Willow knows his words are true. She has seen vampire hunters under that weighty stress with her own eyes. Her mind flashes with images of taut expressions and shaky hands. She quickly pushes those memories aside.

If only those stupid bloodsuckers never came to America, Willow thinks bitterly. *Maybe then we wouldn't have had all these massacres.* Modern weaponry, like Willow's reinforced Glock with digital magazine counter, did little to protect against the wicked-fast and equally cunning vampires many faced.

Willow's blood boiled when she learned in school that the death toll skyrocketed after the vampires immigrated. Not even establishing a border appeased them. That is why Willow is part of the government force known as Vampire Hunters. She will protect the civilians from the beasts that lurk on the other side of the border.

Region Commander Dube, or Rei-Com Dube for short, leads her back through the forest. "Another training mission complete with nearly perfect marks," he notes. "And I am particularly impressed with your focus. You will make a good initiate someday."

"Thank you, sir," she replies, not missing the word *someday*.

It's Willow's dream to become an initiate. It's the highest rank any vampire hunter can achieve without hitting Region Commander. It's also a heavily praised position, full of espionage, sabotage, and one-on-one combat scenarios, and, to Willow, fascinating historic sites and culture yet to be seen by the human eye.

But at her current rate, Willow guesses she'll have an eternity to wait until achieving her prized rank. She can't be promoted without a fair amount of experience in fighting vampires. Therein lays the trouble. One fourth of the vampire borders cut across Maine, but the vampiric province bordering their small town of Hidden Hill hasn't seen a vampire in over seven years. That's all thanks to the current pureblooded vampire ruling Hidden Hill's bordering province.

Stepping over shrubbery and dodging low-hanging branches, Willow repeats the same mental conversation she's been having for the past four years. *I thought purebloods were supposed to not care who their half-bloods ate? So why is the border quiet? Why hasn't anyone seen a hostile vampire—or any vampire—in the past seven years?*

Part of Willow already knew the answer. But it still made little sense.

"Pre-Initiate Hunter," Rei-Com Dube says, his deep voice breaking Willow from her thoughts. "Has Rei-Com Ashe spoken to you about transferring out?"

Willow pushes a barren branch from her face. "Yes, sir, but..." She flushes, staring off at the evening shadows yawing across the leaf-infested ground. "Region Commander Hunter says I am not ready for the Initiate rank." She could hardly believe the words as they leapt off her tongue. Who needs their dad's permission rather than their Region Commander's for moving up in rank? Sure, her dad is a Region Commander, but she isn't under his command.

What am I, three? Willow thinks bitterly.

Rei-Com Dube *hmms* thoughtfully. He says nothing for a few minutes. "Rei-Com Hunter knows what he's doing. That rank will be yours someday."

There it is again, that word Willow keeps hearing from everyone: *someday.*

As the crunch of dead leaves thins out, the buildings of the Vampire Hunter Foxhound branch thicken. Asphalt roads weave past metal ammunition depots, vehicle and training bays, and a smattering of watch towers before stretching under the chain-link fencing and toward Hidden Hill. Vampire Hunters of all ranks crisscross the roads, some alone and some jogging in perfect groups of eight. A few trainees are doing pushups with an ensign supervising.

Rei-Com Dube stops beside the first asphalt road and turns to Willow. "You're dismissed, Pre-Initiate. I will report to Rei-Com Ashe for you."

Willow salutes. "Yes, sir! Permission to ask a question."

He nods and Willow drops her military etiquette—something only the lax Vampire Hunters permit, which happens to be most of them. "Are you sure? I can report to Rei-Com Ashe myself. I have to get my schedule for tomorrow anyway."

Rei-Com Dube waves it off. "No, go back home and get some dinner. You still have homework to do tonight, I heard."

Willow's shoulders slump. The reminder of dull homework is enough to dampen her exciting day. "Yeah, but it won't take long to report."

He laughs heartily. "It's okay, Willow. I will handle it. You are still in high school—you must keep up your studies."

School feels like the least of Willow's concerns, but she knows he is right. Getting good grades is the only way to stay a Vampire Hunter without being over eighteen. "I guess." She sighs, already dreading her awaiting assignments. "I should get back, then."

He nods, pulling out a handkerchief and wiping the sweat from his dark brow. "Wish your father a good evening, Pre-Initiate. And good luck with your work."

Willow thanks him and the two split off.

* * *

Heading across campus, Willow tugs on her dark grey top to let the cool evening air fan her torso. A shower was definitely on her list of things to do. *Right,* Willow thinks, tucking an unruly lock of dark wavy auburn back into her ponytail. *Shower, dinner, homework, then sleep! An almost perfect plan.*

She pauses to let a group of trainees jog past, then continues past some warehouses before turning right. Her gaze absentmindedly jumps from the Vampire Hunters chatting in front of their perfectly aligned one-man homes, to the transport carts whizzing by—which were really golf carts on steroids—and finally stops on her two-story home a few buildings up.

Her steps quicken and her stomach growls at the thought of food. A good meal and a warm shower will prep her for the long night ahead.

"Willow!" a familiar voice gasps. "Your Glocks are missing!"

She jumps and immediately pats her hips relaxing when she finds the two pistols on either side. A guffaw bursts out from behind her. Willow rolls her eyes playfully and turns to find Eric Gregory, an ensign Vampire Hunter with an unusual love for all things camouflage. His brunet hair is buzzed, hazel eyes ablaze with mischief, and wide mouth spread into a grin. Despite the fact that he stands half a head taller than Willow, his face still retains its boyish youth. Today, he is wearing his fraying camo baseball cap, a slightly wrinkled army-green T-shirt, and some baggy camouflage cargo pants with his uniform's lace-up boots.

"I got you!" he teases. "Obviously you're thinking about something. That trick doesn't normally work. What are you thinking about?"

"Food," Willow says simply, not missing the fact that Eric teased her despite her warning against it. He likes catching her off guard for some reason. She suspects it's flirting. But, like most cases, Willow decides to ignore it the best she can. "What are you doing here? Are you on border patrol tonight?"

He stuffs his hands in his pants pockets. "You mean 'aren't *we* on border patrol tonight?'"

"Um, no?" Willow chuckles, cocking a brow. "I have homework tonight. And dinner."

"Not anymore," Eric informs her, trying—and failing—to hide a smile. "The original group assigned for border patrol had to switch to a different task tonight, so us ensigns and you got border patrol tonight."

Willow's world drains of color. Border patrol is a task no one enjoys. Nothing exciting ever happens and patrols pace the border for at least three hours before circulating.

"What…?" Willow protests. The prospect of homework seems heavenly now. "But… I can't! I mean, I have stuff to do."

Eric shrugs. "Hey, at least we get to hang tonight!"

"Yeah, I guess. Um… I've gotta go. I need to talk to my dad about this." She takes two steps backward. "I'll see you around, okay?"

Eric lifts a hand to wave. "See you tonight, then! Don't be late!"

Willow smiles half-heartedly and turns around, trotting toward home. She hopes with all her might she won't see Eric tonight—not because she has something against him, besides his teasing, but because border patrol is pure boredom.

Moments later, Willow takes the front porch steps two at a time, crosses the short distance to the door, opens it, and shuffles inside. She all but slams the door closed, a bad habit of hers, and hops around while unlacing her boots and calling out, "I'm home, Dad!"

The clink of dishes and clang of pots and pans tells Willow that he's in the kitchen. Sure enough, just down the hall and on the right, Desmond Hunter sticks his bald head around the corner. "Hello, Wills! Dinner is almost ready. Spaghetti with extra-large meatballs!" He shows his teeth, partially hidden under a bushy mustache.

Willow smiles weakly. "Cool… um… Dad?"

Not missing her expression, Mr. Hunter says, "You heard about the change in scheduling tonight?"

Willow lets her second boot *thunk* to the floor. "Yeah," she admits, approaching the kitchen entryway. "I was just wondering if maybe someone else could go? I've got homework tonight."

Mr. Hunter gives her a sympathetic look. "We'll talk about it when dinner is ready, okay? Why don't you take a shower or start on some homework now?"

"Sure just… think about it. Please?" Willow waits for Mr. Hunter to nod before heading around the left corner and up the stairs.

Making a right down the hall and then a left into her bedroom, Willow rummages through her closet and dresser for sweats and a cozy top. She turns to head for her awaiting shower, but her eye catches the photograph resting on the bookshelf near the door, just as it does every time she leaves her room.

Sitting atop a pile of magazines about guns, knives, and the latest anti-puncture clothing is a photo of Trisha Hunter—Willow's beloved, deceased mom.

Mrs. Hunter is gripping the white railing of a boat, leaning back and looking to her side at the camera. Her smile is pleasant, relaxed. Her wavy auburn hair is blown by the sea breeze and her face is shadowed under her broad sunhat.

Willow brushes a hand on the wooden frame. "You would prioritize my homework over a boring patrol, right?" she muses to herself before heading for the shower.

The photo is Willow's favorite picture of Mrs. Hunter. She is happy, smiling without a care, and relaxing on a Florida beach getaway. It was taken two years before her death and only three years after the most horrific vampiric attack Hidden Hill had ever seen.

CHAPTER
THREE

WILLOW VIVIDLY remembers the day of the attack. Her aunt was going through trauma, so Mrs. Hunter packed her bags and headed for the coast to comfort her. But she never came back. Willow had been playing "secret agent" with her dolls when the phone rang. She paused her game, arms going slack as her dad's tense voice drifted up the stairs. Moments later, he appeared. His eyes were watery and red, his nose running, and his face wrinkling with his first deep worry lines.

"Willow." His voice cracked, uneven and changing pitch. "Your mom, she—" He had to take a deep breath. "She's not coming home."

A vampire had attacked her mom and aunt. Neither lived. Their bodies were pale, and their open eyes were staring blankly. Only two clean puncture holes in their necks symbolized the gruesome death.

But the horror wasn't over. Just a year after her mom's death, Hidden Hill fell prey to a *pureblood*—a vampire born as such from a long lineage of perfectly pure vampire relatives. He, like most greedy purebloods, wanted more land, more power, and above all, more humans to feast on.

On a cold Friday evening, the vampire sirens blared their blood-chilling warning. Hordes of half-bloods—humans turned vampire—swarmed Hidden Hill at the command of their pureblood lord. Seventy humans died, the rest were injured or scared out of their wits. But not Willow. She was frazzled and angry. The vampires had ruined her life twice, and she wouldn't allow a third.

* * *

"Willow!" Mr. Hunter calls. "Dinner's ready!"

Willow ruffles her wet hair with a towel. "Coming!" She tosses the towel in her laundry basket and heads downstairs. Shuffling into the combination kitchen and dining room, she finds two plates on the table with a pot of spaghetti and tomato sauce, accompanied by meatballs the size of baseballs. She sits down in her place with Mr. Hunter sitting on her left. An empty chair still rests at Willow's right where her mother once sat.

"Help yourself," Mr. Hunter says, scooting his chair in.

Willow piles noodles and sauce on her plate, then Mr. Hunter serves himself while Willow picks up a meatball with tongs.

"So… ready for an *exciting* night of patrols?" He cracks a teasing smile.

Willow gives her father a funny look. With him being one of the three Region Commanders, Willow can't believe he jokes about the border being uneventful. He *is* all about keeping the peace.

Mr. Hunter clears his throat and his expression turns serious but still soft with kindness. "I understand. Patrols are boring, but they're very important."

"Can't you find someone else for the patrols?" Willow pleads. "I have homework to do!"

Mr. Hunter snorts as he slices his meatball. "Since when have you been so invested in home—Uh, I mean," he quickly corrects himself, "I'm glad you're applying yourself, but some urgent business called those Hunters away, and everyone else is busy or resting from afternoon patrols. I'm sorry, Wills, but you have to fill the slot."

Willow pokes her meatball, mumbling, "Maybe I wouldn't mind border patrol if there were *actually* vampires to protect the border from."

Mr. Hunter asks the question he already knows the answer to. "What do you mean?"

Willow puts her fork down, turning to her father. "I became a V.H. to hunt vampires, not patrol a border where vampires never show their faces. Sometimes, I wonder if there *actually are* vampires over there, besides the pureblood anyway. Maybe they all left after the attack six years ago."

Desmond Hunter's green eyes flash with grief and Willow instantly regrets mentioning it. She doesn't like talking about it either, but she is trying to make a point.

The pureblood who attacked six years ago had escaped the Vampire Hunter's grasp. However, one week later, the pureblood was found and killed—but not by one of the Hunters. A new pureblood had shown up and dragged the body of the previous with him. He presented it to the Vampire Hunters as a peace offering—an action which Willow still thought was pretty medieval-esque. It wasn't long after that that Mr. Hunter's trust toward the pureblood began to grow. But Willow thought their alliance was shady. Even the other Region Commanders thought it was mysterious.

"Just remember," Mr. Hunter says eventually. "Not every job we get deals with hunting down vampires. And there are good reasons why we never see vampires anymore. I told you that this pureblood has no desire for more power, land, blood, or anything else. He specifically keeps his half-bloods away from the border, and I am very happy with that decision."

That is Willow's other problem. The entire length of the border—spreading across Maine and into Quebec—has the same rule: no vampires or humans are allowed to cross the border without permission from either governing force, lest a skirmish between the two sides begin. Most purebloods don't care about the rules. They let their half-bloods cross the border and drink civilian blood to their heart's content. But, in Hidden Hill exclusively, both sides will look the other way over the death, which is also pretty shady to Willow.

"I know you want action," her dad continues. "But the truth is—"

"'Your dad and Hidden Hill could use some peace,'" Willow paraphrases. "I know, I know. But being a Vampire Hunter is supposed to be full of cool missions and fights, not patrols and rules. Plus, I'll *never* get to be an initiate if I don't kill one of those bloodsuckers myself."

Mr. Hunter frowns. "I won't have you using such a derogatory term for vampires. And Being an initiate has little to do with killing. It's based on spying, which is why I encouraged the rank. But being a Vampire Hunter isn't about killing vampires, either. It's about keeping peace between two races."

"I don't want peace with a creature that killed Mom," Willow mutters, stabbing a piece of meatball and shoving it in her mouth.

Mr. Hunter puts down his fork with a soft *clink*. His brow crinkles in seriousness, voice low and quivering with remorse. "Your Mother's death hit me just as hard as it hit you, but blindly killing innocent vampires isn't going to make you happy. I'm not saying you have to love vampires, but killing them like a sport is *not* okay." He gives her a pointed look before saying, "And that resentment of yours is why I won't allow a temporary relocation for your initiate rank."

Willow frowns at the small green flecks of seasoning in her sauce. She knows killing isn't the answer, but a hidden anger inside her says that all vampires deserve to be shot down. They are barbaric, cruel, and demeaning towards humans—sometimes even their own kind. Willow will never understand how her father can wish for peace with such monsters.

"Don't wish for danger, Willow Ashton Hunter," Mr. Hunter continues, right on cue. "You're like me. I used to want excitement, adventure, and vampires to kill for heroics. I thought it was all fun and sport. And look where that thinking put me. It took losing your mom to teach me that kind of thinking was wrong." When this clearly doesn't make Willow feel better, Mr. Hunter says, "I know the peace is boring for you, but hold on. I hate to say it, and I never want to see it, but your day will come—a day when it will be your turn to fight and protect what you love."

Willow continues to stare at her food. The prospect of a fight excites her, the knowledge that she may finally cross the border and see the vampiric world's mysteries enthralls her. But when will that be? It's been six years of complete silence, but she knows that Mr. Hunter is right. "I understand..." she murmurs.

Mr. Hunter smiles. He reaches over and rubs her arm. "Good. Now, you've got patrol group B in thirty minutes, better finish your dinner and get into a clean uniform."

A smirk tugs at Willow's lips, and she can't help but ask, "To fight vampires that won't show?"

Mr. Hunter shakes his head with humor, smiling in reminiscence. "As feisty and persistent as your mom."

* * *

Willow heads to the central point of campus—a forked road called "the crossroads." She gazes around the quiet four-way intersection.

"Where is group B?" Willow wonders aloud. According to her dad, the group will consist of just Willow, Eric, and two ensigns named Josh and Darius. Normally, groups contain at least one fully trained and experienced ensign, but they are short one man tonight—something about him having to take Rei-Com Ashe's training duties because she had important business. So Willow, being the next highest rank, was chosen for the job.

Willow checks her wristwatch for the third time. "It's already nineteen-hundred hours... they're late."

"Hey!"

Willow turns, seeing Eric, Josh, and Darius jogging down the asphalt. She relaxes. *There they are.*

The three come to a halt in front of her. Eric adjusts the MP7 strapped across his chest and grins widely. "We're here!"

"You're late," Willow corrects. "All three of you. It's already nineteen oh five! We are supposed to *leave* at nineteen-hundred sharp."

"Sorry, ma'am!" Darius says, stiffening.

Josh follows suit. "We will be on time for the next mission, ma'am."

Willow nods to them. "Glad to hear it. At ease, men." She turns her gaze back on Eric, who is checking his watch curiously, and also forgetting his military etiquette. "My watch says it's eighteen fifty-nine."

Willow wonders, and not for the first time, how he has made it this far in the V.H. Sure, their branch is more relaxed than the actual military, but failing to salute or stand at attention will still get you in deep trouble. Not to mention that Eric had just technically talked back to his superior. And then... there is his outfit. "Eric... your uniform is off again. You *can't* wear camo pants while on patrol."

Eric frowns, looking down at his collared black uniform, combat vest, and baggy camo pants with combat boots. "But I blend in! Besides, it's just us. I thought you wouldn't care."

Willow gestures to her own uniform. "Standard issue top tucked into dark grey pants. *No* camo. And yes, I do care. We are the V.H. and we want to look it."

"At least my shirt is tucked in," Eric mumbles.

Willow huffs and checks her watch again. Nineteen oh six. "We're late, so I'll let the pants slide. But just know, you'll be sorting the ammo bay for *weeks* if anyone finds out."

Eric cringes. He didn't consider that.

The ammunition bays are a mess twenty-four to seven, so all the trainees and those who disobey orders get stuck reorganizing it. That means hours of crawling on the cold, hard concrete floors picking up tiny stray bullets that roll away and organizing bins of every bullet type known to man.

"Alright, let's head out!" Willow strides past the three, taking the lead. But as they head for the West gate, Willow hears Eric say, "Border patrol, here we come!"

Oh boy… Willow thinks unenthusiastically.

* * *

The border is perfectly quiet, as usual—no sign of vampires, just some owl hoots and cricket chirps. The four stride along the forest edge and watch the shadows cast by the partially covered moon.

Quiet though the border may be, Willow feels a small tingle of excitement at standing so close to another world. Just two steps to her right and a mile or so out lays the world of vampires. Very few humans have seen it and lived to tell the tale. Most who cross the border never come back. They are either killed or turned into half-bloods, never allowed to live on human lands again. Despite this, some information has been sent back across the border and other pieces carried on from times when humans and vampires held no boundaries. Still, the world beyond holds many mysteries… mysteries Willow intends to see on her future initiate missions.

"No vampires tonight, I guess," Eric says from behind Willow. He turns his sight toward Hidden Hill about half a mile to their left. The soft yellow glow of the town only adds to the serene atmosphere.

"You *expected* vampires?" Willow snorts, sounding more bitter than she intended. "I mean, it's so peaceful up here you could have a late-night picnic!"

"That doesn't sound half bad," Eric muses. "But these six years of peace can't last forever, right? I mean, that pureblood will get bored soon. Then he'll be out for blood!" Eric clamps a hand on Willow's shoulder. "Then we'll *both* get a taste of vampire slaying!" He throws his head back to Darius and Josh following in single file. "Right guys?"

They grin excitedly, and Willow smiles too. There isn't a single ensign or trainee in Hidden Hill who doesn't want a share of vampire blood. Half the town had lost someone during the attack years before, and they still aren't satisfied—not even with the death of the previous pureblood.

The rest of that night's patrol goes on without a word. Group B walks up the length of the border and back again, but nothing interesting happens. As Willow's watch ticks to midnight, the group begins their trek back to Foxhound. Willow can't help but let her feet drag in disappointment. *Nothing. As usual.* Not that she had been expecting much.

Snap!

Willow jumps, pointing her Glock into the forest. Her heart beats excitedly as she sees... a deer. Willow drops her arms, watching it run madly back through the forest.

"Pretty sure that was the most eventful thing that happened this week," Eric says, watching the deer disappear into the shadows.

Darius, who is also tense, slumps his posture in disappointment. "Just a dumb deer. Anyway, should we continue back?"

Willow exhales, turning the safety on and shoving her Glock into its holster. The sight of the deer annoyed her more than it should have. Her mentor, Rei-Com Ashe, had taught her that signs of forest life means no vampires. *"Animals are keen,"* she had said, tapping her temple. *"They can sense the aura vampires emit from a mile away."*

"Yeah," Willow huffs. "Back to—"

BROOOOOOOooooo! The air is split with tornado-like sirens. Willow's heart skips a beat, a chill racing up her spine at the eerie wail. She locks eyes with Eric, hardly believing her ears. "Vampire attack sirens?"

Eric pumps a fist into the air with a silent cheer of joy. Josh and Darius high five each other.

As the sirens continue to blare, more lights turn on in Hidden Hill. Civilians flip on all house lights as a precaution against vampires—since they aren't fond of anything bright—and street lamps are set a few notches higher, a feature only towns by the vampire border have.

The specialized walkie-talkie on Willow's hip vibrates, indicating orders are being transmitted. She pulls it out, clicking the side.

Kssssh. "Two half-bloods were spotted crossing the border on the far west of town. Probability of them being in Hidden Hill is high. All dispatched personnel are to head to Hidden Hill and track it down. Over."

Willow's hand trembles in exhilaration as she clicks the button again. "Copy that. Group B, on the way. Over."

She straps the walkie-talkie to her belt and pulls her Glock out, flipping the safety off again. She takes a deep breath, calming the party going on in her head. "Okay, you guys know the drill. Head into town. Don't leave so much as a grit of asphalt unturned. Try all the doors of any and every house. Make sure they're locked."

Josh and Darius nod, failing to hide grins. Eric grips his MP7, looking like he might explode with joy. "Let's go, let's go, let's go!"

The four of them run toward Hidden Hill. The flicker of black human shapes—Vampire Hunters—already weave between buildings, crouching in shadows and testing doors.

Group B enters the streets, puffing a little, but ready for action. Willow trots down the pavement with her Glock prepped and pointed downward, away from her feet. Josh and Darius keep pace behind her, their semi-automatic pistols aimed down, too. Eric, positioned on Willow's left, holds his MP7 at eye level, ready to fire on any vampire that dares enter his sights.

As they pass other groups of V.H. and check doors, Willow mentally recites the drill she has come to know by heart. *"When the sirens sound, head to Hidden Hill. Check every house and make sure the door is locked for civilian safety. Patrol town, weapons drawn. Be wary of any and every movement. Continue patrols until vampire is found and shot down. In the event of hearing fire from fellow Vampire Hunters, head to their location and assist immediately."*

Willow tries to wipe the giddy smile off her face. She wants to look professional, but her facial muscles betray her. Secretly, she hopes she'll be the one to kill both the half-bloods, but Willow knows that isn't realistic. So long as she gets to kill one, she feels she will be set for life.

That initiate rank isn't far off now, she thinks to herself.

Stepping lightly and cautiously, Willow approaches a house she knows to belong to her best friend, Martha Heartwood. She jiggles the handle, locked. *Good,* Willow thinks. She moves on.

The silence in Hidden Hill is almost on a haunting level. No wind ruffles the trees, no cars rumble down the streets, just the low breath of Vampire Hunters and the seemingly loud *clink, clink,* of locked doors can be heard. However, the more the silence draws on, the more Willow wonders if the sirens are a false alarm. Annoyance makes her trigger finger twitch, a terrible habit she is trying to get rid of. *If this is a false alarm,* Willow thinks, *I'll find the one who set it off and punch the snot out of him!*

Group B nears the town center, a beautiful park lined with birch trees and benches. Willow is aware of another V.H. group in her peripheral vision. They disappear down an alley. Willow signals to group B with her hand. *Inspect the park.* They nod and take their scouting one step at a time. Willow's eyes switch from tree to tree, searching the dark branches of green for any movement. All is still, as if the entire town is holding its breath.

A soft breeze rustles the tree tops like a mother hushing her baby. Willow's grip on her Glock tightens. There has been no wind all night, yet now a single breeze has blown through. She recalls something her mentor told her, *"Sometimes, vampires move fast enough to disturb the air and cause a breeze, but it's only possible when there is more than one."*

Willow inhales and exhales deeply through her nose. *So, the two are together. No problem, I'll just take them both out.* But even as Willow thinks those brave words, her shoulders become tense. A cold prickling sensation spreads across her back. She is being watched.

Willow turns toward Eric, Josh, and Darius. The three are spread out a few feet from her, checking bushes and aiming guns up the trunks of trees. They all look in Willow's direction as another breeze rustles the treetops. They nod, understanding the situation.

Willow signals with her hand. *Keep sharp. They're close.* But she has hardly finished the signal when a flicker of black catches her attention. Her eyes dart to the right, fixed on a tree twenty feet away.

Vampire, three o'clock, Willow signals. The group creeps toward the tree, Willow in the lead. She steadily raises her Glock, aiming up at the branches and waiting to spot movement again.

Fifteen feet... thirteen feet... ten... eight. Willow nears the tree, another light draft sailing past.

Six feet... four... two...

Willow stares up the tree trunk.

BANG!

Willow whirls around, looking to her teammates. They all return confused expressions. Willow looks to each one of them, whispering, "Did one of you shoot?"

BANG! BANG! BANG!

Pata-pata-pata!

Willow's eyes widen as she realizes where the sound is coming from. Eric beats her to the words. "The alley!"

Willow doesn't wait. She tears across the park and toward the alley, but she stops dead on the park's edge. Across the road, two human shapes emerge from the shadows. Their eyes glow a blood moon red.

Blood smears the lips and left cheek of an athletically built half-blood. The deep crimson is stark against his terribly pale skin. He slings a half conscious V.H. to the pavement, grumbling to his brawny, dark toned partner. "Too weak. We need a better one." His eyes snap up to Willow and group B. He smiles. "Oh... one of them might be *perfect!*"

"Young, bloodthirsty, full of energy," the brawny half-blood agrees quietly. "They will settle this."

They flash toward Group B. Willow sucks in a breath and whips up her Glock, but she's too late. The athletic one and his companion are no longer at the entrance to the alley. They appear overhead, darting from tree top to tree top in confusing zig-zags.

Group B rushes into formation, wrongly following Eric's lead to position themselves in the center of the trees. Willow presses her back into the circle, watching the pale and dark brown streaks of vampire dart among the treetops. Eric sprays bullets along their trail. Darius keeps changing where he is aiming, but never fires a shot. Josh fires aimlessly at trees the vampires have long left.

Willow's mind scurries to keep up, to remember what she has to do. *This formation is bad! Should I warn neighboring Vampire Hunters? No. I should help my teammates! Or, do I get help...?*

The brawny one drops from the trees, catching Willow by surprise. He darts at her, arms outstretched. Willow grits her teeth and fires.

PABAM! PABAM! Miss. He leaps up into the trees again. The other swoops down, making a grab for Eric. He tumbles out of the circle as the vampire misses and leaps back into the trees. Darius takes a step out, hoping to break away in search for backup that is supposed to be coming, but the athletic one dives, forcing him to squish back into the circle.

They aren't hitting the half-bloods and they're stuck. Willow's heart rate climbs, soon beating faster than the vampire's movements.

BANG! BANG! BANG!

Pata-pata-pata-pata-pata!

KABOOM! KABOOM!

Gunfire and Willow's pulse pounds in her ears. *Relax,* Willow scolds herself. *Just call for backup... you can do this.* Hands trembling, she kneels and sets down her Glock and pulls out her walkie-talkie. "We need reinforcements!" she shouts above the noise. "Come in, come in!"

Eric, Josh, and Darius shift around Willow, providing better protection as she attempts to get help. But no one is responding. "We are surrounded!" Willow yells, voice trembling. "I repeat, we are surrounded! Central Park, both vampires, send back—"

"Back up?" says an equally panicked voice from the tree tops.

Willow jolts, dropping her walkie-talkie and snatching her Glock. Too late. Both half-bloods stop their dashing and land on opposite sides of the group. They swerve between shots and Willow is positive she hears one say, "The girl?" And the other reply in assurance, "The girl."

Eric receives a swift kick to the side, rocketing him away from Willow and slamming him into a tree. Josh is easily thrown thirty feet away, skidding and tumbling across the grass. Darius manages to dodge one swing before being punched hard enough in the gut to black out.

In those events, which lasted barely half a second, Willow has almost raised her Glock. The athletic one smacks it from her hand. The Glock goes flying, and before the sharp pain in her hand can register, he swiftly chops her neck's pressure point.

Willow flops onto her side. The last thing she hears is the distant echo of her dad's voice over the walkie-talkie.

"Group B, answer! Status report! Answer! Willow? Willow are you there? Willow!"

She blacks out.

CHAPTER
FOUR

WILLOW ISN'T sure which part of her body to complain about first. Her head throbs, her back aches, and her hand stings. To top it off, Willow's backside and legs are stiff from the cold cement floor. However, her mind is more focused on the conversation that tickles her waking senses.

"… can she do it properly?"

"She has to. She's the only chance we have."

"Look, she's waking!"

"About time."

Willow swallows a moan, blinking at the shadowy darkness. Two pairs of glistening red eyes watch her from above. She lurches and opens her mouth to yelp in surprise. A freezing hand stops her.

"*Shh!*" the athletic one, Gavin, whispers. "Do you want him to hear you?"

Willow glares, slapping his icy hand away and scooting away from the two. Her heart is beating wildly again. "Him?" she whispers. "Who's him?"

"An intruder," Gavin growls. He nods to the Glocks on her hips. "Use those and help us exterminate this monster—before he destroys us all!"

Willow slowly takes her eyes off the half-bloods to look down. Surprisingly, both Glocks are still there. The half-bloods should have taken them. For that matter, Willow should be dead. "What's going on? Where's the intruder? What do you guys want from me?"

The two stand, yanking Willow to her feet before she can ask more questions. Gavin grabs her arm with an unnaturally firm grip, directing her toward a metal door which is open a crack. The brawny, dark-toned one, Thomas, slips up to the partially unhinged door. He peeks through the slit emitting a soft orange light. "The intruder is in there," he confirms. "And his accomplice."

A quiet voice like a slithering snake confirms it.

"... take these," the intruder's slithering voice whispers. "Use them when I tell you to."

A second voice, muffled and unrecognizable, whispers something in return, but Willow misses it.

"They will help you," the intruder promises, his tone hiding a secret and desperate coldness. "Everything will change for your own good."

The muffled voice replies again but is drowned out by the loud creek and scrape of the metal door. Thomas enters the room first and Gavin forces Willow to follow. It isn't until she emerges into the large, deeply shadowed space that she recognizes it.

"The Batch warehouse..." she breathes, referencing the twice a year procedure where death row criminals are sent across the border as food, or rarely, turned into half-bloods. When not used for The Batch, the warehouse is littered with anything the Vampire Hunters don't need: old armored vehicles, flatbeds covered in various junk, dented iron barricades, and many other kinds of broken tools.

"What... is this?" The intruder's voice emerges from the corner closest to them.

Willow startles, despite the gentle tone, and her eyes lock on the corner where a stack of old shipping containers rest. Beside them, a vampire is poised in the gloomy light of a lantern. His shoulder-length blond hair glows golden in the light, pulled back loosely at the neck. His tall frame is regal, yet relaxed. The calm and controlled expression on his face makes his worn dress shirt, scuffed vest, and stained wool pants look almost deliberate.

Willow catches her breath, realizing that this is no ordinary vampire. His eyes are half cobalt blue in the lantern light and half gold in the dark. Only pureblood eyes are two-toned like this, and only the French and Russian purebloods possess that stunning golden tone. There is also his presence: it coils around Willow and her skin prickles in response.

The intruder regards Gavin and Thomas in faux confusion. "Why did you bring a Vampire Hunter here? I'm afraid I do not understand."

Gavin shoves Willow forward as if expecting her to do something useful. But what could a pre-initiate do? Rei-Com Ashe hadn't taught her how to deal with purebloods. Their strength varies from five to ten times that of a human, their speed unmatchable. That doesn't even account for the power which every pureblood possesses—a supernatural power, which only makes defeating them all the more complicated.

Every nerve in Willow's body screams at her to flee and never look back.

"You're a Vampire Hunter," Gavin whispers through his teeth. "Kill him!"

Willow snaps her head around, eyes wide. "What?" she hisses. "I-I can't—"

"Oh… I see," the intruder says, pacing a step closer. "You think this little human child will get rid of me?"

Thomas steps forward boldly. "Yes," he says in a deep voice. "So leave!" He looks pointedly at Willow.

She stares at him in horror. *What? I can't—there's no way.* She puts the words into her expression.

The intruder smirks, eyes drifting from Gavin and Thomas to Willow. "Well… are you going to shoot me, dear?" His words wash over Willow like an icy wave. She can't move… can't breathe… can't do anything. Her brain refuses to work, all logic fleeing her.

The intruder tsks, those blue-gold eyes holding Willow like a snake slithering up to a cornered rabbit. "I thought not," he says softly. He glances over his shoulder, addressing a shadowed figure Willow missed all together. "Leave us," he commands.

The figure, who is the muffled voice from earlier and the accomplice Thomas mentioned, shifts away to signal their exit. Gavin and Thomas ball their fists and rush after the figure.

"Wait!" Willow calls, suddenly wanting them to stay.

Gavin pauses. "We will handle that one. You finish *him* for us!" Then he disappears into the darkness with Thomas.

Willow swallows, trembling and feeling terribly alone.

The intruder spreads his arms. "And now for the early start of act two!" He strides over to Willow.

Now she whips out her Glock, hands visibly shaking. "W-What are you talking about? Stay away!"

"Poor thing," the intruder croons, still approaching. "Frightened, alone, cornered. Do not fear, I will make this quick."

Her heart rate doubles in speed. Tears of terror prick her eyes. Her feet remember how to function as she does what she was told never to do.

She backs away.

How could she hold her ground against a pureblood? She can *feel* his power and his blood lust curls around her like poisonous gas.

"I am going to brew a revolution, my dear. And you shall be the start of it."

Willow can hardly process what he's saying through the panic. Her back presses against the cool wall. "Me…? What—"

The intruder instantly looms over her. He rips the Glock from her hand and casts it aside. Willow's hand, already hurt from the inhuman slap that sent her Glock flying earlier, burns in agony. She gapes, her hand cradled against her chest.

"My dear," the Intruder whispers, reminding Willow of his presence an inch away. She looks up, startled. His long blond hair tickles her cheeks. His now fully golden irises imprison her will. Slowly, he traces a frigid hand down her cheek. "Save your words, my dear. They will not change a thing."

Something clicks in Willow's mind. As her thoughts race along with her heart, her muscles recall the self-defense techniques her conscious brain refuses to remember. She grips his upper arms, wraps a leg around his, and shoves hard. The intruder trips backward with flailing arms and slams against the concrete. By that time, Willow is already halfway to the door in a mad run. She reaches out to grab the doorway but a cold hand snatches the door first and slams it shut. The metal bends, preventing anyone from opening the door again. He grabs her head and cracks it against the metal. Her vision blackens for a second.

"Feisty, little thing. You should know that outrunning me is pointless."

Willow rips her spare Glock from its holster.

PABAM!

PABAM!

Both shots drill into the intruder, but not in lethal places. Willow bolts away but the intruder hisses in irritation and lunges after her. In one heartbeat, he catches up and twists Willow's Glock from her hand, nearly breaking a few of her already-inflamed fingers. He shoves Willow to the floor, her shoulder crashing into the concrete.

"You should not resist—"

Willow flops over and snatches the jagged nozzle of an old pistol. She drives it into his calf. He hisses and grabs for her hair but she rolls and kicks at his injured leg, knocking him down. Willow scrambles to her feet and runs into the maze of rusted armored vehicles and junk.

Her senses detect every speck of dust, every shift of dark shadow. Her mind pulses in fear as the intruder's furious howls reverberate off the metal walls and chase her past piles of soiled tires. She skirts around a slumped transport cart and rams into a door. A chain goes taut on the other side, leaving no more than a handbreadth of space.

CRASH!

Willow jumps and checks over her shoulder. The rear end of an eight-wheeler raises into the air and smashes to the floor in a cacophony of crushing metal.

"Come out, my dearie..." the intruder's voice slithers toward her.

Willow races along the wall, wide eyes searching the deep shadows for another exit. A figure lurches from the shadows.

"Found you!"

Willow's scream is cut off as he snatches her arm and sends her flying into a pile of sodden crates. The wood snaps under her weight, splinters digging into her arms and jagged spikes ripping across her legs. Willow moans and coughs as she struggles for air. Through her hazy vision, she is scarcely aware of the intruder strolling closer.

I have to escape! she thinks desperately. *I can't die!*

Gripping his wounded arm and smiling pitifully down on Willow, the intruder says, "Much better. I do not have the energy to hunt you down, so please stay still."

It's almost unbearable to move. Every inch of Willow screams in acid-hot pain. "Stay... stay back!" Willow gasps.

"Sorry, my dear." Quicker than a gunshot, the intruder snatches a handful of Willow's shirt, lifting her up.

Willow's calves feel as though they'll tear under her weight. Her ribs press in on her lungs. She grits her teeth, prying weakly at the intruder's hand. Her heart threatens to leap from her throat. She knows what's going to happen next.

"This is how it must end for you. Your mangled corpse will ignite the fire I need."

Needle sharp fangs stab into her neck. She screeches. Her life force drains into the fangs of the intruder. Her heart beats painfully fast, her strangled breath coming in desperate gasps.

Then her heart and breath slows down... slower... slower. Willow's eyelids lull. She fights to stay conscious, forcing her eyes open whenever they shut. But what's the point? This is the end of Willow Hunter.

As she loses her sight and her eyes close, Willow's mind drifts. *Is this what Mom felt?* Her chest heaves in sadness. *What about Dad? I'm leaving him... No, I can't leave him alone! Fight! Fight...! Fight...*

KA-BANG!

Willow's consciousness drifts back. *What was that?* Her attempts to return to full awareness are like pushing a boulder uphill. One moment she is making progress, the next she is skidding backward.

The faraway pops and bangs grow louder and closer. Her eyes slit open as she drops to the concrete. The grey and black room explodes with brightness, forcing her eyes shut. She blinks lethargically, trying to peer through the blinding light. Several smudgy figures race into her blurred view, yellow splotches flashing.

What's going... Willow's thoughts trail off, half from exhaustion, and half from the shape that has stopped to kneel beside her.

"... low... okay?" the fuzzy shape asks.

What?

The shape picks her up, hands shaking terribly and mumbling something indistinct.

So tired... Willow's eyelids close and darkness consumes her.

CHAPTER
FIVE

HUSHED WHISPERS accompanied by soft *clinks* slowly bring Willow back to consciousness. Something cottony and soft lays under her fingertips, something warm and comforting across her chest. Her head rests on a plush and cozy object. But with all the pleasantries comes a mild, yet pounding, ache in her torso, legs, and arms. Fatigue nearly sends her deep into the darkness again, but a mysterious force urges her to wake. She's forgetting something… something important.

With each conscious moment, Willow feels a little stronger. Finally, she summons the strength to open her eyes a crack. She closes them, then opens them a little wider. She is met with a dim, golden yellow light. Somewhere in the recesses of her mind, a voice tells her that means it's probably the afternoon. But the more she looks around, the more confused Willow feels. This place isn't anywhere she knows.

An elegant canopy of crimson hangs above her and trails down the rich oak bedposts. A matching comforter embroidered in warm gold thread blankets the bed. Smooth, ivory walls, bordered with intricate baseboards showcase baroque vanities, dressers, nightstands, and work desks—all crafted in fine oak to match the bed. The room, easily twice—if not three times—the size of Willow's bedroom in Hidden Hill, is finished off with grand, floor-to-ceiling windows draped in woven, ivory curtains.

As if the extravagant decor isn't strange enough, Willow is now aware of the peculiar cluster of servants who have surrounded the bed. They are dressed like typical English maids, except that their white aprons are embroidered with navy blue thread—roses and little blue birds resting on branches—and their calf-length, navy blue dresses have white frills peering from the hem and cuffs. The servants stare at her, eyes wide in pleasant surprise.

"I'll let him know," one says, then rushes from the room, disappearing through wooden double doors.

Willow's gaze switches from servant to servant, brow slightly scrunching. "Um… where am I?" Her voice is hoarse.

"You are safe, mistress," a servant with one frosty blue eye and one velvety red eye says. "There is no need to worry. Your father is on his way."

"*Mistress*?" Willow asks skeptically.

"Yes," replies a voice from the doorway. "It is how partially changed vampires, such as black-bloods, and servants are to refer to those higher than themselves."

The servants fan out and make way for the young man standing in the doorway at the foot of the bed. They all bow their heads and curtsey before leaving in perfect, single file lines. Willow studies the young man, who can't be more than a year older than herself, and wonders why something feels horribly off about him. The feeling isn't because of his peculiar looks: neatly trimmed black hair, glassy dark bronze irises, and pale creamy-tan complexion. It's not his choice of clothing either—midnight blue frock, black vest with curving silver zipper, white collared shirt, and black trousers. Willow realizes that it's his *presence*. This presence feels like swimming over the deepest, blackest part of the ocean. No one can say what may lurch from that darkness and drag her into the depths. She could pass by, unharmed, or meet her death within an instant.

This guy is… Willow lurches forward, squeezing the covers in her fists. "You're a pureblood!" With the word and the panic comes Willow's memories. They rush into her brain, bombarding her with recollections of a pureblood's pitying expression, and pain… so much pain.

Willow doubles over, gripping her sides as they punish her for daring to move. In the blur of the moment, cool hands grab her shoulders firmly, but not threateningly. They slowly help her lay back, and when the throbbing ceases, Willow releases the breath she wasn't aware she was holding. She warily turns and sees the pureblood beside her. She nearly jumps out of her skin again.

"I mean no harm," the pureblood promises, taking a step back.

"Yeah right," Willow retorts, glaring. "Where have you taken me? What do you plan to do?"

"Willow," says a familiar, steady voice from the door. "Calm down, it's alright."

Willow's eyes snap toward the door, then soften. "Dad!"

Mr. Hunter smiles, sadness tucked away in a corner of his expression as he walks across the room. He kneels beside her and gingerly pats her hand. "Everything is going to be okay. And don't worry about him." He angles himself toward the pureblood. "We can trust him."

Willow looks between Mr. Hunter and the pureblood. They both share a calm and undoubting air with one another. *Wait a minute… could he be…?* Willow chews her cheek.

"Oh, right. Introductions." Mr. Hunter straightens, clearing his throat. "Willow, this is Hanas Blackwell. He's the pureblood ruling over the province next to Hidden Hill. And this is his manor." He gestures around before continuing. "You owe your life to this young man. He gave you blood from his storage when I brought you here after the—well, the attack."

Willow catches the agony in Mr. Hunter's eyes. He nearly lost another family member to a vampire attack. She wants to hug him and cry, telling him all about the nightmare of a night. She wants to reassure him that she is here, and not gone like her mom–but her mind is still replaying the sentence before his hurt words: *you owe your life to this young man.*

"No offense, but I don't owe my life to *him*," Willow says, stealing a glance at the silent pureblood. "Just like you said, you're the one who found me and stopped that pureblood, the intruder."

Mr. Hunter frowns. "I thought you might say that. Willow, I know how you feel about vampires—"

"This isn't *just* how I feel about vampires!" Willow snaps before she can stop herself. "We *don't* trust purebloods. Ever. And after what just happened to me...?" She can't think of a good way to finish that sentence.

If this pureblood thinks they owe him, he'll ask them to do something crazy, and when they refuse, he'll start a skirmish as revenge. A fresh attack on Hidden Hill will begin and more people will die. It has happened in other border towns. Hidden Hill is no different.

"This is crazy," Willow decides, fear and anger taking over as she grabs her comforter. "Let's go back to Foxhound."

"Unfortunately, you are in no condition to move or be transported anywhere," Hanas, says evenly. "You have severe bruising in several places and require rest for your body to reproduce blood. Honestly, it is also a wonder that nothing in your body is broken."

"Mr. Blackwell is right," Mr. Hunter says before Willow can jump in. "You have to rest here. The black-bloods serving under Hanas are all very well trained in medicine and the human body." His brows rise as he looks to Hanas. "I'm very impressed at their medicinal skills."

A small smirk of pride tugs at Hanas' lips.

The sight makes Willow's blood boil. She looks away, staring at her chest instead, and suddenly notices her frilly white nightgown. *This is a nightmare in itself,* she thinks miserably.

"Anyway," Mr. Hunter continues. "I don't want to carry you back across the border just yet. It's only a thirty-minute hike, but the Rogue is still on the loose and I want to be absolutely sure he's gone off radar before I help you back. Unless, you found him?" He looks hopefully to Hanas who shakes his head disappointedly.

"Seemingly gone without a trace… again," Hanas confirms.

"The Rogue?" Willow butts in. "Is that the pureblood intruder who—" she doesn't want to say it. Admitting in front of a pureblood that she nearly died at the hands of another pureblood is humiliating. She also doesn't want him to think she's weak. Although, Willow is coming to realize, she might actually be.

"Yes," Mr. Hunter says quietly. "This might come as a shock, so prepare yourself. You've been unconscious for three days." He pauses, letting that sink in. "And those three days Mr. Blackwell and I have been trying to gather clues and search for your attacker: the Rogue."

Hanas rakes his bangs to one side, knitting his brow in frustration. "Yes, the Rogue of Vampires. He is a mysterious pureblood who has appeared only once before in our records. Several years ago, he murdered a family of vampires and vanished. Now, he is back and causing trouble in my province."

"And you can't find him?" Willow clarifies, hardly believing it. "Vampiric provinces are big, but they're usually ninety-eight percent forest. So they don't have *that* many hiding places, right?"

"You would be surprised," Mr. Hunter says.

Willow shivers at the thought of her attacker lurking behind any tree or bush, or maybe it's at the reality she has been plunged into. She is currently sitting in a bed in vampire lands, woken after three days, and watching her dad talk with a pureblood like the vampire won't kill or betray them later. "Anything else you'd like to add to this nightmare?"

"I am afraid so," Hanas replies grimly. "I spoke with some of my half-bloods, the ones you may recall who kidnapped you, and they say the Rogue has an accomplice of some sort."

"And," Mr. Hunter takes over, "if he has an accomplice, that means he has a plan." He stares at Willow pointedly.

"What? You think *I* know who the accomplice is?"

"Or perhaps the Rogue slipped when you were with him?" Hanas suggests. "Possibly gave away a clue as to what his plan is?"

"I don't—" She stops. Something tickles her mind. *No, there was something...* Then a single word drifts back, *revolution.* Willow frowns. *What was that even supposed to mean? What kind of revolution?*

Mr. Hunter leans in and Hanas' eyebrows shoot up in surprise. Hanas asks, "Do you recall something?"

"Yes…" Willow whispers. "I don't remember what he said exactly, just something about… a revolution?"

Hanas and Mr. Hunter exchange confused and worried looks. Mr. Hunter states the obvious. "That's not good."

"He said nothing else you recall?" Hanas checks.

Willow shakes her head slowly, bewildered by her own words.

"And you are absolutely positive that was the exact word?"

Willow glowers at him. "I speak English, don't I?"

Hanas shares a brief look with Mr. Hunter. "Apologies, I must notify the Vampiric Council." He strides briskly from the room without another word.

Willow unconsciously watches him go. She wishes, absentmindedly, she had remembered that word sooner, but she also wishes she hadn't remembered that uncomfortable and old-fashioned word: revolution. Clearly, the pureblood is trying to change something. Just thinking about it, Willow realizes the change could be many things. Does the Rogue want to change his own kind or humans? Peoples or government? Does he want to change something for the good of vampires or the good of humans? Willow guesses the first is more likely.

"Revolution…" Mr. Hunter murmurs, breaking Willow from her thoughts. He is having the same misgivings. He sighs and kneels beside Willow again. "Willow... I think you should know the seriousness of this. Although, you probably already understand part of it." He stares sadly at a purple bruise peeking from under her nightgown's sleeve. "If this pureblood wants revolution against *us,* things are going to get very dangerous very quickly. Even if he wants a fight with Mr. Blackwell alone, we may be pulled into it. And—" he raises his tone to cut off Willow, "not because we're indebted to him for saving your life. I want to help him of my own volition. Mr. Blackwell is... well... different. There are certain circumstances that give me a good reason to trust him. And I think you should too."

Willow's face twists in annoyance. She can't imagine what "certain circumstances" he means. Is there *ever* a good reason to trust a pureblood? "Dad, he's just a good-for-nothing bloodsucker!"

"He saved your life!" Mr. Hunter snaps. "I almost lost you, Willow." His voice cracks a little. "I don't know what I would have done if Hanas hadn't shown up. I'm not asking the world of you to trust a vampire—"

"A vampire killed Mom!" Willow barks back.

"I know!" he shouts. "I know that, Willow. Vampires have been tearing apart our family connection for years, but you can't let the words of others and the actions of one vampire force you to hate an entire race."

Willow angrily picks at the gold thread on her blanket.

Mr. Hunter sighs and pinches between his eyes. "Willow... I know what you're going through, but your attitude *needs* to change. Hating vampires isn't going to get you somewhere significant in life."

"Rei-Com Ashe hates vampires," Willow mumbles.

"And she's lost her entire family and still makes terrible choices because of it." He points out. "In a way, I lost my family, too, when I left home to become a Vampire Hunter. They told me I was walking into my own grave. Even your mother broke off with everyone but her sister. They told her she was insane to marry me and even more insane to live along the vampire border." He takes Willow's hand to earn her eyes again. "We have all suffered because of vampires, either emotionally or physically, but hating them and wanting to kill them won't get you anywhere. But trusting them when it's right, that will gain you a lot."

"And for you, that was six years of peace?" Willow asks, a bitter edge to her voice.

"Yes. I can't force you to trust Mr. Blackwell. But I think you would be wise to."

"I don't know…" she says.

"Think about it," Mr. Hunter recommends. "And let's hope this issue with the Rogue is small. But if it isn't, then you know what you need to do. Whether you like it or not."

Willow frowns up at the crimson drapery. "Yeah… sure."

Mr. Hunter stands and heaves another sigh. "I'm going to get an update from Mr. Blackwell's servants on your condition. I'll be back soon. Remember, think about it."

But as Mr. Hunter leaves the room, Willow finds it impossible to consider. Between her chilling memories of the Rogue, her current predicament, and a quiet voice rising inside her that says defeating a pureblood is impossible, Willow doesn't give the idea of working with *that Pureblood*—she decides to call him—any consideration. But then again, she doesn't have to. Willow already knows. *I will never help a pureblood.*

CHAPTER
SIX

A DAY later, the servants decide Willow is healthy enough to go home. Willow couldn't be happier. The past two days have been filled with short conversations between Willow and That Pureblood as he tries to keep her up to date on the Rogue. But there is never much to say. No new clues of the Rogue or his accomplice's whereabouts are found. It's as if he just vanished, exactly like he had after the murder That Pureblood mentioned.

But even stranger than the Rogue's disappearance, is Willow's waning enthusiasm. With every passing minute, she finds herself less and less energized by the thought of hunting a pureblood—much less a revolution involving them.

As Willow changes behind a divider, happily casting off the white frilly nightgown, a small, distant bubble of dread forms in her stomach. The attack with the Rogue has scared her more than she likes to admit. Willow finds herself extra jittery around vampires now, and an uncomfortable thought lingers at the back of her mind. If she continues initiate training with the V.H., there will be a day when she has to fight a pureblood. Willow isn't sure what she thinks of that, not anymore.

Tucking the nasty thought away, Willow gingerly pulls her black uniform over her head and shimmies into fresh combat pants and boots. The servant with odd colored eyes, who Willow learned is called Adabelle, told her she had mended the tears and washed out the bloody stains.

Willow walks around the edge of the divider and jumps. A small squeak of fright escapes her lips. She forgot that Adabelle was still present.

"I am sorry, Mistress Hunter, I did not mean to frighten you," Adabelle says with a small curtsey.

"No, it's fine," Willow replies awkwardly, massaging the ache from her arms. Adabelle is nice, timid, sweet, but Willow isn't sure how to interact with her. What's more, she's partially a vampire too. That single red eye reminds Willow of the half-bloods who kidnapped her, and what ensued shortly after. She finds herself avoiding Adabelle's gaze.

The servant smiles genuinely and raises a delicate arm toward the door. "Whenever you are ready, I will show you to main entrance. Master Hunter is waiting for you there."

Willow nods uncomfortably and follows Adabelle out the doors of the bedroom for the first time.

The rest of the manor is just as extravagant as the room Willow stayed in. They walk down a baroque hall with aging wood floors, ivory walls, and your occasional mahogany side table with either a vase of roses or an aging leather globe. They pass many doors leading to varying sitting rooms, guest rooms, and studies cluttered with objects older than Willow thinks That Pureblood is.

She remembers that wealth comes without a price for vampires. In her Intersentience class in high school, Willow learned that the vampiric economy works not by cash but by influence and the caste system.

A realization strikes Willow. *That Pureblood arrived at this province seven years ago. He didn't inherit it. And even though he killed the previous pureblood, the Vampiric Council didn't say that was illegal or they would have arrested him by now. So how did he get his hands on a province? And at such a young age?*

And where are his parents? Eighteen-year-old purebloods don't own provinces and waltz around without parents or guardians. *Something is definitely shady about him,* Willow decides.

Adabelle directs Willow to a grand staircase on their right. Her muscles and still-healing bruises ache with each step. She grips the polished, wood railing beside her, subtly leaning against it as she steps down. The fraction of weight taken off her muscles lessens the uncomfortable creaking sensation.

Adabelle keeps a steady pace with Willow, wringing her fingers as though she wants to offer help but worries it may come across as offensive. In this way, the two descend slowly.

As the walls pull away and the grand staircase curves into a larger room, Willow hears the murmur of quiet conversation. Of course, as the room spreads around her, she catches sight of the speakers: Mr. Hunter and That Pureblood. She is not thrilled over the latter. But her gaze on the two is stolen by the room itself.

The ceiling rests high above, and a massive bronze chandelier with shimmering glass orbs catches the light from two windows on the wall opposite Willow. As though to give a better opportunity to ogle at the monstrosity of lustrous wonder, a balcony, with entryways on either side of the second floor, curves around the outer perimeter of the room. The tall ivory walls are inlaid with the same framing designs from Willow's room. On the oak floors, elaborately embroidered carpets rest under velvety arm chairs, chaise lounges, and coffee tables—all ivory and lined in dark browns. Everything, down to the woodwork on the windows and the double-door entrance, is extravagant and purposeful in design and color. Willow may have zero artistic talent or sense, but she doesn't need any to know that interior decorators would go insane with envy in this room alone.

As Willow's boots reach the floor, her eyes reluctantly return to the two standing by the entrance. They converse with one another casually, but Mr. Hunter is doing most of the talking, which consists of many thank yous and promises Willow knows will only inflate That Pureblood's head.

Willow glares in disapproval, looking from one to the other. They both turn as she stiffly crosses the room with Adabelle and stops beside them.

That Pureblood smiles courteously. "You appear to be in good condition today."

"I wouldn't be going home if I wasn't," Willow replies sharply.

The two eye her in irritation, although That Pureblood conceals his well. Willow, despite the danger, carries a sense of pride over chipping away at That Pureblood's guise. Poking at a pureblood is a bad idea, but over the past few days, Willow found that exchanging those brief conversations made That Pureblood annoyed and caused him to leave quicker. She hopes he is getting the hint that she will *never* consider herself in debt to him. Maybe it's childish and rude, but Willow doesn't care. She already faced a cruel and demeaning pureblood once–she wasn't going to subject herself to that again or be forced to do his bidding just because he saved her life.

"Be polite, Willow," Mr. Hunter warns.

Willow looks away, content to judge the rich decor and suppressing shivers from the presence That Pureblood gives off.

"As I was saying before," Mr. Hunter continues. "Thank you again for your hospitality and kindness."

That Pureblood nods. "I only hope that we can find the Rogue before he causes more unpleasant experiences for either of us."

Mr. Hunter runs a hand over his bald head. "Yes. We will find that rogue, no matter what." With a quick look to Willow, as though hoping she will thank him too, Mr. Hunter continues, "Well… we better get back to our side of the border. I don't want Willow expending any extra energy."

That Pureblood steps aside and Adabelle skirts the group to open the front door. Mr. Hunter makes an *"after you"* motion to Willow, who is all too happy to leave the manor. With some final farewells, Mr. Hunter follows Willow out the door and into the warm and sunny clearing. A short way out is the forest circling the manor, beyond that is nothing but layers of tree trunks and a floor of twisting roots. The sight takes Willow by surprise, stopping her on the front porch. She already knew that Border Nobility tend to live in seclusion. Their followers, half-bloods, usually lived in small towns nearby. But even then, there are roads leading to those places or at least obvious paths through the forest. Here, there is nothing but forest caging the manor in. It's almost like Hanas wants to live completely alone and cut off from others.

"Everything alright?" Mr. Hunter asks, coming around to face her. His eyes linger on the part of her neck where the Rogue bit.

Willow subconsciously rubs it. "Yeah, I'm fine." She steps off the concrete slab, following Mr. Hunter to the forest and the border beyond. "It's just… I know you don't want to hear it, but something is off about that guy. I mean… where are his half-bloods? I don't see any trails to the towns. And we both know that purebloods don't rule provinces at—" She pauses, trying to do the mental math. *Ten times older than he looks… and he looks eighteen…*

"One-hundred and eighty," Mr. Hunter supplies, not sounding particularly concerned. "If you go by his physical appearance, which looks around seventeen or eighteen to me."

Willow doesn't miss his tone. "And you aren't concerned because…?"

"I told you, he has certain circumstances."

"Which are…?" Willow drawls.

Mr. Hunter peeks at her from the corner of his eye. A playful smile spreads under his mustache. "I can't tell you. If you want to know, you'll have to ask him yourself."

Willow rolls her eyes. "Daaad! I can't just straight out ask him! That's rude, since it seems personal, and I *don't* want to talk to him again."

Mr. Hunter brushes a low-hanging branch aside as they enter the forest. "You know, part of that initiate rank you want deals with vampire communications. There will be times when speaking directly with vampires is necessary."

That doubtful voice echoes in the back of her mind and fear of fighting a pureblood turns her hands clammy. "I'll cross that bridge when I get to it," Willow says, swallowing away her nerves. "Besides, what he doesn't know you shared won't hurt him."

"*That,* Willow Ashton Hunter, is how you get a pureblood to turn on you. I have spent the past seven years building a relationship of trust with Mr. Blackwell, and I won't destroy it for your curiosity." He eyes Willow, who trudges along beside him, twinging every so often from a particularly sharp ache. "Trust is something you should learn if you want to be an initiate."

The uncomfortable voice whispers again, but Willow waves it away. "I *do* trust people. Just not vampires. They don't deserve it."

"Not even when they save your life?" he says in warning.

"He *didn't save my life!*" Willow snaps, then flinches at the sharpness in her tone. "Sorry. Just forget it."

Mr. Hunter huffs. "Does that mean you've made up your mind about trusting and helping Mr. Blackwell?"

Willow nods. "Yes. I just can't do it."

Mr. Hunter sighs. "I hope you will change your mind."

"Don't count on it," Willow mumbles.

* * *

Thirty minutes later, Willow and Mr. Hunter near the border. The trees become sparse, the metallic V.H. fence, a few feet from the border, peeks between the trunks and greenery. Willow is all too happy at the sight of human land. The deathly silent forest is giving her the creeps.

"Finally!" Willow exclaims, but flinches and quiets her loud tone. "The border! You can cut this air with a knife it's so thickly silent."

Mr. Hunter smiles at Willow. "You'll get used to the quiet, one day." He pauses, then adds, "Are you still doing okay? We're almost there, but I can still carry you."

"No thanks," Willow says with a stiff smile. "I *really* don't need that humiliation."

Mr. Hunter gives her a pretend look of hurt.

Willow rolls her eyes, a smile tugging at her lips. "Like I said ten minutes before, and ten minutes before that, and ten minutes before that: I'm seventeen! I don't need to be carried like a baby."

"Alright, alright!" Mr. Hunter says, holding up his hands. "No carrying the big girl!"

"*Daaad!*"

"I'm just kidding," he reassures.

As the trees pull away and turn to fresh green grass, Willow and Mr. Hunter approach the north entrance of Foxhound. But before the gate rattles open, Willow spots a crowd huddled near The Automobile Garage. At the clinking of the fence, the crowd turns.

"She *lives*!" Eric yells, throwing his head back in a shout to the world.

They break into applause and cheers.

Willow stares in surprise. Her gaze sweeps the crowd of at least fifty Vampire Hunters of all different ranks. They clap, whistle, and cheer. Some jump, others holler greetings. Many of the V.H. are just acquaintances, which makes Willow wonder about all the enthusiasm.

"W-what is all this?" Willow breathes.

Mr. Hunter pats her shoulder. "Everyone was worried about you."

As the cheering continues and Mr. Hunter leads Willow into the crowd, she stares at each face in turn, completely mystified, until her eyes find a girl beaming through her tears. Willow's heart skips a beat and she pushes toward her. "Martha!"

Martha Heartwood, Willow's best friend since kindergarten, holds out her arms and hurries to Willow. The two meet halfway, locking in a tight embrace. The crowd breaks into a collective *"aww!"*

Martha lets go of Willow after a few minutes, tears dripping down her dark cheeks. "Eric told me *everything*. I was so worried! I don't know much about vampiric medicine, but my mom says it can be iffy."

Willow's gut lurches. Somehow, it never clicked that the medications used to heal her were created by vampires. She rubs the puncture mark on her neck uneasily. "Everything vampiric is iffy. But I guess it did the trick."

Martha nods her agreement, though she scans Willow up and down warily. Martha aspires to be a nurse, following the medical line like her mom. Knowing her friend well, Willow guesses that Martha is doing a mental checklist for any bad signs from the vampiric medication.

"Anyway," Willow says, hoping to take her friend's gaze away before she spots a huge bruise. "I'm sorry you were so worried. I hope Eric didn't milk the story."

"Don't be," Martha insists, shaking her head. "I'm glad he told me. I don't want to be left in the dark about my best friend."

"Alright everyone," Mr. Hunter interrupts, raising his hands for attention. "Thanks for the cheers, but I want Willow to get some rest."

The crowd reluctantly disperses, returning to their jobs. A few give last bits of congratulations before turning to leave. That makes Willow cock a brow. *Congratulations? For what? Surviving?*

Eric walks up to Willow, beaming. "Man, I'm so jealous of you! Taking on a full-grown pureblood and sending him running."

Oh... that's *why everyone was saying congratulations.*
Willow kicks at the grass, embarrassed and ashamed. "I didn't
fight him or send him running. As a matter of fact... I'm the one
who got pummeled and was trying to run."

"Oh..." is all Eric says.

"We've all had our fair beatings from purebloods," Mr.
Hunter says softly. "Don't be so hard on yourself."

Martha smiles. "You're alive and that's what counts."

It certainly doesn't feel that way to Willow. All those years
of saying how she wanted a fight, how she would win, and now
she got what she wanted... and lost. The realization rolls across
her mind, grey and heavy like a rumbling storm cloud.

Martha notices something is wrong. She opens her mouth to
say something, but Eric beats her to an attempt of lifting spirits.
"Hey, someone is waiting for you at your house! And she will
agree with me on your heroics wholeheartedly."

"Who—" Willow's freezes, not needing to finish the question. "No way... no way. I can't see her!" How did she forget
who she was coming back to? Maybe the vampiric medicine was
affecting her after all.

Mr. Hunter takes the lead, making an arm scooping motion
at Willow. "Come on. It won't be as horrible as you think."

Willow doubts that. How is she going to face Rei-Com Ashe
after having her rear end handed to her by a vampire? Rei-Com
Ashe is not only one of the three Region Commanders for Hidden
Hill, but is also the best Vampire Hunter in all of Maine—the
Chancellors' Directorate had awarded her themselves.

Willow is half-pushed, half-dragged home. That doesn't
help her aching limbs, but she is more focused on what Rei-Com
Ashe will say. Will she be disappointed? Mad? Maybe she'll
tell Willow that she doesn't have what it takes to be an initiate,
though Willow may heartily agree.

Once on the front porch, Martha and Eric bid their farewells.
They don't want to barge in on the conversation between father,
mentor, and pre-initiate.

Mr. Hunter and Willow enter their home. Holding her breath and dreading each moment, Willow follows Mr. Hunter down the hall and to the living room.

"Look who I brought!" Mr. Hunter announces, standing in the doorway.

Willow pauses beside Mr. Hunter, trying, and failing, to not hang her head in shame. Across the plush carpet sits a woman with legs crossed and arms spread across the back of the couch, somehow managing to take up the entire space with her singular frame. Her eyes lock on Willow, expression stern and calculating.

Willow shifts uncomfortably, fearing any wrong movement will make Rei-Com Ashe pounce like the cougar she so strongly resembles. Rei-Com Ashe adorns an '80s biker look. She's in her early thirties. Her hair is jet black and bushy with bangs cut straight across. Her lined, almond colored eyes slowly narrow at Willow, her berry painted lips ripening into a challenging smile. She stands up and folds her tattoo sleeved arms.

Willow opens and closes her mouth a few times before managing, "Rei-Com Ashe... I'm so sorry, I—"

"Hallelujah and pass the mashed potatoes!" Rei-Com Ashe shines her pearly white teeth. "There she is! My vampire-butt-kicking girl!"

Willow's insides do a backflip. She frowns, despite the surprise, and says, "I keep telling everyone, I didn't—"

"Nonsense!" Rei-Com Ashe hops over the coffee table, standing before her pre-initiate. "You didn't kill the pureblood, which is a shame, but you bet your hot latte that you lived to tell the tale! Not many can say that, girly. Besides, everybody takes at least one beating from a pureblood." She winks. "It's a sign of you becoming a true Hunter. Sheesh, girl stuff—didn't your dad tell you that?"

"Yes, but—"

"Then don't question it!"

"But—!"

Rei-Com Ashe gives her the evil eye.

Willow sighs in defeat. "Yes, ma'am."

"Atta, girl!"

"But seriously, I really didn't do anything! I didn't even touch him… the Rogue just chucked me around the room until he got hungry."

Rei-Com Ashe shrugs, unconcerned. "They say you've gotta feel the lowest of the low before you can shoot high. Understanding just how powerless you are compared to vampires is the first step to achieving what you need to defeat them."

Willow glowers at her boots, recalling the rush of fear at both the Rogue's and That Pureblood's presence alone. "I definitely felt powerless. Makes me wonder if killing purebloods is actually possible for me."

Rei-Com Ashe smirks and pats Willow's head. "When I was your age, I thought the same thing." She knits her brow. "Wow… that made me sound old. Look what you're making me say! No more pouting."

A little smile tugs at Willow's mouth, but it disappears quickly. That nasty thought returns, and this time it won't go away. *What if I can't fight purebloods?*

Rei-Com Ashe's brows shoot up and Mr. Hunter's worry lines appear.

"You're worse off than you look…" Rei-Com Ashe mumbles. She pats Willow's shoulder, accidently hitting the spot where Willow had been bitten. "Get some sleep, girl stuff, because…" Her voice goes an octave higher as she tries to get Willow excited. "When you get better, I'll teach you the tricks of fighting a pureblood. You won't be far from that initiate rank afterward!"

Willow shrugs half-heartedly. Mr. Hunter takes the cue. "Why don't you go change into some sweats? I'm going to update Rei-Com Ashe."

Willow nods and trudges toward the stairs. Being back at home, and not in the strange, almost fantasy world of vampires, reality slams down hard. Somehow, Willow will have to face what happened and overcome it.

But what if I can't?

CHAPTER
SEVEN

IT'S SATURDAY, the day when Willow should catch up on due homework. But her mind is far from worrying about late assignments. All she can think about is her future... and the Rogue.

He almost killed me, Willow thinks again, hardly believing it. *I couldn't fight. I couldn't do anything. I was just... useless.* She was a fool for thinking that fighting a pureblood, or any vampire, will go as planned.

A soft knock sounds at the door. Willow spins lethargically in her swivel chair, meeting her dad's gaze in the doorway.

"How are you doing?" he asks.

Willow shrugs and looks away.

Mr. Hunter seats himself on the bed, leaning forward to rest his elbows on his knees. "Are you still thinking over what happened?"

Willow turns her chair from side to side. "Yes," she whispers.

"Everyone of high rank has felt this before," he reminds her. "You're mad at yourself, a little scared, and in your case, you're angry with me, right?"

Willow's mouth tugs at the corner. "I still can't believe you let a pureblood save my life."

"I know. But he *is* our ally," Mr. Hunter says, fixing Willow with a serious look before continuing. "I just want you to know that what you're feeling is normal. You'll get through this–all Vampire Hunters do, so don't beat yourself up."

"I'll try."

"Good. Let's get started then!" He jumps up, startling Willow. "Rei-Com Ashe is waiting for you in the lecture room. She's going to start teaching you the ins and outs of Initiate level pureblood hunting."

Willow tries to not visibly cringe. Taking out a pureblood is not at the top of her list anymore. In fact, it's hard for Willow to imagine she ever wanted to. She feels weak, incapable, afraid. Before she can stop herself, the words slip out: "Do I have to?"

Mr. Hunter smiles sympathetically. "Yes, Willow, you do. The sooner you get this information after an attack, the better. It will boost your confidence, and help you if something like this ever happens again."

Willow swings a thumb over her shoulder. "But I have home-work."

"It can wait. I'm going against my word, but right now your Initiate training is more important than school work."

Willow sighs and pushes herself to her feet. "I wasn't getting much homework done, anyway."

"That's my girl," Mr. Hunter laughs. "Change into uniform. Your lesson starts in fifteen minutes."

* * *

"There's my vampire buttkicking girl!" Rei-Com Ashe announces as Willow sulks into the room. "How you feeling?"

"Same as before," Willow admits, pacing to the front row of padded chairs, then slumping into one at random. She had barely summoned the energy to pull her uniform on–how will she be able to retain any of this information if even getting dressed is ambitious?

"I'll spare you the 'we've all been there before' lecture," Rei-Com Ashe says, noting Willow's less-than-lively appearance. "I'm sure Rei-Com Hunter has already given you that."

"Yes, ma'am," Willow sighs.

Rei-Com Ashe cocks a brow, pursuing her lips. "You're a piece of work, aren't ya? Well, let's see if some instructions and overly detailed charts can fix that!" She spins around to face a smart screen, tapping its edge with two fingers. The lights dim and the screen changes from plain white to bullet-pointed text.

"Okay, girl stuff, you know the basics." Rei-Com Ashe turns toward the screen and scans it, reading quickly and half-heartedly through the list. "Vampires tend to follow an English/Victorian way of life and manners, their society is a monarchical oligarchy, watch their facial expressions, body language, and tone because they put on a lot of facades, yada, yada, yada. *But...*" She pivots on her heels, lips pulling into a challenging smirk. "What do you know about this deathly aura they emit—their *'presence'* as they call it?"

"It can be dangerous to be around," Willow replies automatically. "Especially if you have a weak heart or other similar medical problems since the aura causes fear, anxiety, stress, and strain. It's a natural ability all purebloods are born with, like a marker indicating that they're the top of the food chain, even though they aren't."

"You got it, girl stuff! But, it's also the downfall of a pureblood," Rei-Com Ashe says pridefully. "If you can feel your target pacing one room away, you'll be able to plan where you need to be for the fatal strike. What's more, you won't have to search a bunch for the target either. They'll be right there, sittin' like a duck roast."

Willow shifts in her seat, folding her arms. "That sounds great and all, but... what if I *can't* fight a pureblood? I never stood a chance against the Rogue—!"

"A-but-but!" Rei-Com Ashe holds up a finger. "I don't want to hear that. You're beaten, defeated, so what?" She turns up her palms. "You'll get back in the game, I promise. So…" she flips to the next slide. "You're facing a pureblood, tell me what you do."

Willow decides the answer "scream and run" is probably not what her mentor is looking for. Instead, she sighs heavily. "I keep calm and aim for the vitals."

"Which are…?"

"Center of the chest," Willow drones on. "But hitting the organ itself doesn't cause fatality so I have to hit the veins shooting off from the organ. Except those are pretty small, so I should aim for the vital veins near the neck or collar bone—Rei-Com Ashe, this feels really useless. Is this rehashing and tip-giving *really* going to help me?"

"Never debunk those small facts, girl stuff. They can save your life. Remember the basics, too. Now," she taps the screen, and it shows two figures, ready to attack, surrounded by a lot of text. "When facing a pureblood, speed and accuracy is always key. No one can outdo a vampire in swiftness, but if you assess the situation quickly and move equally fast, your chances of success strengthen. But what do you do when actually caught by the bloodsucker?"

Rei-Com Ashe flips to another slide. "You use these one-on-one combat tips! You remember that you should almost never run from your target, right?"

Willow nods. "Yes, ma'am."

"Well, that doesn't apply when physically caught by a pureblood. They're significantly stronger than us, annoyingly, so you have to run in order to succeed." She slips a glance from her peripheral vision, waiting for the question Willow already has on her tongue.

"But that doesn't make sense—um, ma'am. You can't run if they already have a grip on you."

"Exactly!" Rei-Com Ashe beams. "That's where the fun comes in. You have to twist yourself from their grip, slip right out from under them! It isn't easy, and ya don't always come out clean, but the look on their faces when you get away is *priceless!"*

A small part of the old Willow wakes with a gleeful bounce. She can almost see the look of bewilderment on the vampire's face. Or would they be furious because a "lowly human" escaped their hands? The spark is gone as quickly as it came, replaced by the image of the Rogue's pitying blue-gold eyes.

Rei-Com Ashe shifts her weight. "Almost got a reaction," she mumbles to herself. "You'll get to learn those things after tomorrow, because you first need some experience."

Willow doesn't like the sound of that. She tries to hide a grimace and loses her military etiquette in the process—not that it was strongly present before. "What kind of experience?"

A grin slowly spreads across Rei-Com Ashe's berry-colored lips. "Specialty one-on-one combat experience… across the border."

Willow's eyes go large. *"What?"*

"You heard me. Rei-Com Hunter somehow got permission for us to use the front half of Pasty Boy's province—you know, that Blackwell guy. I've got an idea for some realistic training. I'm going to hide somewhere and you have to find me and fight me. But don't expect me to hold back, either. You're gonna have to outwit me with technique."

Willow is suddenly very awake. Her mouth opens and closes a few times before she makes out, "Me? Go back across the border? But… no, no, no. The Rogue is still running around somewhere! And what if this is a trap? That Pureblood could have us surrounded and killed!"

Rei-Com Ashe snorts. "I said the same thing. But Rei-Com Hunter says Mr. Glossy Eyes won't pull that on us. They're gonna be busy having some important meeting on the province." She shrugs. "Besides, if any half-bloods do show, killing some bloodsuckers might be useful for your training."

Willow shakes her head, gut twisting in anxiety. "I don't think I can do this…"

Rei-Com Ashe saunters closer, putting a hand on Willow's shoulder. "This is a once-in-a-lifetime experience. How many other initiates can say they trained on vampire lands? C'mon, I know you're nervous, but you've got this!"

Willow bites her lip, images of the Rogue's sickly-sweet smile flashing in her mind. "I don't think I can... I just... I don't know."

Rei-Com Ashe winks at her. "Hey, don't sweat the details, girl stuff. Once you've done it, you'll be bragging to everyone you know. Plus, being across the border is good for you to adjust to. It's your work field as an initiate, right?"

Once again, Willow questions her choice of pursuing the initiate rank. A very miniscule part of her urges her forward, but the mass majority tells her to slink back and be content with the ensign rank.

"Are you scared of him?" Rei-Com Ashe asks abruptly, resting her fists on either hip.

Willow looks up. "What?"

"I said, are you scared of him? That pasty bloodsucker?"

Willow blinks and slowly shakes her head. He's uncomfortable to be around, that's for sure, but Willow isn't really *scared* of him so much as she's wary.

"Then what's there to worry about?" Rei-Com Ashe challenges. "So this rogue gave you a scare, showed you what a pureblood can really do. So what? If you can face Hanas Blackwell, you can face any pureblood." She shrugs one shoulder. "He's an average pureblood. The Rogue's a notch higher. We'll work you up there."

Willow chews her cheek. Rei-Com Ashe has a point—an annoyingly accurate point. She still isn't sure about all this, but her lips betray her. "Do you *really* think this will help?"

"Worth a shot."

That's not exactly the answer Willow is going for, but that's how Rei-Com Ashe is. She heaves a sigh. "Okay... let's do it."

* * *

The following evening, Willow shifts nervously by the north gate. She gazes through the chain-link fence at the forest gaping before her. *Am I really going to do this?* she thinks. In that moment, Willow doesn't know what she wouldn't give to be doing homework instead. *No!* she chides herself, scowling. *Remember what Rei-Com Ashe said? If you aren't scared of That Pureblood, then you don't have to be afraid of any pureblood!* Too bad those words aren't much comfort.

"Someone's excited." Rei-Com Ashe strides up, pausing beside Willow with a grin. "Look at you, getting here early!"

Excited is not the word Willow would choose—maybe horrified or anxious. Willow says, "I just want to get this over with."

Rei-Com Ashe gives Willow her signature half-smile. "Let's get going then, girl stuff—er, Pre-Initiate Girl Stuff. Gotta keep that military formality, yeah?" She flashes her commander logo, a piranha chewing an MP7, to the gate guard and the man in the guard box nods and presses a button. The chain-link fence shudders then begins to roll away with a warning of *chink, chink, chink-chink.*

Rei-Com Ashe leads the way through the gate and toward the forest's edge. They pause, staring at the thick of shrubbery, towering trees, and crisscrossing twigs. Willow feels for her Glocks, knowing they won't help much with BBs for ammunition, but feeling comforted by the weapon's familiar weight.

"Alright, so here's the mission," Rei-Com Ashe says, pulling a map from her back pocket. She unfolds it. "This is the area we've been given by Mr. Glossy Eyes. Memorize the parameters. You won't always have a map to study or the time to pull it out." She points to some sparsely located old buildings. "And these dots here are where ya might find me. It's your job to find me without *me* detecting *you*." She hands the map over to Willow and pulls out some ear pieces from her shirt pocket. "I'll be wearing these hearing amplifiers to make the mission realistic. After you find me, you have to take me out using that wit your mom gave ya." She winks and gives Willow an encouraging smile. "Got all that, Pre-Initiate?"

Willow nods. "Yes, ma'am!"

"Remember, no holding back. We're using BBs instead of real rounds, so I want you to go all out."

"Yes, ma'am!" She drops her eyes, scanning the map. "Ma'am, may I ask a question?"

"Sure."

"Are you really sure this is safe?"

"No."

Willow's attention shoots up and Rei-Com Ashe chuckles. She slaps her playfully on the back. "You've got this, Pre-Initiate. Alright! I'm headin' out. You have forty-five minutes to study that map and make a plan. When time's up…" she shows her teeth. "You better come find me, if ya can."

The minutes pass by faster than Willow likes. She studies the map, tries to bet where her mentor will hide, and think of a plan to sneak up and shoot her undetected.

But Willow's focus is elsewhere. Even with her Glocks as back-ups to her BB gun, in the event that a vampire shows, Willow still feels vulnerable. She still feels weak… afraid.

All too soon, her digital watch changes to o' five-hundred hours. With a deep breath to calm her tingling nerves, Willow folds the map and stuffs it in an empty compartment on her belt. Her best bet is to head northeast where a small cluster of abandoned buildings sit. It's the perfect place to hide with lots of cover and possibilities for an ambush.

"Here we go," Willow breathes. She crosses the border at a walk, chills tickling her spine, and soon proceeds into a steady jog. Foxhound slowly vanishes bit by bit between the yellowing greenery as the world of vampires expands around her.

Willow's ears fill with the rhythmic crunch of boots against the leafy floor. Her breath comes in steady and practiced. *You can do this. You can do this,* she reminds herself. *It's just like hunting practice with Rei-Com Dube. Only… across the border.*

The forest is as quiet as ever, making Willow wonders if anyone gets used to such eerie silence. In the least, the lack of forest life makes her job easier. Any snaps or rustles not caused by Willow can only be caused by one other being, a vampire. The more Willow progresses the more she realizes, to her immense relief, she is alone.

Something large looms through the trees ahead and Willow slows her pace. A new heavy silence weighs on her—but not a perfect silence. It is punctured with creaks and groans. She paces forward, unconsciously drawing her BB gun and eyeing the wrecked, abandoned homes in awe. Her mission turns to a distant buzz in the back of her mind.

Nature has taken over most of the area, showing signs of the struggle between humans and vampires many years ago. The land belonged to humans before they were attacked and driven out. Little is left to the imagination of what transpired among the shambled homes.

The gallant windows of the old colonial style residences are smashed in. The shutters on the windows hang crookedly or lay in mossy heaps at the home's base. On closer inspection, dried blood can be seen staining the white front columns, crumbling front doors, and white porches. On some structures, frighteningly large chunks of wall are missing. Oddities of the homes are strewn everywhere—crushed chairs, outdoor tools, and bonfire piles of what used to be dining tables.

As Willow paces among the homes, she can almost hear the screams of horror, the crackle of fire, the snapping of wood and smashing of windows.

A chill caresses her spine. She keeps moving, blocking out memories of the Rogue's searching voice and his fangs sinking deep into her neck. To Willow, this is more evidence of why vampires can't be trusted—why they are animals just waiting for the kill.

Okay, focus Willow, she thinks, realigning her thoughts. *You have a mission to carry out. Don't let this distract you.* She checks her watch's compact compass, adjusts her heading, and focuses on the task ahead.

The houses become more densely packed until Willow crouches at the edge of the small cluster. Rei-Com Ashe will be hiding nearby. She must be quiet, focused, stealthy. In order to win, she must find her target and initiate a surprise attack.

From behind a tree, Willow scans the old homes. Memories of the damage done to Hidden Hill six years ago threaten to resurface, but Willow shoves them down and forces her attention on the smallest of details. First, she must find fresh signs that someone is here. Her eyes scan the first house, taking in the chips in the wood, the glass shards littering the porch, the mosses and grasses sprouting from the porch and windows. When she finds no evidence of recent activity, she stalks closer to the home and peeks in the windows.

There is no sign of recent activity in the first home, which would be prominent in this case with the age of the house. Willow skips the second, since it's no more than a hill of rodent homes, and moves on to the third. She hunkers down in the tall grass, checking the home at a distance again. That's when her eyes catch it. The moss on the doorway is scuffed.

Willow smiles, a little of her old self slipping back once more. *Targeted location reached.* She scans the old grey building one more time, keeping a particularly keen eye on the second-floor windows, and begins her hunt.

One carefully placed foot at a time, Willow inches forward. She keeps her breathing slow and gentle, her heart steady and calm. In a minute, she's at the front porch.

Slow and easy, Willow reminds herself. *Test one board at a time.*

She lifts a boot and gingerly presses the farthest side of the first step. Rule number one in climbing old stairs: keep to the edges where possible creaking will be less noisy.

The first stair is safe, so Willow puts her full weight on it. She tries the second, then the third, and up she goes. Finally, she's reached the porch. She pauses by the door frame, pressing her back to it and sliding her head around the edge carefully. All clear. Willow enters and lets the old home swallow her.

Checking her surroundings again, she looks for details that may indicate someone is here. The ivy climbing up one wall is untouched, and some toppled couches sprouting the remains of mouse homes tell nothing. She studies some peeling wallpaper, eyes a few cobwebs lacing the stairs' railing, and examines the doorframe to the sitting room.

Willow bites her cheek in frustration. Rei-Com Ashe has left a hint to which home she's in, intentional or not, but any other signs of her don't exist. *I'll have to check the rooms one by one,* Willow grumbles to herself. *This will take a while.*

Creeeak.

Willow freezes, ears perked. The sound came from above somewhere. Someone had shifted their weight. Willow's smile returns and she silently heads for the stairs. Taking it one step at a time, Willow works her way up. She glances through the rails part way up, checking the three rooms in her immediate sight. There is nothing of importance, just some moldy beds, smashed lamps, and—Willow's heart misses a beat.

There, visible between the space of the floor and bed, protruding from a pile of stained brown bedding is a skeletal hand.

Willow's heart begins to pound. Her mind dives into a sea of memories. She sees her mom's pale corpse, motionless in its casket. She hears the cries of the restaurant staff falling prey to a half-blood. She sees the Rogue's dark figure lurching from the shadows.

Creeeak.

She whirls on the stairs, catching a glimpse of Rei-Com Ashe before losing her footing and plummeting back to the first floor.

"Curses!" Rei-Com Ashe growls, vaulting the railing and slamming down on the stairs.

CRACK!

She vanishes through the wood followed by a loud crash. Willow has just enough time to pick herself up and aim her BB gun as Rei-Com Ashe kicks open the cupboard door and stumbles out with her MP7 at the ready.

Willow spins around, looking for the Rogue, then fires as movement catches her attention.

PABAM! Miss.

She has no time for a second shot. A line of BBs splays toward her. Willow ducks and rolls to the right, then straightens up for another attempt. Her heart is now racing, her mind flashing in and out of her previous fight with the Rogue.

A figure surges around the corner, already firing at Willow. Sharp pangs explode on her shoulder and leg. She grits her teeth and bolts into a sitting room, diving behind an overturned coffee table. She steels her nerves, trying to force her memories of the Rogue from her mind. She jumps up, aims at the doorway and—

PABAM! PABAM! PABAM!

Two hits, one miss. But none hit the desired spot, the artery.

Willow ducks back behind the table, preparing to run as she scolds herself for not focusing. Another loud crack echoes through the room. Willow pops back up and nearly forgets to shoot. Her enemy has one foot stuck in the floorboards and is yanking it hard, but with no success.

PABAM!

The figure stops struggling and sighs. "Ya got me, Pre-Initiate. Right in the soft spot."

Willow blinks, confused at seeing Rei-Com Ashe with her foot stuck in the floor. She suddenly remembers that breathing is important, but her BB gun stays up. A groan sounds behind her and she whirls, firing into the wall thoughtlessly. Her hands tremble. *Nothing is there...where is he? Where is the Rogue? Where's—*

"Willow."

She snaps around, BB gun trained.

Rei-Com Ashe gives two more yanks before pausing her attempts to look at Willow. Her brow knits. "Hey, I said it's okay, girl stuff. You've won. No one is here but you and me."

Willow lowers her BB gun, chest heaving. Her heart pounds in her ears, but at least it slows now. *I did it…? I won…?*

Rei-Com Ashe eyes her. "Are you okay, girl stuff?"

It takes several moments for her words to register. "Um… yeah."

"Great! Help me out, will ya?"

Willow shifts forward unconsciously. She bends down and pulls at the wood, helping her mentor pull free. Reality slowly slips back as her mentor mutters something about dumb old houses.

"I won?" she whispers.

"Yeah," Rei-Com Ashe says, wiping some smeared blood off her forehead. "But not cleanly and you had some help… is this mine?" She checks herself, frowning.

"I messed up," Willow sighs. "I saw something and—"

"The memories came back?" Rei-Com Ashe guesses. "I thought they might. Which is why I chose this house. I was betting you'd see that skeleton, it'd trigger you, and you'd have to fight through a daze. But you feel better now, don't ya?"

Willow stares at a plant stalk growing in the corner. "I guess I kinda do…"

Rei-Com Ashe slaps her on the back. "Atta girl! See? I told you this would be good for you. We'll get that fear worked out of you, no problem!" She grins and Willow can't help but return it. A small amount of courage has leaked back into her.

"Now, let's get out of this place. Gives me the heebie-jeebies." She looks around with a scrunched nose. "And I'm bleeding from a few light scratches. Let's go before I attract something *really* nasty."

* * *

The hike back to the border is tiring in more ways than one. Mostly, Willow is exhausted mentally and physically, but there is also Rei-Com Ashe's lecture. She went into explaining Willow's lack of a plan, the missteps when she panicked, how she needs to stay calm even when she sees something horrifying, and how she must stand and fight when caught in one-on-one instead of running. They are all good tips, but Willow's heart still isn't completely in it. Instead, she focuses on how amazing ice will feel on her growing BB welts.

Those thoughts are obstructed when a strange noise vibrates her eardrums.

"… You're gonna see lots of unpleasant things on initiate missions," Rei-Com Ashe is saying. "So you have to learn to keep calm and—hey, are you listening to me?"

"Do you hear that?" Willow frowns, turning her head toward the low rumble.

Rei-Com Ashe pauses, listening. "Yeah… sounds like—but it shouldn't be…"

Willow glances to her and they both drop to a crouch.

"It shouldn't be anything too dangerous," Rei-Com Ashe decides, lowering her voice. "So this is good training for you. Let's go see what's up, yeah?"

Willow swallows nervously and nods. Her courage diminishes again, but a flicker of it stays—just enough to keep her going.

They pick their way toward the sound, eyes focused ahead and alert for movement. Her mind warns her of what could be waiting, probably vampires… or the Rogue. But Rei-Com Ashe isn't concerned, so maybe she shouldn't be either.

The rumble grows louder. Willow looks to Rei-Com Ashe for confirmation then reaches out and pushes a slumping branch aside. Her eyes go wide. Rei-Com Ashe huffs beside her.

"Thought so. It's just a car. Wonder whose it is, though…"

Sitting before them wasn't anything Willow would call *"just a car."* It's sleek black and styled like a Rolls Royce with silver hubcaps. Its engine hummed quietly, creating the strange noise Willow had heard moments before. Willow would have thought an old car to make a much louder and more jarring noise than the silk this machine emits. However, considering it was designed by creatures with sensitive hearing, its quiet engine isn't so odd after all.

Rei-Com Ashe shakes her head in disgust. "Let's move out, pre-initi—"

"When I lent part of my province to you, I said you may borrow it, not bleed all over it."

Willow practically jumps out of the shrubbery as that gaping trench presence wafts around her. Rei-Com Ashe just rolls her eyes and stands lethargically.

"And I came here to get work done, not have a tea party and a casual chat," she snaps.

That Pureblood, Hanas Blackwell, paces around the bend in the dirt road. He ignores her snarky response. "I stopped my car when I smelled fresh blood. I feared something was wrong because I was told the two of you were training on my land, not cutting each other up."

"It's none of your beeswax what we do for training," Rei-Com Ashe says.

Any formality That Pureblood tried to use with Rei-Com Ashe melts at her sharp words. "So you admit to it, you *were* slicing each other for training." He smiles mockingly. "Truly barbaric, Ms. Ashe—"

"HA! You call us barbaric? That's cute coming from a blood-sucker."

Willow's gaze flickers between the two like a tennis match. Even though she's annoyed that That Pureblood felt obligated to check on them like children, she knows a fight isn't a good idea right now… or ever.

"Why don't we all just stop arguing," Willow interjects. "And go our separate ways."

"Ms. Hunter is correct," That Pureblood agrees before Rei-Com Ashe can speak. "It is a petty argument and without a point." A little of his polite etiquette spreads back across his features. "Actually, I was hoping I might have a word."

Willow steps back without meaning to. "What do you want?"

"Nothing that will harm you, I promise," he says, clearly noting her jitters. "I spoke with your father moments ago and I think we both came to an intriguing idea."

"Get on with it!" Rei-Com Ashe says impatiently.

That Pureblood's eyes flicker red in irritation. "I will, if you would kindly keep quiet. As I was saying, we came to this idea that you may be exactly what we need to help track down the Rogue. Your father can give you the details, if you are interested. The main part of the job includes some spy work in my province. The task is much like this rank I hear you are trying to achieve… initiation, I believe he called it."

Willow's cheeks burn red, but she can't tell if it's from anger or embarrassment. Her dad went and told That Pureblood about her dream to become an initiate like she was a three-year-old wishing to be a princess. "It's called *initiate*. And, let me get this straight. You want a Vampire Hunter… running loose in your land… to spy on stuff you wouldn't normally want anyone to know?"

"I never said anything about running loose," That Pureblood clarifies. "And I do not believe you will get into anything secretive I would rather humans not know, but yes. We are at a loss for finding the Rogue and some new areas need thorough searching. Needless to say, I could use an extra pair of skilled eyes."

"I'm sure you have plenty of half-bloods for that," Willow counters, folding her arms.

That Pureblood shifts uneasily. "That is… part of the problem."

"Oh really?" Rei-Com Ashe pries.

That Pureblood gives her a level look. "Yes," he says simply before turning back to Willow. "What do you think?"

Willow's insides conflict for a moment. One part of her wants nothing to do with purebloods and nothing to do with the Rogue, but another part—that miniscule part of her that won the match with Rei-Com Ashe—says differently. This would be like an initiate mission, allowing her to cross the border and spy on vampires, where she can learn secrets and see the things some historians would kill to see. Maybe she will even discover why That Pureblood lives in seclusion. Plus, if she found clues leading up to the Rogue, she wouldn't have to fight him—she could leave that to the professionals.

But clue searching across the border would also mean working with a pureblood—a pureblood who may already think she owes him.

Willow wants to say no. She intends to. But her mouth betrays her. "I don't know. I'd have to think about it."

That Pureblood nods. "Think on it as much as you need. If you agree, let either myself or your father know. Now, I must hurry off, as should the two of you. It is getting late and nearing an unpleasant hour for humans to be found on this side of the border."

Willow glances up at the sky. Sure enough, the sun is beginning to set. When her eyes come back down, That Pureblood is already in his car. He smiles pleasantly and says, "Good evening," more to Willow than Rei-Com Ashe, then drives away.

CHAPTER
EIGHT

WILLOW FINDS that That Pureblood's words stir her mind more than she likes. All the way back to the border, Willow was unable to focus on Rei-Com Ashe's words—which partially included a miniature rant on That Pureblood. She couldn't figure out why her mouth decided to say she would think about it. She would *never* work with a pureblood, or any vampire for that matter. Yet the offer still intrigued her. As a result, the offer was all Willow seemed able to focus on, even as that day ended and the next began.

"Ms. Hunter?" A pair of blue scrubs shifts in front of Willow.

Willow blinks from her trance and looks up. A familiar nurse stands in front of her, smiling comically. "The doctor is ready to see you."

Willow blinks again as reality sets back in. "Oh! I'm sorry." She stands, remembering she has a check-up due today, which is why she's sitting in the hospital waiting room. Willow always thought it was odd that she had to go to a hospital for check-ups involving vampire wounds, even after Martha explained that it was because that expertise went beyond family doctors.

"Right this way." The nurse leads Willow through a large white door and down a hall. She gestures for her to take a seat inside an empty room. A moment before Willow can slip back into her mental tussle, a friendly face walks in with a warm, kind smile.

"And how are you, Ms. Willow?" Dr. Heartwood asks, closing the door behind her.

Willow isn't sure how to answer that question anymore, but she tries her best. "Well, physically, I'm still a bit sore. Mentally…? I honestly don't know."

Dr. Heartwood writes something down on her clipboard. "Healing from a vampire attack isn't always just physical," she says in her clear, motherly voice. "Make sure you take care of yourself up here, too." She taps her head. "Now, is your bruising getting better? Worse?"

"Better," Willow says. "My bite mark doesn't bother me much either. It's almost gone, if you can believe that." She tugs on the collar of her shirt, showing it to Dr. Heartwood.

Dr. Heartwood walks closer, feeling the mark and examining it. Her eyes widen a little and she takes notes on her clipboard again. "That vampiric medicine you took is no joke. I don't think I've ever seen a wound heal so fast. Which leaves me to ask, do you have any abnormal symptoms? Cravings? Pains? Heightened senses?"

Willow shakes her head.

Dr. Heartwood takes more notes. She listens to Willow's heart, then lungs, then checks her blood pressure and shines a light in her eyes. "Well, your father will be happy to hear that you're perfectly healthy! I'm still not seeing any signs of vampiric poisoning. Your blood tests came back normal, too."

Willow smiles a little. "Always good to know I'm not turning into a black-blood."

Dr. Heartwood leans against the small counter space. Her soft brown eyes fix on Willow as she smiles gratefully. "That it is. I'll tell you the truth, Willow, I was ready to pack some medical supplies and march right across that border when I heard what happened. I don't trust vampiric medicine."

"Martha said the same thing. She checked me from head to toe when I came back."

Dr. Heartwood beams. "That's my girl. She kept pacing around the house after we heard you were attacked. I told her, 'Child, you're wearing a path into the carpet!' She finally sat down after that."

Willow chuckles. She can picture it perfectly. Ever since they were young, Martha would always pace around when she was nervous or anxious. Once, she told Willow that one of the worst parts of the attack six years ago was that she couldn't pace around to calm herself. She had to stay hidden during the attack and close to her parents afterwards.

"Sounds like Martha to me, although Eric apparently went over the top about what *actually* happened. He had all of Foxhound thinking I'd bested my first pureblood." The words sting her chest as she says them. *Too bad I can never beat a pureblood.*

But you won against Rei-Com Ashe yesterday! another voice counters.

Out of sheer luck.

Willow tries to not let her disappointment show. But that's pretty hard to do since Dr. Heartwood is like a second mom to Willow.

"You're going through a lot," she observes with a gentle smile. "Don't push yourself or you'll come back to me sick from stress."

Willow manages a smile. "I'll figure it out."

Dr. Heartwood rests one hand in her coat pocket. "Alright, that should do it for now. I'd love to chat, but I have other patients. It's good to see you again, Willow."

"You too." She stands as Dr. Heartwood opens the door.

"If anything happens or you feel strange, come straight here. And if it's not a medical emergency, you know my number." She gives Willow an encouraging grin.

Willow nods. "I will. Thanks again, Dr. Heartwood."

But as Willow heads back down the hall, her mind slides back into twisting thoughts and feelings.

* * *

"I'm home!" Willow announces. Her day at school had been just like her doctor visit that morning: full of people telling her to "hang in there" and saying they were happy to see her again. Meanwhile, her brain would go through loops of, *I can't work with the creatures that killed Mom!* and *But this goes beyond that, it's like your first initiate mission!* during class.

"Hello! I'm in the office," Mr. Hunter calls.

Willow kicks off her shoes and heads down the hall, swinging around the corner into his double-door office. "Hey," she says a little breathlessly. The day had really taken the energy from her.

Mr. Hunter looks up from his laptop and smiles. "Hey, Wills. I heard from Dr. Heartwood this morning. She says you're healthy as a horse! Not in those words, but you get what I mean."

"Yeah. So, I can stop going for visits until something is actually wrong, right?"

Mr. Hunter goes back to his work, frowning a little. "Vampiric medicine isn't completely safe, Willow. You'll go as many times as Dr. Heartwood feels is necessary."

Willow frowns and leans against the doorframe. "It's such a hassle. I almost wish That Pureblood didn't use any medicine."

"You mean Mr. Blackwell?" he clarifies and corrects her. "You should be grateful. That medicine is what helped you bounce back so quickly. You might still be across the border without it." He pauses, typing something, then continues. "By the way, Mr. Blackwell and I were discussing something during our meeting yester—"

"He already told me about it," Willow interrupts him. When he looks up at her in surprise, she leaves her backpack by the door and drops into a chair in front of his desk. "We ran into him yesterday on our way back to the border."

"Is that why you look more lost in thought than usual?" Mr. Hunter asks. "I thought you were still upset over initiate training."

"I still don't know what to think of initiate training," Willow admits. "But I also don't know what to think about this offer. I mean… I want to say no. But I somehow ended up saying I'd think about it instead!" Willow puts her hands on her face and pulls them down, stretching her skin.

Mr. Hunter stifles a laugh. "You'll look like me if you keep doing that: wrinkly and old."

Willow ignores the comment, deciding she has no energy to figure out a response.

"I can't tell you what to decide," Mr. Hunter sighs, leaning back in his leather office chair. "But I can tell you what I think would be a wise choice. You already know that spiel, though."

"I want to help," Willow says, staring at the pile of papers on Mr. Hunter's desk. "But I can't work with That Pureblood. And I don't know if I can handle being across the border, not yet anyway."

"I understand," Mr. Hunter says solemnly. "Well, in the meantime, you could help me with some work that Mr. Blackwell and I have split. You wouldn't technically be working *with* him, but it would still help us with uncovering the Rogue's whereabouts."

Willow eyes him. "What sort of work?"

"Desk work," Mr. Hunter clarifies. "I know it's not your favorite, but field work is saved for if you accept Mr. Blackwell's offer. You also won't be let in on a few details because you haven't agreed to join us."

Willow chews her cheek. Desk work is mind-numbingly boring, but field work doesn't sound appealing, either. She shrugs. "What's there to lose? I'll help, I guess."

Mr. Hunter smiles. "Maybe we're finally getting somewhere…"

"Don't count on it."

He laughs and spins in his chair, unlocking a metal safe behind him. He pulls out a tan folder with a stack of ivory paper inside and hands it to Willow. "These are all written accounts from Mr. Blackwell's half-bloods. Most of them saw strange activity from an unknown person that we think is the Rogue's accomplice."

"So we're searching for his accomplice now?" Willow asks skeptically.

Mr. Hunter sighs. "We can't find the Rogue, so this is our next best bet, and we would have to track down his accomplice sooner or later."

"That's simple enough," Willow decides, flipping open the folder to glance at the different scrawlings. "We'll have the accomplice pretty quick, then he can spill whatever he knows!"

"Not so fast," Mr. Hunter warns. "If it were that easy, Mr. Blackwell would have gone through those papers himself and apprehended the crook. You see…" he pauses, choosing his next words carefully. "Mr. Blackwell's half-bloods all have different stories and different descriptions, and when I say different, I mean *very* different. You're going to have to find which stories and descriptions are most common and hope those descriptions are correct."

"Okay, so that complicates things more. Still, it's not a huge deal," Willow objects.

Mr. Hunter's features crinkle in an expression Willow can't read. "You'll understand soon."

Willow cocks a brow. "Okaaay. On that ominous note, I'm going to drop my bag off upstairs and shower. You cooking dinner or am I fending for myself?"

Mr. Hunter turns back to his work. "I think there are leftovers in the fridge and a few things in the cabinets."

"Cool." Willow turns to leave, taking the folder with her. She glances at her dad from the corner of her eye before grabbing her backpack. His face is now drawn into a wary, tired expression.

Willow hefts her backpack onto her shoulder and heads upstairs, vowing to murder the Rogue for sucking the life from her dad, too.

* * *

Tuesday comes in like a second Monday. Willow reluctantly wakes after a long night of assignments, both late and due, and sifting through accounts on the Rogue's accomplice. She spends the day in classes that make her eyelids lull and is less than thrilled to find she has more initiate training when she gets home. To top it off, her dad has both asked and ordered her to an important meeting that night.

Willow's body slams against the blue mat. Rei-Com Ashe stands, huffing a little, and paces back a step or two. "Again," she orders.

Willow puts her hands on her face, biting back a groan of agony. She had been trying to break from Rei-Com Ashe's grip for the past two hours. She has little energy or motivation to better herself in one-on-one vampire combat.

"C'mon," Rei-Com Ashe urges. "The sooner ya understand this, the sooner I can go home and feed Jerome."

Willow pushes herself up, limbs aching and throbbing. "Your pet piranha is going to starve. I just can't do this!"

"You want to be an initiate, don't ya?" Rei-Com Ashe counters, her tattooed muscles bulging as she puts her fists on her hips.

Willow is really starting to hate that question, along with *How are you feeling?* "I don't know anymore, okay? I seriously just don't!" She rips her hair from its messy bun and begins to tie it up again.

"You're frustrated, I get ya. This will all be worth it, though, I promise."

"It better be," Willow growls, finishing her hair. She still feels that she can't back out of her initiate training. The small win against Rei-Com Ashe stops her every time, yet she can't imagine anything more frightening than having to fight a pure-blood again.

Willow stands and faces Rei-Com Ashe, tugging down the bottom edge of her black tank-top and taking a deep breath.

Rei-Com Ashe grabs Willow's left shoulder with one hand and her right wrist with the other. "Here goes again."

Willow twists her wrist and drops down, but Rei-Com Ashe squeezes her pressure point and keeps a firm grip on her dominant hand. She follows Willow down, slamming her against the mat. Willow pulls her knees up and jabs one into her commander's stomach. Rei-Com Ashe's grip loosens and Willow yanks a hand free. She clamps it onto Rei-Com Ashe's neck, pressing where it won't hurt a human but will create something similar to suffocation for vampires.

Rei-Com Ashe smirks proudly as she loosens her grip on Willow's shoulder. "Atta girl! Just like I taught ya."

Willow kicks Rei-Com Ashe in the side, dumping her off. She quickly darts the opposite direction to gain space, but Rei-Com Ashe snatches her ankle and she face plants. Within seconds, Willow is pinned again, but this time she can't move at all.

Rei-Com Ashe stands again and wipes the sweat beading on her forehead. "You're gettin' there."

Willow just lies on the mat and stares up at the metal beams the light fixtures hang from. She feels like she is no closer to breaking from Rei-Com Ashe's grip than when they first started.

"That's enough for today," Rei-Com Ashe decides, walking to the edge of the mat. "You'll get the hang of it. We'll just keep working at it. Before ya know it, you'll be on to the next grip hold!"

Willow's head lulls to the side. "You mean there is more than *one*?"

"Course!" Rei-Com Ashe says, sitting down to lace up her boots. "There is more than one way to put someone in a lock, isn't there?"

Willow decides she isn't getting up; she has no motivation to.

Rei-Com Ashe chuckles when she turns to see Willow spread eagle where she left her. "Up and at 'em, Pre-Initiate! You've got a meeting with Rei-Com Hunter and Mr. Sparkle Eyes."

"Don't remind me," Willow begs, pushing herself up and crawling to the edge of the mat where her boots sit.

"He's not exactly a package of fun," Rei-Com Ashe sympathizes.

"And he's a vampire," Willow adds.

"Yeah, but you agreed to search through his half-blood notes. Of course you gotta report your findings to the two of them..." she frowns. "Wish I didn't have to refer to them together."

"They're so chummy," Willow agrees, tugging her laces harder than needed.

"Hey, I got my eye on that pureblood," Rei-Com Ashe assures, folding her arms. "I won't let one destroy your family again."

Willow decides to not remind Rei-Com Ashe that it hadn't been a pureblood's fault her mom died, it was his half-blood's, but right then, she doesn't care. She just wants the day to be over.

"You finished scoping out those reports pretty fast," Rei-Com Ashe says. "Weren't there at least two hundred of them?"

"Yeah, but some of them were just a few sentences long." She stands, slipping her grey, collared top on. "Plus, the sooner we find the Rogue's accomplice, the sooner we can stop the Rogue." She buttons up her shirt and tucks it into her pants.

"I hear ya there. Freaky bloodsucker."

Willow stands at attention. "Permission to be dismissed, ma'am."

"Granted. Get your butt outta here." Rei-Com Ashe smiles, giving Willow a playful push. "Have fun tonight!" she calls as Willow leaves.

"Tell Jerome I said hi," Willow calls back, then she pushes open the door and steps into the night.

* * *

When Willow approaches the Strategy House, she finds her dad waiting outside. He stares up at the dark sky, the moon covered by thick clouds. Worry sets in. Willow hasn't seen him stare off like that since her mom died. Was the Rogue really starting to bother him that much?

"Hey." Willow stops in front of him. "What are you looking at?"

He slowly turns his gaze down on Willow. "Nothing. Just thinking."

"About the Rogue?"

"I don't like how things are turning out," he says vaguely.

Willow cocks a brow, glancing down the paved road like there might be an answer somewhere out there. "What do you mean? Nothing has happened lately. It's, well, back to normal."

Mr. Hunter shakes his head and a cool wind buffets the two of them. It smells of an oncoming storm, of rain. Willow shudders as Mr. Hunter murmurs, "I don't like how this is all adding up. Something is happening, whether we see it or not."

Mr. Hunter has put some pieces together that Willow has not. She is about to ask for more clarity when that gaping pit presence lurks near. She glances over her shoulder to see three figures appear on the road. That Pureblood is flanked by two ensign Vampire Hunters, both with standard AR15s at the ready. When they near, Mr. Hunter smiles apologetically.

"Sorry about the escort, Mr. Blackwell. It's for your own safety, even though you probably don't feel like it is."

That Pureblood smiles politely. "I understand the need, Mr. Hunter." He turns to Willow and nods. "Evening, Ms. Hunter."

Willow gives him a one up and eyes his excessively warm-looking, black wool jacket before saying, "Hey."

Mr. Hunter tries to hide a smile, pleased by the small exchange, and jerks his head toward the two-story, square building beside them. "Let's get started on Willow's findings. She'll probably need to get home soon after a long night going through them all."

"Yes," That Pureblood agrees. "I was not only surprised to hear you were willing to work with my documents, but also shocked at how quickly you worked through them."

Willow shrugs and shoulders past them into the building. "Yeah, well, I work quickly when I'm extra focused."

Mr. Hunter orders the two ensigns to stay by the entrance then gestures for That Pureblood to go in first before he follows suit.

The three of them enter a square room with a square table at its center. The table itself is covered in layers of topography and road maps, strewn pins, markers, red string, and pressed-open books on general vampire-related knowledge. The walls are covered in dusty bookshelves that hold cups of more markers and pens, stacks of newspapers, piles of old and new maps, askew books on everything from vampire psychology to Vampire Hunter tactics, a few guns, some spare ammunition, and lots of other junk. All of it makes Willow eager to write out plans of espionage… until the crooked smile of the Rogue flashes in her mind.

Willow pauses at the far end of the table and Mr. Hunter stands across from her. That Pureblood takes the side between the two, glancing at an open book on vampiric economy. He smiles comically before turning his gaze away.

"Sorry, it's cramped in here," Mr. Hunter apologizes, brushing some pins aside. "But we won't be bothered in here and we have anything we might need."

That Pureblood nods in understanding. "I am sure it is better suited than any place I can offer."

Mr. Hunter gestures to Willow. "Alright, what do you have for us?"

Willow slips a slightly crumpled piece of paper from her pocket and unfolds it. She lays it in front of That Pureblood. "A lot of the descriptions were vague, but these are the recurring features for this accomplice. Short or medium height, male, chin-length hair, and either blond or brunet."

Hanas picks up the paper, scanning it. He shakes his head and hands it to Mr. Hunter. "No one in my province matches this description."

Willow frowns. "Well, maybe the accomplice isn't one of your half-bloods."

"No," Mr. Hunter sighs, the worry lines returning to his features. "We are positive the accomplice is one of Mr. Blackwell's half-bloods." He turns his attention to Hanas. "You're sure this isn't even remotely close to anyone in your province?" When That Pureblood assures him, Mr. Hunter sighs like he's eighty years old. "Another dead end, which is what I was afraid of."

Willow's eyes flicker between the two of them. "Why are you so sure the accomplice is one of your half-bloods?"

"That information is classified," That Pureblood states. His glassy eyes fix on Willow. "Unless you agree to assist Mr. Hunter and myself."

Willow crosses her arms in defiance, returning That Pureblood's level gaze. "I can't. Not right now."

"Then you can go back over the accounts again," Mr. Hunter says as he tosses the paper back to Willow.

She stares at him. "What? Why? The same common features will just come up again."

That Pureblood rests his hands on the table, studying a road map of his province before it became vampire land. "You can probably pull out some more minor details from those accounts. However, there *are* other less dull tasks you could be doing. But you must be willing to work with us first."

Willow glares at him. Mr. Hunter must have told him how much she hates desk work. "Are you trying to back me into a corner?"

He looks up, a small smile tugging at his pale lips.

Willow knits her brow and shoots a look at her dad. *Do something about this!* she silently pleads. *He can't push us— me—around!*

Mr. Hunter just watches and says nothing helpful. "You did promise to think about helping us."

Willow can't believe what she's hearing. She wants to slam her findings on the table and storm out, but what good will that do? It's not very professional, either. She struggles to keep her voice calm as she says, "Why is this such a big secret? Is it *really* so a big deal that you can't tell me anything unless I work with you? I'm a Vampire Hunter, for Pete's sake! I'm sworn to keep this stuff secret from the public if need be! *Why can't you just tell me?*"

That Pureblood glances to Mr. Hunter who stares back silently.

Willow glares at the two of them. How can she do her job if they won't give her crucial information? They set her up, and Willow knows it. She hates every inch this charade, but she feels that small voice urging her forward—the voice that won against Rei-Com Ashe and pleads her to be the initiate she dreams of.

Willow huffs, eyeing the worry lines creasing her dad's brow, and makes her decision. *I'll do it for you, Dad, to get rid of whatever is sucking away your energy.* She drops her eyes to the collection of black and red markers in front of her. "Fine. I'll… help you. But I want answers here and now!"

Mr. Hunter smiles proudly as That Pureblood says, "Your assistance is much needed and appreciated, Ms. Hunter."

"Just Willow," she grumbles. "I'm not an old woman. And don't think too deeply about me helping, got it? I don't have a choice and you two bullied me into it."

That Pureblood nods. "Using 'miss' shows equality in my culture, but if it offends you, then I will call you whatever you please."

Willow averts her eyes from him, not even attempting to form a response to that.

"I don't know about, 'bullied,'" Mr. Hunter muses. "But I am glad you're helping, Willow. Mr. Blackwell isn't just being polite when he says we need your help."

"So," Willow sighs, feeling increasingly uncomfortable and irritable. "Answers?"

"To address your previous question," That Pureblood begins reluctantly, "we are certain the accomplice is among my half-bloods because they have all been acting... well, odd." He pauses, looking ashamed.

"I'm listening."

"His half-bloods won't give him clear answers." Mr. Hunter takes over, "even when he commands them, which we both know isn't something half-bloods can refuse easily. They just won't talk. They only give us vague pieces of information, like the accounts I asked you to look through. Believe me, Willow, I've seen it myself. These half-bloods know something, but they won't share it with Mr. Blackwell or even me."

Willow narrows her eyes. "So, they're dodging the question, big deal. The accomplice probably threatened them into silence."

"It is not that simple," That Pureblood says, tone deepening in remorse. "Half-bloods are... a different kind of entity. They are loyal to their master and are not easily swayed. For them to withhold information from me means..." He trails off as if the realization has just struck him.

"It means you're not in control of them," Willow finishes. Mr. Hunter shoots her another warning look and she clamps her mouth shut.

That Pureblood clears his throat, attempting to regain his composure. "The accomplice must be someone they know. Half-bloods will guard other half-bloods' secrets to the grave, at times, especially when it is something big."

"Like a revolution," Willow says, recalling the odd word. It gives their modern air an unsettling vibe.

Hanas doesn't respond, contemplating her very real suggestion.

Mr. Hunter leans forward on the table, staring intently at the map of Hidden Hill. The worry has drawn itself fresh on his face. His expression slowly makes more sense to Willow as she puts the pieces together. *If the Rogue is starting some kind of revolution… and the half-bloods are in on it… and no one can control them…* After a few seconds, she voices the fear they're all thinking.

"Hold on, if what you're saying is the case, then there isn't much stopping the half-bloods from attacking us." She finds herself looking to That Pureblood, her anger melting away and then bubbling up, double fold, at the horrible realization. "That's why those half-bloods were able to cross the border and kidnap me… you can't control them anymore…"

"Willow…" Mr. Hunter warns.

"You can't control them, so there was nothing stopping them from running into Hidden Hill! They brought me like some humiliating sacrifice to the Rogue—I almost *died*—and now my life is a confusing mess, and now we have some crazy revolution on the horizon, all because you can't control a lousy bunch of half-bloods? Or were you ever able to control them in the first place?"

"I was never meant to rule half-bloods!" he snaps, and Willow knows she's hit a nerve. That Pureblood locks her under his now fiercely sharp eyes. "You and that accursed Region Commander sneer at whatever I say and do, yet you have never once sat at the head of a province to dictate what is and is not simple. Tell me, how can you easily blame me for something you cannot accomplish yourself?"

Willow steps back in surprise, her hand clamping on her Glock.

"Willow," Mr. Hunter warns again, eyeing her hand and then looking to That Pureblood. "Let's all calm down."

But That Pureblood plunges on, and it's all Willow can do to not make the situation worse by whipping out her Glock.

"You think this is a game of mine?" Hanas shouts. "That I want my half-bloods to be slinking away from me? Just like you, I am not safe until this Rogue is found. At any given second my half-bloods could turn against *me*! And unlike you, I cannot retreat farther into my race's land if they overrun me! I live here and I may very well die here if this Rogue is not stopped!" He suddenly comes to an abrupt halt and blinks, realizing he'd been advancing on Willow.

That Pureblood slowly backs away and pinches between his eyes. "Apologies," he says hardly louder than a whisper. "I should not have lost control like that."

Mr. Hunter gives Willow an accusing frown before saying, "You're stressed, Mr. Blackwell. Don't worry about it."

Willow looks everywhere except at That Pureblood and Mr. Hunter, connecting pieces of information. *He can't run farther into vampire land? Why not? Is he a criminal? Is he sentenced to run a province as jail time or something? And if he is afraid of being overrun by his half-bloods...* she can't finish the thought.

"I'm sorry," Willow breathes unconsciously. She didn't even stop to consider his feelings. In fact, Willow never considered vampires to have feelings or be under stress. They always seem so cunning, so calculating, that they never need to worry or stress.

"I think we're all under a lot of pressure," Mr. Hunter concludes, making an *all clear* sign at his side. Willow notices the ensigns in the shadowy entrance for the first time. They slip back outside. "Why don't we conclude here for tonight and search for new clues in the morning?"

That Pureblood nods. "I think I need to get away from my dead-end office work. I will check up on the half-bloods tomorrow and see what I can find."

"You should go with him," Mr. Hunter says. It takes Willow a few heartbeats to realize he means her.

"What? Me?"

"You said you'd work with us, so you start tomorrow. Go start your first unofficial initiate mission." He smiles encouragingly.

"But I have school tomorrow," Willow says, wondering why that has become her new countermeasure. Plus, if That Pureblood blew up on her deep in his province…

Willow quickly dismisses the thought.

"You can head over to Mr. Blackwell's place after school," Mr. Hunter says. "Would that work for you, Mr. Blackwell? About five-thirty or six pm?"

He straightens himself and nods slightly. "Yes, that will work. And I promise I will not yell at you," he adds to Willow. "Apologies, I am not sure what came over me."

Willow chews her cheek, not liking how this is turning out at all. "Is it… you know… safe? I mean, not to bring the subject up again, but…"

"There are certain dangers," That Pureblood confirms. "But I will be there in the event anything does happen."

"Comforting," Willow says sarcastically, although not meaning to sound rude.

"I am glad you think so."

Willow can't tell if he's being sarcastic or didn't understand her own sarcasm.

"Alright, I'll send her over after she changes into uniform tomorrow," Mr. Hunter decides before Willow can object. "Follow me, Mr. Blackwell. The ensigns will escort you back to the border."

Willow silently trails the two outside where they say final goodbyes before heading home for the night. As That Pureblood is led back across Foxhound, Willow catches her dad staring up at the cloudy, night sky again. A soft rumble echoes in the distance and Mr. Hunter ushers Willow home with remarks of being caught in the rain.

Something really big was coming, and it wasn't just a physical storm. Willow could feel it now too, the oncoming dread of what was to come. But, at least for the evening, all Willow can do is accept her fate.

CHAPTER
NINE

"*KRRSH,* COME in Willow, over."

Willow blinks and turns to Eric. His hands are cupped over his mouth to make walkie-talkie noises. "What?"

"I asked why you weren't eating your pizza," Eric says. "Is it that bad?"

"I'm just not hungry." She is still exhausted from yesterday, and by the bleary-eyed look Mr. Hunter had, her dad wasn't feeling any better. She spent most of her walk to school thinking about that… and the Rogue… and the revolution… and her information search with That Pureblood later on.

She pushes away the cafeteria pizza. A few students stare at her and whisper uneasily, but Willow tries to ignore it. Some of the huge worry warts fear she'll turn into a vampire because she was attacked. Willow wishes they would understand that that's just not how it works. Vampiric poisoning is deliberate, and the Rogue *definitely* hadn't been planning on letting her live as a vampire or a human.

"You've been zoning out a lot lately," Martha observes. She leans closer, her whisper barely audible over the high school cafeteria racket. "Should I call my mom?"

"No," Willow says. She had been zoning out all day, lost in thought and just plain tired. It wasn't anything to worry about. "I've just got a lot on my plate."

"You do?" Eric eyes her plate jokingly.

Willow gives him a look. "You know what I mean."

Martha takes a bite of her carrot, still studying Willow carefully. "Are you trying to track down the vampires that kidnapped you? Is that why you're spacing out?"

Willow glances around, catching some more kids whispering. "I'm not allowed to say what I'm doing. It's Vampire Hunters only," she apologizes. "But... my dad has been acting spacey lately."

"Fatigue from overwork?" Martha guesses.

"I think he's worried about something, but I'm not really sure what." She leans in and whispers, "He hasn't acted like this since mom died."

Martha chews thoughtfully on her sandwich.

Eric shifts his tray around. "That's not good," he mumbles to himself.

After a moment, Martha says, "You should do something to cheer him up. Maybe make him something he likes for dinner or something along those lines."

Willow sighs. "Can't. I've got work right after school."

Eric gives her a sympathetic look. "More initiate training?" He shakes his head. "I don't know why you want such a crazy rank."

"I don't have initiate training tonight. Not officially, anyway. Again, sorry, but I can't tell you what I'm doing."

"Don't apologize," Martha says with an understanding smile. "It's your job. There are things we can't know as the general public."

"Hey, I'm not the general public," Eric reminds them.

Willow smiles at Eric's pride, admiring it for the first time. Once, she was proud to be a pre-initiate, but that felt like a long time ago. "It's still classified," she says, spinning her cup on the table.

"Well, keep us updated as much as possible," Martha says after taking a drink of water. "And if you need some time away from whatever is happening, just call me. We can have a sleepover and a rematch of *Operation Surgery*. My hands have gotten steadier." She tilts her chin up proudly.

Willow smiles, reminiscing the late-night tournaments and little zaps to her fingers. "I'll keep that in mind."

As Eric launches into some rant about a grade he got on his history quiz, Willow finds herself shifting back into a normal mood. She wishes she could spill all her troubles to Martha and Eric, but just expressing her worries about Mr. Hunter has left her shoulders lighter. For the remainder of lunch, they laugh about Eric's reasoning for why he should have gotten an A on his quiz. Willow corrects the brief facts about vampire history that Eric thought he had gotten right, and for a moment she forgets all about the Rogue, her initiate training, and the impending horror of working with That Pureblood. However, the reprieve is brief. She is snapped back into reality when the end-of-school bell rings.

* * *

It doesn't take Willow long to get ready. She pulls on her dark grey, collared top, tucks it into puncture proof cargo pants, and laces up some black combat boots. Next, she fastens her X shaped belt around her hips, pushes her dual Glocks into their holsters, then ties back her auburn waves. With a huff, she heads downstairs to face what's coming.

Mr. Hunter sits at the dining room table with a cup of coffee, taking large gulps in between squinting and frowning at various charts and a map of Hidden Hill. He looks up when Willow pauses in the doorway. "Heading out?"

"Yeah. Are you sure about this?"

Mr. Hunter goes back to his map, marking something with a pencil. "Mr. Blackwell will keep an eye on the half-bloods. If they do anything suspicious, he'll bring you right back."

"It's not the half-bloods I'm worried about," Willow mumbles, although she partially is.

"Just do your job," he glances up with a grin. "And bring me back some new information!"

"I'll try," Willow sighs.

"Do you remember how to get to Mr. Blackwell's mansion?"

Willow slips a paper from her pocket. "Got a map just in case."

"Do you have your Glocks?" Mr. Hunter asks, writing on a chart.

"Yes."

"Spare ammo?"

"Yup."

"Puncture proof uniform?"

"Yeah."

"Pepper spray?"

"Daaad!"

Mr. Hunter laughs. "I'm just kidding. Head on out, Pre-Initiate."

* * *

Willow takes her time crossing Foxhound. She's in no rush to reach her destination. But all too soon, the chain-link fence comes into sight, and suddenly, Willow finds herself on the other side. She stares at the grass that thins out into a bed of forest leaves. She looks up to the looming trees that drip with the day's rain.

Willow takes a deep breath, her heart pounding a little. "Okay... let's get this over with." With one steady foot in front of the other, she presses through the low branches and thick shrubs.

On the other side, Willow is surprised to find a man-made deer path. Brown roots arch up in random places, dead tree sprouts spreading a few sharp twigs across the way. The path twists and zigzags through the tall pine and oak trees, heading out of sight.

"How did I miss this path before?" Willow wonders aloud. She must have been too preoccupied with her own thoughts and missed it entirely when she hiked back from That Pureblood's mansion with Rei-Com Ashe. Either way, it doesn't matter now. Steeling her nerves, Willow begins her walk through the hauntingly silent forest.

The walk only takes about thirty minutes, but every twig that snaps underfoot and every rustle of leaves against Willow's pant leg sounds louder than bulldozing a tree down. It puts her on edge as she fights to keep the Rogue's mocking tone out of her ears and the thought of red eyes lurking behind the leaves from her mind. As a result, seeing That Pureblood's stone mansion ahead sends a wave of relief over her until she remembers who waits inside.

Willow warily looks over the colonial mansion's two stories. It sits in a small, eerily peaceful clearing, with healthy and well-watered vines climbing one side. The curtains in the floor-to-ceiling windows of both stories are drawn aside to welcome in the gloomy light.

Walking up to the front doors, Willow makes a note to be extra careful on overcast days—the soft, dim light must be perfect for the nocturnal eyes of vampires. This caused her to wonder why she was even meeting with a Pureblood when it was still light outside. *Shouldn't he be asleep?*

Willow swallows and raises a clammy fist to knock on the door. A moment of silence passes and she wonders if even a vampire can hear a knock in such a large house.

A second later, there is a small click and the door swings open. The servant named Adabelle appears in the doorway, her mismatched eyes alight with joy. "Mistress Hunter! It is wonderful to see you again."

Willow smiles awkwardly. "Hey."

Adabelle beams. "Please, come in. Lord Blackwell has been waiting for you." She graciously sweeps an arm to the inside waiting room.

Willow steps into the ivory room, feeling overwhelmed by all the rich decor again. *This is still too fancy,* Willow thinks in annoyance. *It's like a five-star hotel!*

A footman Willow didn't notice closes the door behind them. The soft *klunk* makes her jump and look over her shoulder.

"I will show you to the parlor, Mistress Hunter." Adabelle's words make Willow flinch back around. "Please, follow me."

Willow follows Adabelle and scolds herself for being so jumpy. *Calm down. You have your Glocks if anything goes wrong.*

Adabelle shows Willow through a doorway between two grand staircases and down a forked hall. Continuing straight, they emerge into a room that makes Willow's eyes widen. The walls stretch nearly one-third of the mansion's width and shoot up past its second floor. Two ornately decorated balconies rest on the wall, ferns and teardrop flowers spilling over walnut wood railings. Walnut beams shoot out of the ivory walls and crisscross high above in the rafters. The ceiling and far wall are clear glass, presenting a view of a patio and the forest beyond.

The room itself hosts many segregated seating arrangements, all skillfully carved from walnut wood and cushioned with rich red material. Small cocktail tables are scattered around the room. Vases sprouting vibrant, green plants provide privacy among couches, and the room is divided with elegant, walnut separators containing a pattern of finger-sized holes.

The mansions in movies and pictures Willow has seen suddenly pale in comparison to this. She stares at a cushioned chair that she assumes is probably worth more than she is and scoots away. "I don't want to touch anything in here," she murmurs to herself.

"By all means, please do," a male voice behind her says.

Willow jumps and nearly knocks over one of the fancy separators. She almost missed the presence he gives off, which makes her worry she will get too used to it.

Willow sighs and glares as That Pureblood paces out from behind a tall vase. She is starting to see a pattern of him randomly appearing.

"I do not like this room," he continues, running a hand along the wood rim of a couch. "The furniture is nice, I suppose, but the room itself is too open and large. I'm not fond of these plants, either. They belong outside."

"We *can* remove them for you, my lord," Adabelle chirps.

"The room would be doubly empty, then," That Pureblood replies distastefully. "Might as well leave it the way it is."

Adabelle curtseys respectfully, but a comical smile sweeps her lips. "Will you be needing anything else, my lord?"

"That is all," That Pureblood confirms.

Adabelle bobs a curtsey again before leaving.

That Pureblood spreads out an arm to indicate their walk toward the patio, and Willow stiffly falls into pace beside him.

"So, where exactly are we headed? Searching the entire forest for clues seems a little impossible," Willow says, looking everywhere but directly at the pureblood beside her—although she keeps note of his movements in her peripheral vision.

"We will head to Vamstadt and ask my Head Half-blood if anything new has risen first. I doubt there will be any news to tell, so we will head to some of the abandoned human residences I have yet to check afterward."

Willow peeks at him, cocking a brow. "Vam-what?"

"You will see."

They reach the glass wall and That Pureblood pushes open a glass door. The two head across the patio to the left and Willow stops dead in her tracks. Waiting beside the patio is the black and silver car Willow saw him driving two days ago. *No. No, no, no. I am so not driving in that old thing.*

"Something wrong?" That Pureblood asks, noticing she's stopped.

"Are we... driving in that?"

"Yes." The corner of his mouth tugs into a partial smile. "Unless you would rather walk for thirty to forty minutes."

"No, but... is that thing even safe? Didn't old cars like that used to flip easily and, you know, crush people?"

"This car is not as old as you think," he says, walking up to it and patting the hood. "It may look similar to the cars of your history, but I assure you it is completely different and safe."

Willow scrunches her face, eyeing it skeptically. She can't imagine sitting in a vampiric car and trusting a vampire at the wheel. If they got into a convenient crash, That Pureblood would walk away alive but Willow wouldn't.

Not like I have much of a choice in the matter.

Still, she felt the need to say *something*. "Is there even a road to drive on?" She scans the forest with no signs of so much as a deer path. "I mean, are we planning to plow through the trees?"

"There is a road," That Pureblood promises. "You saw me driving on it once already." He walks to the other side of the car to open the passenger door and gestures to the empty leather seat.

Willow hesitates a second longer before striding over and plopping in. That Pureblood closes the door and slides into the driver's seat beside her. Producing a skeleton key—which Willow tries not to stare at—That Pureblood slips it into the ignition and turns it until the car rumbles gently.

"Are you sure you can drive this thing? You can't tell me you have that much driving experience with next to no roads out here!"

"I have driven plenty of times," he assures, pressing the gas and carefully steering the car away from the patio. They gain a little speed, heading straight for a low-hanging canopy of leaves.

Willow pales. "Stop the car..." she says, barely louder than a whisper.

The canopy grows closer. Five feet. Two. One.

"Stop the car!" she yells and throws her arms up as they crash through the canopy. The branches swish all around and snap and creak, then only the soft hum of the car is heard.

Willow lowers her arms, heart pounding. They are gliding along a smooth dirt road.

She blinks and twists in her seat, the wall of canopy growing smaller and smaller. She sits forward and is immensely annoyed to find That Pureblood grinning.

"What?" she demands, although she already knows why he's making that face.

"Apologies. I have never seen anyone react in such a way over a secret road."

She huffs, glaring out her window at the forest zipping by. "Where I come from, we don't just plow into the forest."

That Pureblood chuckles, then attempts to get his demeanor back in order. He clears his throat. "It will not take long for us to reach Vamstadt. Sit tight, if you would, for a while."

Willow does just that, sulking in the passenger seat. But as the minutes tick by, she finds her sulkiness turns to nervous restlessness and a very slight twinge of excitement. Here she is, heading deeper into vampire lands than most humans have ever gone. If something goes wrong, she's a goner. No Vampire Hunter can come to her aid out here.

Yet, silly as it is, she is excited to be seeing what others haven't. The trees aren't normal trees, they're trees that vampires have passed hundreds of times. The dirt road isn't carved out by human hands, but by vampiric ones. The adventurous part of herself she thought to be dead has been roused from its sleep.

"I feel I must apologize again."

Willow turns away from the window. "Huh?"

That Pureblood doesn't take his eyes off the gently winding road. "I should not have yelled at you yesterday evening. I even went as far as to advance on you, which I assume is quite intimidating. I sincerely did not mean it."

Willow runs a finger along the stitches in her seat. "I yelled too. So we're even. But you *did* corner me into joining you. So I guess you're in *my* debt. That means you have to protect me today, no matter what."

That Pureblood glances to her, a playful smile tugging his lips. "I like how you think, turning the tables. Very well, I am in your debt today."

Willow can't help but smile too. "Good. So, don't you dare try flipping this car. Where did you get this thing, anyway?" She was having a hard time imagining vampires in fancy suits building cars in a warehouse.

"It was my father's," That Pureblood replies.

"Where are your—" she immediately stops. The last time she asked an insensitive question, she nearly had her blood drained. "Never mind," she says instead, scolding herself for forgetting that vampires have *very real* feelings.

"You were going to ask about my parents?" That Pureblood asks her, then adds to himself, "Looks like my situation is strange even in the eyes of humans." He glances at her then focuses on the road again. "We are partners now, so we should not keep secrets from each other. If we are to trust each other, then we need to settle any misunderstandings between us."

Willow holds up her hands, forgetting momentarily that she is supposed to hold on for dear life. "No, no, no! It's okay. We don't need to get all weirdly deep and personal."

He smiles a little. "I know humans better than that. How does your saying go? Curiosity killed the cat?"

"My curiosity is not going to kill me."

"So, you admit you're curious?"

"No!" Willow snaps. "I mean… ugh!" She grips her head, sinking in her seat.

That Pureblood chuckles. "My circumstances really are not a big secret, only my whereabouts—thus why I cannot travel back to the capital, Bloodlust."

Willow bites her tongue before she can say, *"So you're not a criminal?"*

"I live on the border, hidden, because it is safer for me here. My mother mysteriously went mad one day, and my father and elder brother vanished shortly after she did. I am being kept hidden until the whole ordeal is settled."

Willow's eyebrows arch. "Whoa. So, if you came here to hide, then your family has been missing for six years?"

"They've been gone ever since I was thirteen." He pauses, then clarifies. "Thirteen in vampiric years."

"Oh…" is all Willow can think to say. There is no sound but the grumble of the car for a few minutes. "So… anything about me you're curious about?"

"Not particularly. In truth, your father told me most of anything that would be mysterious." His expression saddens a little. "He told me your mother was murdered in Sir Vitya's province."

Willow shrugs, looking back out the window. Mrs. Hunter's death is the last thing she wants to talk about with a vampire. All she can think to say is, "Yeah, well… junk happens."

The conversation dies. Willow can't decide if she's happy or sad about that—maybe she could have gotten more information out of him.

As the car rumbles on, Willow spots burnt tan, baby blue, and moss green shapes flickering between the trees. She straightens. "What is…" She can't finish her sentence as they round a bend. The dirt turns to bumpy cobblestone accompanied by quaint, colorful Tudor buildings.

That Pureblood pulls his car into an overhang beside a long cobblestone street. Willow hardly notices him shut off the engine and step from the car as she gapes at the expanding town.

"Do you like it?" he asks, making her jump as he opens her door.

Her mouth flops open and closed a few times. "It's… it's… Vamstadt is a *town*?" Her eyes drop from the buildings to the people walking the streets. Her heart lurches. "And those are…"

"Half-bloods?" That Pureblood supplies when she doesn't finish. "Correct. These are all my followers, but you needn't worry—I will not let them harm you."

His words are an empty comfort. Willow is terribly aware of how squeamish she looks, but she doesn't care right then, not in the face of a horde of what looks like hundreds of vampires. She considers slamming the car door shut and demanding that That Pureblood return her to the border, but she has a mission and a culprit to find.

Swallowing her nerves, she shakily slides a boot from the car. When she stands, she takes a deep breath and feels for the heavy comfort of her Glocks on either hip.

"W-we are heading to meet your Head Half-blood?" she asks, not removing her gaze from the bustle of red eyes and eerily pleasant smiles.

"Correct," That Pureblood says. "Would you like my arm?"

"You're wha—?" She looks at the arm awaiting a lady's elegant grasp. Willow can't decide if he's teasing her or genuinely trying to make her feel comfortable and safe. Either way, she would sooner be caught dead than hanging off the arm of a vampire. "No. I'm fine."

He gestures toward the town. "Follow me."

Willow stiffly follows That Pureblood, folding her arms to hide her trembling hands, as Vamstadt swallows them. They follow the uneven cobblestone street past colorful, Tudor-style shops that loom to either side of them, and through masses of half-bloods dressed in some form of modern, yet simple, Victorian fashion. They mill around That Pureblood and Willow, a few nodding respectfully toward That Pureblood before eyeing Willow in irritation. She tries to look confident, eyeing them right back, but finds she is always the first to look away. When it happens again, Willow grumbles, "Shouldn't all these half-bloods be asleep? It's still daytime."

"They are more active today because it is cloudy. On a normal, sunny day, they do not emerge until sunset as the light bothers their eyes."

Willow glances to That Pureblood. "What about you? Aren't you nocturnal?"

He half smiles, catching Willow's eyes. "And you say you are not curious."

Willow glowers. "Are you going to say that *every time* I ask a question? Do I amuse you or something?"

"Greatly," he says, nodding to a shopkeeper who tips his baker's hat. "And to answer your question, yes, I am inherently nocturnal, but humans are not. So, in order to work with your kind, I must be awake at or near the same hour as you. And it is not just me," he adds when Willow eyes him suspiciously. "Most border nobility are diurnal or crepuscular."

"Hm." Willow turns back to surveying the crowd, trying to not look like this new information has interested her.

As That Pureblood steers them along, Willow looks from face to face and picks up as many conversations as she can. Gossip is a great way to obtain information, and Willow partially hopes to see someone acting suspicious among the crowd. However, the shoppers pressing past jingling doors and the workers handling goods or repairing shops are all completely ordinary—as far as half-bloods go.

Willow watches a twelve-year-old half-blood with a mail bag slung across his shoulder dart between two vampires in skirts. Her heart twinges in sadness. Even little kids get turned.

Her sadness quickly fades when she catches a familiar face. She stops, staring through the crowd at a dark-skinned man walking with a cheery whistle and two heavy planks on his shoulders. His red eyes somehow find hers and he quickens his pace.

Unconsciously, Willow snatches That Pureblood's sleeve. "Look! That's one of the half-bloods who kidnapped me!" Her brain flashes with memories. "He went after the culprit," she breathes, hardly believing her luck. "We have to stop him! He can give us—" She cuts off when she snaps her head around to see That Pureblood's emotionless expression.

"Thomas cannot provide us with information," he says simply.

Willow's heart sinks. "What do you mean? He *saw* the culprit!"

"Willow, he will not tell me anything."

She deflates like a balloon, recalling that the half-bloods have been refusing to give straight answers. Willow looks back through the churning crowd. That particular half-blood, Thomas, is gone.

"Come," That Pureblood says, glancing down the street before turning away. "We have an appointment with my Head Half-blood."

Willow and That Pureblood follow the street around the bend and make a right down a side street. The crowds thin until no more than five or six half-bloods are strolling every block. The plain, yet colorful, Tudor homes spread out enough for tight alleyways, their simple structures producing supporting beams and other inlaid wood work. Some of the windows are open and Willow dares peek inside at the simple furniture. She would have guessed a town of half-bloods to be no less fancy than That Pureblood's mansion, but even though it's quaint, Willow can clearly feel the hierarchy difference between pureblood and half-blood.

"Here we are," That Pureblood announces.

Willow snaps her attention from a home she'd been watching across the street. She hopes That Pureblood didn't catch her staring into the oddly simple homes.

Willow's gaze turns ahead to find they are at an intersection of three quiet streets. A Queen Anne style home rises two stories in front of them—a stark difference from the half-blood homes. It's an awkward green and has many windows with black curtains pulled over each one. It looks like no one is home, but a loud *THUMP* and *crash* from the inside says otherwise.

Willow doesn't like the look of this. "What's all that noise?"

"My Head Half-blood is... well... you will see."

Willow rests a hand on her Glock, preparing for whatever carnage or craziness might be inside. "If someone is getting murdered in there," Willow mutters.

They walk up the front porch steps and That Pureblood knocks on the door.

An anthem of thuds sound through the door.

Willow tenses. It sounds like a wrestling match is taking place inside. A moment later, the noise stops and the door clicks opened slowly. Soft light pours into the gloomy house, but Willow doesn't see anyone. She squints, then jumps when a voice says, "Lord B-Blackwell! P-please... come in."

That Pureblood steps inside and Willow hesitantly follows. The home is dark and dusty, with mysterious shapes looming all around. The patch of light around Willow and That Pureblood reveals black stains on the floor before phasing away with the soft click of the closing door. Willow turns and faces the outline of a lanky figure by the door, her hand still clamped on her Glock.

"This is my Head Half-blood, Edwin," That Pureblood says from beside Willow.

She blinks, her eyes slowly adjusting to the shadowy room. The figure by the door, Edwin, looks like he's in his mid-to-late twenties. His blond hair is a disheveled, wavy mess, his eyes a calculating red in contrast to his anxious expression. His ivory dress shirt is only half-tucked into his stained slacks, and a pair of suspenders hangs uselessly at his sides.

Willow relaxes a little, taking her hand off her Glock. This half-blood looks about as dangerous as a jittery chihuahua.

"Edwin, this is Willow Hunter," That Pureblood continues. "She will be working with me for a while."

Edwin switches his eyes to Willow, the red glow of his gaze flickering over her uniform and Glocks before studying her face.

"P-pleased to… meet you. B-by work, you… mean helping, uh, locate the accomplice?"

"Yeah. Got a problem with that?"

"No!" he bursts out, then chuckles nervously and ruffles his hair. "N-n-not at… all."

Willow cocks a brow suspiciously.

Edwin looks back to That Pureblood and then abruptly rushes over to a couch, which probably hasn't been sat on in years, and begins shuffling stacks of papers, fountain pens, and newspapers from its stained suede seats. A stack of fresh paper crashes to the floor when he backs into it by mistake. "I w-w-wasn't thinking! Have a s-s-seat."

"Do not worry about that, Edwin," That Pureblood says, his tone calm and reassuring. "I do not think we will be long. I only came to inquire for new information, but I doubt my half-bloods have given you anything new."

Edwin stops, lips pressing into a thin line. "You really… need to s-s-sit, then."

Willow glances to That Pureblood, who returns her surprise. They weave among stacks of books as tall as Willow and sit on the couch Edwin cleared. Willow coughs when dust springs into the air. That Pureblood waits until she's stopped before saying, "What have you found?"

Edwin brushes some empty ink pots aside and sits on the couch opposite them. He is visibly shaking, eyes darting everywhere but at Willow and That Pureblood. "I, uh, you s-s-see, I… found—" he pauses, concentrating. "I w-w-went out in the… woods…" He grips his pants, squeezing his eyes shut.

Willow folds her arms impatiently. *Come on, what did you find? A better description? The place the accomplice lives? The accomplice itself?*

That Pureblood waits patiently, attention unwavering.

Finally, Edwin says, "A b-b-body. I f-f-found a dead… body."

"Aren't there plenty of dead bodies out here?" Willow asks. "I mean, you guys do have whatever's left of The Batch and all."

Edwin twitches when she says *The Batch*. "It w-w-was a half-blood." He shudders at his own words.

Willow's arms slowly uncross as she glances to That Pureblood.

His brow knits in horror. "Who was it?"

Edwin's gaze rests on Willow a moment before landing back on That Pureblood. "Gavin, Lord B-Blackwell."

That Pureblood nearly jumps to his feet, but he grips the arm rest to stop himself.

Willow subtly scoots away as the arm rest groans under his intense strength. "Who is Gavin?"

"One of the half-bloods who kidnapped you," That Pureblood answers in a strained tone. He swallows as if gulping down something bitter. "The accomplice did this?"

Edwin shakes his head. His voice trembles in fear as he says, "I s-s-searched the... body for... DNA. What I... found m-m-matches no one here. It had to b-be the Rogue."

Willow looks between the two, not making the connection they seem to be making. "I don't get it! Why would the Rogue kill a half-blood? And why specifically the one who kidnapped me?"

That Pureblood makes eye contact with Edwin before murmuring. "To make an example. You said the half-bloods who kidnapped you ran after the figure you saw—the accomplice? They must have tried to take the accomplice out, so the Rogue caught the leader of their group and ended him."

Willows blinks, letting that sink in. "Then... if we try to catch the accomplice too..." The Rogue's face flashes in her mind. She grips her wrist until her knuckles go white.

Edwin stares at her hands, either lost in thought or studying her again.

That Pureblood stands, pacing toward the mantle and staring quietly at its contents for a long time.

Now that there has been a death, Willow knows the stakes have gone up, but she can't understand how something as simple as chasing down the Rogue's accomplice would result in death. She thought villains weren't supposed to care about their henchmen, so to speak. Then again, this *is* the real world.

"Gavin, s-s-supported you until the end," Edwin says, barely louder than a whisper. "That's… what Tom told me."

That Pureblood nods and murmurs. "He was one of the few who supported me." There is another moment of silence—one where Willow wonders how long they'll just sit around instead of trying to find the Rogue to avenge this Gavin guy—before That Pureblood turns around and says, "Thank you for the update, Edwin. Willow and I must head out now. There is one more place I would like to check before dark."

Edwin nods, standing. Willow gets up too and follows That Pureblood to the door. Before they step out into the still-gloomy, yet seemingly now-bright afternoon, Edwin says, "I w-w-will b-bury… Gavin respectfully tonight, Lord B-Blackwell."

"Thank you," That Pureblood says. He and Willow head up the street in silence.

CHAPTER
TEN

WILLOW AND That Pureblood are quiet. As they head up the more unpopulated streets of Vamstadt, Willow busies herself with staring at the half-blood homes. This time, however, she doesn't really see what she's looking at. Her mind is far away in thought. *Is this what Dad is worried about? Did he guess that someone would take a hit for hunting down the Rogue's accomplice?* But that doesn't make sense. Mr. Hunter is good at predicting oncoming fights, but the Rogue has no reason they know of for protecting his accomplice to this degree, and they have no information on the accomplice at all.

Something is missing… Willow decides.

In that moment, Willow blinks back into reality. The sudden shift in surroundings causes her to stop, but That Pureblood keeps walking into the forest ahead.

"Um, where are we going?" she finally asks.

That Pureblood pauses before vanishing among the low branches. He was lost in his own thoughts. He turns, his expression distantly confused before returning to a neutral state. "Oh, yes, we are heading to a collective of abandoned homes no has had the chance to search."

"Oh." Willow glances up at the gloomy sky, which is turning ever darker. Her last visit to the abandoned homes hadn't gone well, and she had seen that body. She suppresses a shudder.

"Do not worry," That Pureblood says. "I will return you to the border before nightfall."

Willow's eyes come back down. She huffs, not wanting to say what is actually on her mind. "What? Don't want to keep a 'lady' past dark?"

"On the contrary," he replies as Willow trudges after him. "I do not want you to become someone's... meal." The tease dies on his lips.

Willow chews her cheek, studying the silent forest. Things are not going well. She hopes they will find a new clue before heading back, one that will lighten both their moods. Maybe even one that will put a stop to this accomplice and the Rogue before more harm is done.

* * *

Willow isn't sure if the walk takes forever or no time at all. Other than explaining that no roads lead to their place of investigation, That Pureblood has said nothing. Willow can't decide if his silence is pleasant or unnerving. Either way, she doesn't bother him. He's lost someone close, and Willow has learned her lesson on poking agitated vampires... mostly, anyway. She is just contemplating whether to ask how much farther they have to walk when a breeze brings an eerie groan.

"What was that?" Willow says, the question coming out as a whisper for some reason.

"Our destination," That Pureblood replies, pressing down the branches of a bush with his foot and gesturing for Willow to go first. "Careful, this place is quite old."

Willow glances cautiously to him then steps through. She stiffens. Willow stands in what might have been a clearing once, heavily surrounded by thick bushes and mossy fences, with multiple houses in the center of it all. Some of the wooden fences have spikes pointing out, and the ones that don't are no more than a pile of splintered wood. Farther into the circle, there are sharp metal contraptions made from welded rifle barrels and household objects. In the center, a federalist style home sags, boards nailed over its windows. Beside it is a boarded up shed or maybe a horse stable. All together, the place looks like a make-shift fort.

"It is a historic site," That Pureblood says, noticing her surprise. "Well, for vampires it is. This was the last standing ground for the humans when we established the border so many years before. Many humans clustered here and fought us off however they could, refusing to admit their land and lives were ours."

Willow knits her brow, turning on him. She doesn't like that last sentence at all.

He catches her expression and says, "Only in this area. I am not referring to the land beyond the border." As if that makes it better.

Willow brushes the comment off for the time being. "Okay, that aside, this place is a little too fortified for my liking. I mean…" she paces over to a metal spike and nudges it with her toe. "It's all old and not super good fortification, but it's usable. A little *too* usable." She stares at the boarded-up windows, the dark slits just wide enough to peer through.

Willow automatically sinks into the tall grass. "Did anyone check this area *at all?* This place looks like a great hiding place for the Rogue."

That Pureblood walks up beside her, watching the houses without concern. "There was a general sweep the first time the Rogue appeared. Nothing was found."

Willow really doesn't like the word "general." And how do they know he hadn't just stepped out for a bit when they were searching the place?

"I will go in first, if that makes you feel safer," That Pureblood says. He stalks toward the first home on the right.

Willow snatches for his frock too late. "No, wait—!" she whispers harshly.

He keeps going.

She sighs. They weren't being stealthy when entering the clearing anyway.

She trots up behind That Pureblood just as he crosses the creaking porch and steps through the doorway. She cringes with each piercing creak and tenses when both the home and shed groan in the frequenting wind. A whiff of rain passes her nose as a breeze travels through the dirty rooms.

"If the Rogue or his accomplice were here, then search for signs of anything being disturbed or something fresh they dropped or left behind," that Pureblood says, checking behind a weathered couch, although careful to not touch it.

Willow is suddenly glad Rei-Com Ashe had her do that tracking mission, but she also worries about what they might find upstairs.

She begins to scout the overturned furniture and check inside the holes of the ripped up floorboards, but the more clueless spaces and empty pantries Willow searches, the stupider she feels. *We don't even know enough about the Rogue to know what to look for!* she thinks in frustration, finishing her check of the sitting room. *And who's to say he isn't watching us now and laughing?* She stops at that thought and desperately shoves it from her mind.

A low rumble sounds in the distance, a wave of swishing leaves coming her way. The house moans again and the wind whistles louder between the boarded-up windows. Willow suddenly regrets splitting up with That Pureblood. She gets up from her crouch, deciding to see if he found anything yet, when a groan sounds directly above.

The ceiling caves, raining splinters down on Willow.

THUD!

Willow whips out her Glock, aiming at the body before her. She relaxes when That Pureblood grunts and sits up, gritting his teeth and rubbing his back.

"What're you…?" Willow breaths, holstering her Glock and hurrying forward. "What happened?" Her heart pounds as she checks his back, amazed to find no pieces of wood lodged into it.

"Floor must be corroded," he says tightly. "I should have considered that. But never mind. I found some—" He looks around. "Where did it go?" He swipes his hands around the splintery mess.

Willow watches, still stunned. "You did? I mean, you just fell through the ceiling. Shouldn't we check for, I dunno, giant stakes stuck in you?"

That Pureblood isn't listening. Willow tries to shrug it off and help him search, getting down on her knees and calming her newly jittering nerves. "What are we looking—" Her knee nudges something into a slit of light. "—for?" She stares for a second, then reaches down and picks the glass vial up. Even in the gloomy light, it shimmers. The glass is thick, and three-dimensional diamond designs are protruding from every inch. To Willow, the vial looks like an over glorified test tube from a science lab.

That Pureblood ceases his search when he notices the vial in her hand. "Good. I feared it shattered."

The vial doesn't feel like a terribly monumental clue, but Willow still stares at it in awe. "What do you think it means? If it means anything, that is."

That Pureblood squints at the vial. "I am not sure. But I know none of my half-bloods have ordered vials from craftsmen, so I assume that either the Rogue or his accomplice may be the owner. If I can figure out who created the vial, then I may be able to track down who bought it."

Willow takes her eyes off the shimmering designs to watch That Pureblood. "But there have to be thousands of these things and hundreds more vampires who've bought them."

He looks at her in confusion. "What do you mean? There is only one set like this."

"I'm talking about mass production," Willow clarifies, hardly believing he doesn't know the word. "You know… factories, conveyor belts, hundreds of thousands of copies?"

That Pureblood slips the vial from her fingers, knitting his brow as if the whole idea is absurd. "We are artisans. Everything must be unique and crafted to the individual's taste."

Willow stares in disbelief. She knew some vampires were craftsmen, gaining their place in society through their expert work, but she never thought that *everything* was hand crafted. "Okay… well… I guess that gives us a good start. But whoever made it can't possibly remember everything they've ever made. And they probably have *a lot* of customers."

That Pureblood nods solemnly, tucking the vial inside his jacket. "That is true. But it will give us something to go on— something beyond inaccurate descriptions."

They both stand and another gust of wind whistles through the house, a low roll of thunder following.

"Sounds like that storm my Dad told me about," Willow murmurs. "We better check the shed before—"

"*Lord Blackwell*!"

They both tense, Willow spinning as a series of heavy thumps pound through the house. Willow's hand flies for her Glock when a tall, dark-skinned, and muscular half-blood thumps to a halt in the doorway. Her grip tightens as she recognizes him as Thomas, one of the vampires who kidnapped her.

"Lord Blackwell," he says in exasperation, then adds shyly before continuing, "And miss Hunter. You must go to the border!"

"Why? What's wrong?" Willow asks before That Pureblood can.

Thomas's head hangs a little as he says, "It's the half-bloods… they're all heading to Hidden Hill."

CHAPTER
ELEVEN

DAD WAS right. Those are the only words Willow can focus on. This must be the reason for his sighs and distant looks; he guessed the half-bloods would attack. But Willow still has another question.

"Why...?" she breathes as they speed back to the border. "Why would your half-bloods attack Hidden Hill?"

That Pureblood's grip on the steering wheel tightens. "My guess is that someone pushed them to do this. If I know anything about my half-bloods, it is that they are not so bloodthirsty that they would kill an entire town."

"It has to be the Rogue or his accomplice," Willow says, not entirely buying that vampires could ever not be bloodthirsty. "Maybe one of them encouraged the half-bloods to do this. It's not that different than the Rogue making an example of Gavin."

"We are agreed, then, but we still have another important question to ask. If the Rogue or his accomplice did force my half-bloods into this, presumably using heavy threats, then why did Thomas come and warn us instead of following the others?"

Willow chews her cheek. She hadn't thought of that. Her head threatens to unleash a pulsing headache from all the questions unanswered. She sighs. "I don't know. But right now, I have to get to Hidden Hill and help my dad and the others."

"Do not worry, I am sure that your—" His brow knits as a gust blows against the car. Lightning flashes and thunder follows soon after.

"What's wrong?"

"I smell blood," he murmurs, then adds with a glance to Willow. "A lot of it."

Willow's heart misses a beat.

The car bursts through the wall of leaves and skids to a halt beside the patio. Willow kicks the door open as she jumps from the car, the two jogging around the mansion and hurrying into the forest at a run.

Her heart races all the more when the metallic fence finally peeks through the trees. She slows to a fast walk once across the border, That Pureblood still at her side.

Inside Foxhound, blaring stadium lights glare down on the hundreds of grey uniforms rushing back and forth. Groups of ensigns run for the West Gate, trainees rush in and out of the munitions depot, transit cars speed in between the varying groups, and Rei-Com Dube is shouting orders. So much is going on, no one even notices Willow or That Pureblood.

"I will head to Hidden Hill and do whatever I can to stop my half-bloods," That Pureblood murmurs uneasily.

Willow swallows. "I need to get my orders." The guard shack is empty, so she tugs on the chain-link fence. It doesn't give.

That Pureblood grips the metal and rips a hole just large enough for her. Willow sighs, wondering how she'll apologize for that later, and steps through. "Thanks."

"Stay safe," he says, backing off. "I will return when this mess is cleared. Then we can discuss our next course of action."

"Right. Just don't turn into a blood stain before then," she chuckles weakly.

His glassy eyes shimmer in amusement. "So long as you keep your blood inside you." They share halfhearted smiles before he turns away, a flash of lightning illuminating his back before he vanishes into the night. With that, Willow takes a steadying breath, turns, and heads into the organized mayhem.

Grey uniforms streak by, orders echo from every direction, and distant gunshots pierce the air as sirens wail. Willow focuses on not getting run over as she heads for the munitions depot—the most probable place to find Rei-Com Ashe—but her thoughts slip to flashes of the blood-flecked ground and damaged homes from six years ago.

MEEP MEEP!

Willow jumps, barely stopping in time as a transport cart zooms by. She sighs. *Focus, Willow!*

She weaves into the munitions depot and spots Rei-Com Ashe. She is barking orders over the click of guns and *plink-pink* of dropped ammunition.

Willow halts in front of her, clicking her heels together and saluting. "Pre-Initiate Hunter, reporting for duty."

"At ease." Rei-Com Ashe clicks her magazine into her gun. "Good to see Mr. Sparkly eyes didn't attack you too, Pre-Initiate. Lock, load, and get into Hidden Hill. I want ya to see if you can find who orchestrated this mess." She eyes the doorway like they might appear any minute. "I'm sure whatever punk decided this was funny will be gallivantin' out there with a big smile on."

"And if I find them, ma'am?"

"Try an' take 'em alive. But if you can't, take 'em out."

Willow solutes again. "Yes, ma'am!" She slips between the crowd and back toward the door, running to the West Gate. Narrowly missing a few more transport cars, she spots a heavily armored truck shipping V.H. out. She bolts for it, grabbing the back rung and hoisting herself up to stand on the thick bumper.

"Willow!" a voice hisses beside her.

She jumps, noticing Eric for the first time.

"What are you still doing in Foxhound?" he says, his tone just loud enough to hear over the truck's rumbling engine. "I thought you would be out there already."

Willow holds onto the side, swaying as they lurch into a faster speed. "I was out on a mission, remember?"

"Oh, right," Eric says uneasily, adjusting the AR15 resting on his shoulder.

Eric looks as nervous as Willow feels. His enthusiasm for vampire hunting must be wavering in the moment. She can hardly blame him—she knows exactly how he feels. She glances at the other ensigns lining the truck bed. A few mirror Eric's worried expression; others have gone pale in horror.

"What happened?" she asks. "Did the half-bloods just charge the town? Come in droves? Do we even have a count?"

Eric shakes his head. "I heard the sirens go off, then I went to meet up with my squad. But by the time I had, the commanding ensigns were saying at least two hundred half-bloods had flooded the town."

Willow grips the rung harder, knuckles turning white. Part of her had wondered if some stayed behind, like Thomas had. That hope is lost to the wind, now.

The echoing bangs and crashes grow louder as they near Hidden Hill. When they finally skid to a halt, Willow is engulfed by a horrific mix of blood curdling shrieks, car alarms, and hoarse shouts of orders. She jumps off the truck and rounds the side, the ensigns pouring out behind her. Her eyes go wide as she witnesses the chaos first hand.

"*Take them out!*" a commanding ensign bellows. His squadron corners a group of half-bloods, gun tips flashing. But his men are overwhelmed as five more half-bloods spring down from a roof with stolen guns and pump the ammunition into them.

"*Help!*" a civilian screams, scrambling through a smashed window to find safety. Another civilian lays motionless in the bushes.

The metallic scent of blood stains the wind as half-bloods emerge from ransacked homes or flash out of dark alleyways with blood-smeared lips.

The only sign of pushback from the humans are a few scattered piles of vampiric ash or the smattering of half-bloods sprawled on the ground with unfocused eyes.

Willow's knees wobble a little. *This is so much worse than six years ago.*

The ensigns charge past Willow, taking to the streets in squadrons. They hunker behind smashed cars and overturned dumpsters, firing at half-bloods and securing their parameters. A group of five bloodstained half-bloods come hissing out of the shadows. Fresh gunfire explodes from the squadrons, the half-bloods taking several shots while skittering for hiding places of their own.

Adrenaline pumps through Willow. She yanks out her Glock, rushing toward the car Eric and his teammates hide behind. She presses her back against its dented frame. "There isn't even a safe drop off point," she says in exasperation.

Eric twists up, pouring lead into a plastic garbage can and earning a howl from a half-blood. He drops back down. "I hope my parents are safe," he mumbles.

Willow barely hears him over the rapid fire and shouts. "I'm sure they're perfectly safe." But she isn't so sure herself.

Eric nods absentmindedly.

Willow pokes her head up a little. The commanding ensign is picking his way toward a dumpster. She glances at the dark alley to her right. It looks empty… for now.

"I'll catch you later, Eric. Stay safe."

"You too."

She takes a deep breath and runs for the alley, keeping her posture low and her Glock pointed down. The alley swallows her in echoing yelps of pain and varying pops and bangs. At the other end, she slows down and crouches behind a trash heap.

A half-blood grabs the shirt of a V.H. and slams him into the hood of a car. His eyes bulge as the hood dents inward.

Willow bites back a gasp of horror. She raises her Glock, her muscles doing all the thinking. *PABAM! PABAM!*

The half-blood drops, and Willow can hardly believe it. Somewhere in the recesses of her mind a voice whispers, *You did it! You killed your first vampire!* But the voice is smothered by a heavy onslaught of emotions—the most prominent being horror. But worst of all, she realizes that she had been wrong all along. *Dad was right… this* doesn't *feel good.*

Willow slumps behind her trash heap, watching the Vampire Hunter gingerly sit up and drag himself back into the fight. *We can't easily kill these monsters. I don't feel proud for shooting one down. What's wrong with me? Why am I not enjoying protecting everyone? Why am I afraid of these murderers?* Her head spins. She can't focus.

A half-blood leaps the gap above. Willow holds her breath, sinking deeper into the shadows. It doesn't see her. She breathes again. The momentary scare roots her back in reality. *Right. Focus. Just find the orchestrator of this and it all ends.*

But Willow knows deep down inside that it won't. Still, all she can do is just keep moving.

With a shaky breath, she darts toward the opposite alley. She charges through the darkness again, blood-curdling screams and her own shaky breath stabbing her ears. Before she slows near the alley's end, she slams into something. She lands hard on her rear, hands scraping against the concrete.

The shape stumbles, then whirls around, red eyes glowing in the gloom. Willow immediately goes into autopilot, years of training saving her life. She swings her leg in a panic, tripping the half-blood. He flails and crashes onto his rear as Willow jumps to her feet. She aims her Glock between his eyes, but is launched forward before she can pull the trigger. Willow crashes into the street, dazed, and her muscles remind her to roll over and take aim again.

Two half-bloods pounce from the shadows, one pinning her to the ground and the other ripping the Glock from her hands. She gasps as the second points the gun at her.

Pulling her leg up, she slams it into the side of the half-blood holding her. He tilts sideways, and the bullet pierces him instead. He yelps and jumps off Willow. The other half-blood pales and lowers the gun. He howls a moment later as a barrage of bullets drill into his back. He crumples to the ground, the acidic bullets burning away at his regeneration cells. The first half-blood snarls and charges the oncoming squadron of Vampire Hunters.

Willow army-crawls to avoid being hit by the spray of bullets. Once she reaches the alley, she jumps up and runs again, her mind finally catching up, her heart hammering in her chest. *That was too close.*

She weaves between the alleys, working her way deeper into Hidden Hill. But the farther she goes, the worse it gets. Bodies, both severely wounded or dead, litter the streets, motherless babies scream from inside ravaged homes, Vampire Hunters yell for backup that can't reach them. It takes everything within Willow to not crumple in a corner to cry and tremble in fear. The only thing that keeps her moving is the knowledge that she can't give up. Someone has to fight on the blood-slicked asphalt, to find the orchestrator and accomplice, to stop more children from becoming like Willow—motherless.

She takes a heartbeat to crouch behind an overturned truck and check her magazine, but a cut-off shout pierces the air too close for comfort. Willow crawls to the other end of the truck and peers around its back. A mass of ginger hair rests at the neck of a Vampire Hunter. His head hangs back, eyes staring straight at Willow but not seeing her.

Willow's gut clenches as she presses herself against the truck bed. She squeezes her eyes shut, wishing she could become numb to all of the death.

"Stay away from her!" a male voice bellows.

Willow's eyes fly back open. She knows that voice. She whirls back around, one eye peeking from behind the scraped grey metal. She pales. Mr. Gregory, Eric's dad, stands with one arm protectively around his wife and the other held out defensively. He glares the ginger half-blood down, eyes flicking between her, their dead protector, and a snapped AK47 on the ground.

"You've had your fill of blood. Now leave!"

"You think I'm doing this for sustenance?" the half-blood scoffs. "Ha! Humans really are stupid."

The half-blood flashes forward, snatching Mr. Gregory's arm and tearing him away from his wife. He tumbles across the pavement as the half-blood yanks the struggling wife closer. She nails a good fist in the half-blood's jaw.

Willow surges into action, but this time of her own will. "Drop her!" she yells, and then fires—*PABAM!*—not even waiting for the half-blood to listen.

The half-blood shoves Mrs. Gregory to the ground, dodging the bullets easily. In an instant, the half-blood is in front of Willow, grabbing the nozzle of the Glock. Willow immediately lets go and rips out her secondary Glock. *PABAM!* The half-blood doubles over, gripping her stomach. She grits her teeth and slams a leg into Willow's side. Willow's head cracks against the asphalt, her vision growing spots for a moment.

"That *hurts*!" the half-blood snarls.

Something snaps inside Willow. Her fear boils to rage. She is tired of being afraid. *How dare they kill us like animals! How dare they ruin our peace! How dare they create this stupid fear in me and ruin my life!* She rolls over with a scream of anger, swiping the half-blood's legs out from under her. The half-blood jumps but a shot explodes into her shoulder.

"Your fight is with *me*, bloodsucker!" Willow yells.

The half-blood growls, snatches up the barrel of the broken AK47, and swings it at Willow's head. She dodges with mere centimeters to spare. Willow holds up her Glock, but the half-blood cracks her broken weapon against the gun. Willow's arm flies to the side, but she grips her Glock tight as the momentum spins her around and she drops to a knee.

"Thought you could slap it from my hand?" Willow sneers. *PABAM!* "Like I'm some kid?"

"You missed." the half-blood smirks, swiftly reaching a hand toward Willow's pressure point.

Willow bends backward and grabs her wrist, pulling herself up as she sends the half-blood down. In the moment of passing, Willow slams the butt of her Glock on the half-blood's head. She crashes to the pavement, struggling to regain herself. They've traded places.

Willow aims her Glock for the half-blood's heart valve, the only organ keeping her alive.

"I'm going to enjoy every drop of your blood," the half-blood mutters.

There is a gunshot, the flash of fangs, and the world turns over. The air is sucked from Willow's lungs as a dark shape and something metal glints past. A howl of pain follows. At first, Willow expects the cry to be her own, but then she gulps in air and her senses refocus. The half-blood trembles over her, teeth gritted and very close to her neck. The half-blood tilts to one side and collapses with a grunt, glowering at the figure silhouetted against the bright street lights.

"That will be *quite* enough," the figure says.

Willow blinks at That Pureblood, hardly recognizing him. His frock is ripped in several places, his ivory shirt and black vest are stained with blood. The pureblood's hair is unorderly, and dried blood marks the shallow cuts across his cheek.

"What are you doing?" Willow demands. "I almost had her!"

"Really? It looked to me like you were about to become her snack." He nods to the half-blood. "I stopped her with a second to spare."

Willow turns to glower at the half-blood, but she notices the knife through her throat. Willow's eyebrows shoot up.

That Pureblood kneels down and Willow has to look away as he pulls the blade out. "As for you, Rose, I am getting very tired of your antics."

Willow's eyes shoot back to the half-blood. "She's alive?"

The half-blood, Rose, gingerly sits up, her neck wound healing quickly. "That was a dirty move, *Lord Blackwell.*" She practically spits his name. "One more inch and I would have died!"

"Then be glad my derringer is out of ammunition," he counters, wiping off his intricately designed parrying knife.

Willow pales. "You're armed?" She knew some purebloods carried parrying knives and a few even went as far as derringer guns, but she somehow never thought That Pureblood would carry either one, let alone both.

"Most of us are," he replies dryly before saying to the half-blood, "I have been told you know a thing or two about the accomplice?"

The half-blood slowly gets to her feet, smirking and rubbing her neck. "Shouldn't you apologize first? A gentleman wouldn't stab a lady."

"Spare me, Rose," he growls, and even Willow shivers at his sudden change in mood. "I've seen you take on worse in your petty street fights. Now, I do not have time for your childish mockery and pretense. Tell me what you know of the Rogue and his accomplice!"

Rose, scoffs. "And who told you I know anything? I sent in my report along with the rest."

Willow scowls. "Yeah, and it was as useful as you are." She turns on That Pureblood. "Just let me finish her. She's not going to talk, just like the rest of those bloodsucking murderers."

Rose steps toward Willow, but That Pureblood holds out an arm. "Those 'bloodsucking murderers' are full of currently priceless information, so for just this one moment, I advise you to *step down.*"

Willow glares at the ammunition in her magazine, counting eight shots left. "Fine. But once you're done, I get eight more opportunities to end her after she fesses up." She smiles at Rose.

Rose sneers. "Why don't we test that right—"

"Rose, I will spill your blood if you do not start spilling answers," That Pureblood snarls. "And kindly, Ms. Hunter, only contribute to this conversation if you have useful points," he adds to Willow.

Willow glares and paces a few steps away to reclaim her missing Glock, and stays silent.

"A certain half-blood told me you know something about this mess," That Pureblood says to the half-blood, "and that you have a good reason for doing this. Tell me."

Rose sneers. "Yeah, we've got an incentive. Not that you *oh so superior* purebloods would care."

Willow's ears perk at the word *incentive.*

"I am terribly interested, Rose," That Pureblood says impatiently.

"Yeah, because you want to stop us from getting it. As a matter of fact, you would just *love it* if we stayed at the bottom forever—if we just bowed down like the humble slaves we are. So yeah, we've got something to fight for, and it's freedom from oppressive beasts like you!"

Willow turns back to Rose with a knit brow. That Pureblood looks taken aback too.

"Speechless?" Rose sasses, inclining her head. "You should have seen this coming a mile out."

"You make no sense," That Pureblood says. "What have I done to diminish you? I let you all live your lives how you choose; I have never forced my hand with any of you!"

"This isn't just about you, *Lord Blackwell.* It's *all* of you purebloods."

KABOOM! The city trembles and Willow jumps, checking checks her surroundings. Directly east, beyond the trees, a plume of pitch-black smoke rises into the sky. Willow's mouth drops open.

"Looks like we broke into Foxhound and found the explosives," Rose chuckles. "Later!"

That Pureblood snatches for her, but she's already across the street and hopping from roof to roof. "Rose!" he shouts, then growls when she doesn't return. "I'm going after her. I'll meet up with you later, as planned." He darts off without waiting for an answer.

Mr. and Mrs. Gregory walk up beside Willow and say something about getting to safety, but Willow barely hears their words. Adrenaline pumps in her ears, her anger numbing her. She has to run. She has to do something. "No way. *Dad…!*" She takes off for Foxhound.

* * *

Thundering across town, a new set of noises follows Willow. The shouts and gunshots still echo around, but now the half-bloods swarm toward Foxhound like a pack of hyenas, whooping and laughing. They drop down from the roofs every so often to crush a Vampire Hunter. Pistols pop and machine guns rattle as half the V.H. in town scramble to protect Foxhound.

Willow weaves among fallen allies and the rain of half-bloods. She sees the chaos, but can't process it. Her brain is racing with questions—*What was Rose talking about? What could the Rogue offer her? What about Dad? Is he okay?* She tries not to trip over tussling V.H. and the occasional pouncing half-bloods. By some miracle, she arrives at Foxhound with only a few scratches. Except, now she wishes she had never come.

Ammunition rolls from the munitions depot in the hundreds, half-bloods scattering the bullets like maniacs. Nozzles flash with gunfire as V.H. barrage the half-bloods. Nearby, the transportation warehouse is spitting flames, gasoline trickling from inside and threatening to set the grass ablaze. A few transport carts lay on their sides, serving as shields. Everywhere else is uncontrolled mayhem. The place swarms with bloodied and dirtied bodies, screams and orders, explosions and death.

Before she can regain her composure, Willow is slammed to the ground. She slips in slick grass, then pain explodes in her shoulder. She gasps and grabs her attacker's shoulders, throwing the half-blood to the side and changing their positions. She aims the Glock, point blank, at his artery, then fires.

PA-BAM!

The half-blood goes limp.

She checks her shoulder, breathing heavily. Her uniform has saved her. Puncture proof. She had forgotten all about it.

Willow blinks several times, the weight of battle pressing down on her. She takes a shaky breath as her muscles remind her to stand up and find a new target. Before she can race to the aid of an ensign group, an annoyingly familiar voice screams overhead.

"Mission accomplished, boys! Head out!"

Willow's gaze shoots up, along with hundreds of others.

Rose stands on top of the munitions depot, her ginger curls a disheveled mess and her hands stained red. She jumps down from the depot and races for the forest with all the other half-bloods in tow. They leap over and tear through the fence, but no V.H. follow them. The Vampire Hunters just watch, too torn, wounded, and confused to chase. It's not worth it anyway. More men would be lost if they ran across the border, chasing the half-bloods into the comfort of their own land.

The half-bloods are gone as quickly as they came.

The silence that follows is punctuated by soft moans, the crackle of fire, and drifting thunder. A commanding ensign rushes from the direction of the living quarters. His eyes are wild as he shouts, "Rei-Com down!"

That spurs everyone to action. Willow's skin feels clammy as she moves to run toward the commanding ensign, too. More V.H. follow, while the rest hurry to put out the fires and tend the wounded. A more-controlled chaos descends as everyone rushes to fix the damage.

Willow runs behind the commanding ensign, whisking past broken homes. Her eyes lock on the road ahead, one word pulsing in her mind: *Dad!*

When they near her house, Rei-Com Ashe is standing outside. She is just about to enter the home when she spots the group.

"I heard a Rei-Com was down," Willow says firmly. "Show me."

The commanding ensign leads the way inside, but Rei-Com Ashe grabs Willow's arm before she enters. "Hey... prepare yourself."

Willow swallows and nods, stiffly stepping pass the threshold. Rei-Com Ashe leaves her behind, thumping down the hall and up the stairs. Willow, on the other hand, has a hard time getting past the living room.

It looks as if someone put the room through a garbage disposal. The windows are broken, the front door torn from its hinges, furniture smashed in two, and bloody splinters, shards, and every other manner of object littering the floor.

The kitchen is no better, almost completely visible since it's missing an entire wall. The dining table lies on an angle with two missing legs—both of which protrude from the refrigerator. The cabinets and stove are peppered with bullet holes while the floor is a mosaic of broken dishes.

"Medic! This is an *emergency*! We need a medic *now*!" Rei-Com Ashe's muffled yell comes from somewhere above.

Willow jolts from her trance, summoning what little energy she has left to jog down the hall and toward the stairs. She halts beside her Dad's office, the red catching her eye. Her world drains of every color except the red of blood dripping on Mr. Hunter's documents.

A new burst of adrenaline carries Willow up the stairs and down the hall. She halts in her Dad's bedroom.

Rei-Com Ashe's hands are slick with crimson as she presses on a man's chest... Rei-Com Dube's. Other ensigns crowd around, tearing bedsheets for bandages and applying what little first aid they carry.

Willow wants to punch herself for feeling a twinge of relief. *It's not Dad. But then…*

"Stay with me, Dube!" Rei-Com Ashe breaths. "Where're those cursed medics?"

Willow can only stare, her stomach churning. "Where's Dad?" The words escape her before she can stop them.

Rei-Com Ashe jumps. "You scared me! Hurry up and help rip some bandages!"

But Willow can't move. She hardly remembers how to breathe. The horror of losing Mr. Hunter, of losing another family member, dumps down on her. He should have been fine, should have fended off the vampires and stayed safe, like Rei-Com Ashe has. So why is Rei-Com Dube bleeding out? Why is her Dad not here to help?

"Willow?" Rei-Com Dube croaks. "I'm… sorry—"

"Don't talk, Daniel; focus on staying alive," Rei-Com Ashe instructs.

Rei-Com Dube moans and shakes his head ever so slightly. "No… you must hear this. It's… about Desmond."

A lump swells in Willow's throat. "What? My Dad, do you know where he is? Is he okay? Is he alive?"

"I-I don't know. I joined him… after they chased us." Rei-Com Dube grunts as Rei-Com Ashe presses fresh bandages against his wound. "I helped fight them off, but they chased us here… cornered us… took Desmond!"

"Who? The accomplice? The Rogue?" Willow asks desperately.

"The accom… plice…" Rei-Com Dube's head lulls.

"We're losing him!" Rei-Com Ashe's voice is strangled.

Willow takes a step back, unsure of what to do. All her emotions collide together and shoot up in an explosion of tears. Her vision blurs, her surroundings losing focus. *Dad! No… no!*

Vampires never take hostages to keep them alive. The hostage always is turned into someone's meal.

Somewhere distant, Rei-Com Ashe checks Rei-Com Dube's breathing. "Great Gatsby, don't do this Daniel!"

What's happening?

Rei-Com Ashe puts both hands over his chest and pumps.

There were no vampires almost a week ago.

"Where are those uselessly slow paramedics?"

Now they're here… and they're killing and ravaging…

A voice echoes in her mind, stern and horribly right, *"Don't wish for ill fortune, Willow Ashton Hunter."*

Everything sucks away, replaced by silence. The words come again. *He was right.*

Paramedics appear in the stairwell and hurry past Willow in a blur. Rei-Com Ashe is by Willow's side then, leading her out of her home—or what used to be her home. They walk back down the street, V.H. whisking by, their mouths moving as they call for aid or explain the situation to an onslaught of paramedics. Ambulance lights swirl, gurneys wheel in every direction, civilians limp into Foxhound with tears streaking their cheeks as they cry for their fallen loved ones.

But Willow doesn't hear any of it. It's as if her brain has shut off her hearing, not allowing for any more trauma to invade her numbness.

The world stays like this until she enters the crossroads and spots That Pureblood slumped against the guard shack. A little of the world slips back as she breathes, "Oh no…" and runs to his side.

"What happened?" she demands, looking over his hunched form. "Are you okay?"

He unfurls himself a little, and Willow can see he's gripping his side where a massive red stain bleeds into his shirt. "It looks worse than it actually is," he reassures, though his voice suggests otherwise.

"Do you need—like, a bandage or something?" Willow says, unable to tear her eyes from the stark blood against his pale fingers. "You look terrible."

"It is already healing," he says, straightening himself with a grunt. "Internal wounds are harder to heal than outer, so it merely takes a moment longer."

"Well, what do we have here?" Rei-Com Ashe strides up. "Come to apologize, bloodsucker? Or maybe you think we'll give ya shelter from your out-of-control freaks?"

"Watch your tongue," That Pureblood growls. "I am in a rather foul mood."

"What happened with Rose?" Willow cuts in before the two can start another fight. "I saw her call back the half-bloods like..." her words trail away as she sees the anger and maybe even a little hurt in his eyes.

"Like she was ruling them," he finishes for her. "I did not see it, but I heard. Just before her little declaration, she managed to lead me into a trap. She, along with some of her other cronies, jumped me and did this to me." He lifts his hand, showing where his vest and shirt are torn, revealing a deep and festering red gash. "She took off before I could attempt to pry for information—or do anything for that matter."

"So, let me get this right, m'kay?" Rei-Com Ashe says. "You think this bloodsucker knows something, from my point of view she may even be the accomplice, and ya let her go *stark free*?"

That Pureblood pushes himself up, leaning on the wall heavily. "Next time you take a parrying knife to the gut, inform me if you are able to chase down the half-blood who did it."

"You're a bloodsucker," Rei-Com Ashe says flippantly. "I'm sure ya can handle it."

That Pureblood's eyes flare red, lips curling in a snarl that reveals needle-sharp fangs. He looks ready to replace the blood he just lost. Sensing this, Willow steps in.

"We don't have time to argue! We need to find Rose and—"

"Get off our land," Rei-Com Ashe snaps, her sharp eyes never breaking from his.

Willow gawks at Rei-Com Ashe, and even That Pureblood is shocked.

"I think you need to take pause and think this through," he says carefully, but firmly. "You are upset, as we all are, over this tragedy. I am here to help—"

"By doing what?" she hisses. "You aren't controlling your bloodsuckers, ya haven't found clues, and now you're tellin' me ya can't even catch some bloodsucker who duped ya?"

"We *have* found clues!" Willow says, not entirely sure why she's siding with a pureblood. "Just before the attack, we found a vial—"

"*Ha*! A vial? What're we going to do with that?"

"We can use the vial to track the Rogue via purchase history—"

"Perfect! Evidence of where the Rogue shops!" Rei-Com Ashe hollers, earning the attention of a few ensigns hurrying by. "Completely useless! I don't want his grocery list—I want the accomplice! Actually, I want the Rogue's head on a platter!"

Willow frowns. "And you think we *don't*? Listen, if we can identify the Rogue's identity with the vial, then we can do that!"

Rei-Com Ashe holds up a hand, silencing them both. "No. This attack is the last straw for me. We can't afford something on this scale again. We can't trust this bloodsucker. We are gonna solve this problem ourselves, starting with a timer set on Mr. Sparkly Eyes here."

Her words sound foreign to Willow, they send a chill down her spine. "What're you—"

"Listen well, *Blackwell*. If you don't find that Rogue soon, you'll be dead from starvation. I won't be letting any more Batches over the border until you get me that Rogue."

Willow's mouth drops open.

That Pureblood's eyes widen. "Ms. Ashe, you do not have the permissions—"

"I'll do what I want, *bloodsucker.*"

Willow can hardly form words for several moments. "What... but that's... I mean... that's the stupidest thing I've ever heard!" She chuckles a little, saying, "If he doesn't have the Batch for blood, they'll have no choice but to attack us again for sustenance!"

"And we'll be ready." Rei-Com Ashe smirks challengingly.

That Pureblood blanches. He is at a complete loss for words, silenced by shock.

"You can't do that!" Willow explodes in his place. Her anger at all of this rises from the depths again, threatening to send her into an emotional outburst.

Rei-Com Ashe rolls her eyes, turning to Willow. "We can't trust him! You *know* that, Willow!"

"He fought alongside us today! We managed to find clues to the Rogue's plan *and* find the half-blood who might be the accomplice!"

"Which he still never caught, mysteriously. He's a pureblood, for heaven's sake, he could catch a half-blood if he wanted!"

"Not while wounded!" Willow gestures to his bloodied hand still covering his gash. "We're running out of allies, Rei-Com Ashe." Her eyes sting.

"Which is why we need to cut our ties with loose ends, like him!"

"*My dad is gone!*" Tears blur Willow's vision. "Rei-Com Dube is dying, and everyone else is dead or wounded! Without Hanas, there is no chance of finding the Rogue *or* my dad." The name feels strange on her tongue, but she presses on. "We need his help to search his land *and* question his half-bloods. And he needs *us* to back him so he can get rid of the Rogue *before* all his half-bloods turn on him!"

"We can do it without him!" Rei-Com Ashe growls. "We don't need a pureblood! We're Vampire Hunters—hunting 'em down and killing 'em is what we do!"

Willow can hardly see through her tears. Her anger, hurt, confusion, and sadness are all melding together. "You aren't even listening to me! Your anger is clouding your logic!"

"Alright, look, you've got two options," Rei-Com Ashe plows on, her tone dangerously calm. "Stay with me, and we'll figure this out. We'll get your dad back no matter the cost. Or you can side with *him*, and you'll be banished from Foxhound until further notice."

Hanas cuts in. "Ms. Ashe, you are not thinking—"

"I'm the only Region Commander around, so what I say is final!" she snaps, looking between the two and daring either one to challenge her.

Willow's shock drops into a glare. She's tired of all this. Tired of people changing her life at the snap of their fingers, be they vampire or human. She's tired of losing things, like her love for initiate training and her desire to take out the creatures who took away her mom and now her dad. She can't stand any of it. Not the fear, not the hurt, not the confusion. *It all ends here and now.*

"Go with her," Hanas murmurs. "I will find a way to resolve this mess and keep you informed on the Rogue's ploy."

"No!" Willow says. "You can't go on your own. We'll find the Rogue, his accomplice, *and* my dad together!" She whirls around, storming toward the border.

"Willow," Rei-Com Ashe shouts. "You'll be goin' against your dad if you leave!"

That stops Willow in her tracks.

"He was such a wreck, I thought he was afraid of another fight with a pureblood. But after the half-bloods attacked, and you were nowhere to be found, I realized he wasn't afraid of a fight. He was afraid of losing *you*!"

Willow bites back a sob. Was that why he wanted her to team up with Hanas? He knew an attack would happen, and she'd be safer with him at her side? *Either way, that was a terrible plan, because now* I've *lost* you, *Dad.*

"I'll have to stand by what he wanted, then," she says, trying to sound firm and strong. "And he wanted me to help Hanas find the Rogue, so that's what I'm going to do." She continues on, not daring to look back.

Hanas hurries after her, glancing between the two women.

Now Rei-Com Ashe is at a loss for words for a moment, but when Willow is almost at the border, she calls, "If you cross that border, you'll *never* become an initiate!"

"Fine." Willow calls back. "I don't know if I want the rank anyway."

With that, the forest looms closer and Willow exchanges no more words with her mentor. Hanas leans close, as if worrying Rei-Com Ashe might hear, "Are you positive this is what you want?"

"No," Willow sniffs. "But this is the best I can do."

CHAPTER
TWELVE

FOR ONCE, Willow is thankful for the quietness of the forest. Out in the freeing silence, away from the shouting and destruction and loss, it's as if she can breathe again.

Her mind is still a train wreck of thoughts, but the farther she gets away from the chaos of Hidden Hill, the more at ease she feels. She hates herself for it, but it's almost as if the problems are no longer her own. She just has to find the Rogue, his accomplice, and her dad. No training, no uncertainty about her future, no school work piled on top of missions and border patrols or anything.

Of course, Willow still keeps it fresh in her mind that she can't fully relax. She's on enemy land, banished from Foxhound. *Where am I going to go now?* She thinks of Martha first, but Willow can't stomach going back and seeing the mess the half-bloods caused. For that matter, Willow doesn't even know if Martha's house is still in one piece. *And Dr. Heartwood will be tired and busy at the hospital. Mr. Heartwood won't be any less busy, reconstructing the town and all.* There was no way she was going to stay with Rei-Com Ashe, and Eric was out of the question—*that* would be much too awkward.

Willow's eyes slide toward Hanas. He is lost in his own thoughts, his expression is scrunched in frustration. As much as the thought unsettles her, Willow *has* stayed in his mansion before and there doesn't seem to be another option at the moment.

She wipes her nose on her sleeve and dries her eyes again, resolving to not cry anymore—particularly in front of Hanas. "So… what do we do now?"

Hanas blinks from his thoughts, turning his blood-red eyes on her. "What indeed…"

Willow chews her cheek, looking everywhere but at Hanas as she casually asks, "So… mind if I crash at your place?"

"Crash?" he asks in confusion.

He's not making this easy, she thinks in exasperation. "I mean I don't have anywhere to stay. My house is kind of a mess and, well, there's the whole thing with Rei-Com Ashe…"

Hanas's features lift in understanding. "Ah, yes. You are more than welcome to stay at my manor. In truth, it may become easier to work together this way."

Willow nods, having to agree, but still feels uneasy about *living* across the border—easier or not.

Hanas winces as he lifts up a low branch allowing entry into the clearing.

"Don't hurt yourself more," Willow says warily, glancing at the drying blood under his ribcage. She leaves out her worry of him deteriorating to the point of taking her blood for replenishing.

"I'll live," he promises again.

They head for the stone mansion, its tall windows casting warm light across the dewy grass. It almost feels comforting, if in a foreign and strange way. Willow suspects that any place still intact would seem homey after tonight's events, though.

The two wearily trudge into the entryway and are swarmed by black-blood servants.

"Are you alright, my lord?"

"He's bleeding! Get the medicine and bandages!"

"My lord, is there anything we can help with?"

Hanas waves a hand and they all go silent. "I will debrief you later. For now, please see to Ms. Hunter's needs. She will be staying with us for some time."

The servants all bob their curtseys and bows before splitting off to begin their work of finding medicine, bandages, and blood, fixing up a room for Willow, and doing whatever else is needed. A handful stay behind to tend to Willow and Hanas.

"Shall we discuss our next course of action in the morning?" he asks Willow, for once looking his age.

"Yes," Willow says, feeling like she's aged a few hundred years herself.

"Ask the servants for whatever you need. Evening to you." He nods politely and heads off to his own room up the stairs on the right.

"Are you good to walk?" a servant asks.

"Yeah," Willow says, although her feet ache.

"Right this way, please."

* * *

A comforting and familiar sensation blankets Willow. Half awake, half asleep, her mind wades through sunny memories: Mr. Hunter piling warm and wet sand into fortress walls, Mrs. Hunter insisting they make a sand castle instead of a sand fortress, blurry smiles and exciting conversation around a candlelit table, and a cool breeze blowing Mrs. Hunter's hair while Mr. Hunter shows Willow how to take a photo. Mrs. Hunter's smile lingers, then morphs into Mr. Hunter's. He fades back until he is no more than a picture on Willow's bookshelf. Willow reaches out, her fingers just an inch shy of reaching the picture, and then it falls. It smashes on the ground into a hundred shards.

Something uncomfortable wakes Willow, something in her chest. Then her mind slips from the dream, focusing on the dark of her eyelids. That pain in her chest rises, and warm, wet tears stain her pillow.

Her eyes crack open after groggily moving an arm to brush away the tears.

She recognizes the warm room she sleeps in: smooth ivory walls, warm crimson canopy and bedding stitched with gold, oak bed posts, immaculately designed baseboards. But it is also different, Willow realizes with a sinking heart. The gauzy curtains don't let in warm light, just the cold, cloudy, and filtered rays of distant happiness. The cold, dark reality sets in—Mr. Hunter is gone. This time, he won't burst through the door to ask if she's okay.

Willow sits up in her new bed. Her muscles plead for her to lay back down and never move again, but Willow knows that sleep won't visit her—and if it does, it won't be pleasant. With a heavy sigh, she rubs her bleary eyes and tosses off the covers. There is a slight chill in the air which nearly sends her back under the cover's warmth, but the sight of her clothes sends her hurrying for the wood separator in the corner.

No! No frills! She *will not* be seen in a frilly white nightgown—not again—but Willow is dismayed to find her dirty uniform is no longer crumpled on the floor where she left it. Even if she had been exhausted and easily swayed, Willow should have never changed out of it. She groans, checking under the carpeted chair and pulling out drawers filled with horrifyingly girly under things.

Now, what—? Her eyes land on a neatly folded pile resting atop the dresser. She pulls them down reluctantly, reading the gently written note resting on top.

> *To: Mistress Hunter*
> *I spotted your uniform this morning and feared the stains would never come out unless it was cleaned immediately. I hope this does not anger you, but if it does, then please notify me. If*

not, then I have left an outfit to wear in your uni-
form's stead. I remember that you are not fond of
the skirts and dresses worn by the vampire ladies.
So, I have brought you an outfit I hope will suit
your liking. If not, then I will diligently search for
a more fitting outfit.

Sincerely, Adabelle.

"I'm not a Mistress," she says to no one in particular. Willow lays the note aside and holds up the clothes to look them over. She sighs. "Guess this will work."

A moment later, she is dressed in coffee-colored slacks, suspenders with hand-etched buttons, and a beige, button down blouse. She ties her hair into a relaxed ponytail and sighs. Everything feels like too much effort today. And why wouldn't it? Her world had practically crumbled to dust within the past several hours.

Her stomach growls, demanding the food it never had for dinner the previous night. Willow rubs it, looking doubtfully around the room for sustenance. To her surprise, a silver tray sits on the writing desk across the room. A cloche covers something warm, a glass of orange juice waits to quench her thirst, and despite the gloomy light, a fork and knife shimmer on a freshly pressed napkin.

Willow crosses the room, the soft thump of her boots sounding noisy in the quiet mansion. She picks up another delicately written note beside the polished tray:

Breakfast for the Mistress.

From: Adabelle

"I'm *not* a mistress," Willow grumbles again. She puts the note aside and gingerly curls her fingers around the cloche's immaculate handle. She's almost afraid of what might be underneath, being prepared by a black-blood and all, but she is pleasantly surprised to find a hearty helping of sausage, an omelette, and two pieces of perfectly golden toast. To the left of the dish are the options of peach jam, butter, or honey—all in dainty glass bowls with mini cloches on the top. There is also a strangely shaped piece of silverware that Willow assumes is for the butter, since it's sitting next to it.

Willow humphs, impressed, and takes up the fork. "Maybe I am a mistress."

After a filling breakfast, which she wolfed down in minutes, Willow leans back in the soft Louis Chair with satisfaction. Her somber mood and world lightens a little, allowing a small glimmer of hope to flicker into existence. Maybe living here for a while wouldn't be so bad. Maybe she would find her dad quickly. Maybe the Rogue would turn up soon and this would all be over.

Willow rocks her chair, staring at the crumbs on the white and blue china plate. *Maybe this won't be so bad. Better than being in Hidden Hill.* She allows herself a smirk. *Take that, Rei-Com Ashe!*

A knock sounds at the door.

Willow pauses her rocking, chair leaned back. She forgot that part of staying in this mansion meant being around That— *no, Hanas,* she reminded herself—at all hours.

"Come in," she says, voice quivering awkwardly.

To her slight relief, Adabelle steps into the room with a dainty curtsey. "Mistress Hunter, I am glad to see you have found my notes. I hope they were not offensive or assuming?"

"No, they're fine," Willow says, not daring to move. She feels vulnerable and out of place, even dressed in vampiric clothes and having eaten vampiric food.

"Do your clothes fit you well, Mistress?" she inquires, her tone as light and feathery as ever.

Willow looks down as if to ask the clothes themselves. "Maybe a little baggy, but I don't mind. And, uh…" She sets all four legs of the chair down. "You don't have to call me Mistress. Just Willow. I'm not your mistress or anything like that. Just a… well…" She heaves a sigh, Rei-Com Ashe's words ringing in her mind: *you'll be banished from Foxhound until further notice.* "Just an outcast, now."

"Not in our eyes, Mistress," Adabelle says, her words like a temporary blanket of comfort. She smiles proudly at Willow. "If I may… Master Blackwell explained the situation this morning, and I think you did what was right—not because Master Blackwell is my master, but because I believe that only the two of you can stop the Rogue."

Willow's eyes widen. "Really? You believe that?"

She nods. "I think your father would be proud."

Willow's lips twitch with a weak smile. "I hope so."

"If you would, Mistress Hunter, Master Blackwell asks for you. He says he wants you present to help question Ms. Rose on the Rogue."

Willow blinks, sitting up straighter. "He's got her already? Didn't she like, I dunno, run for it?"

"She may be defiant, but Ms. Rose is still required to obey Master Blackwell," Adabelle says.

"Still…" Willow objects. "I can't see her coming here without a fight."

Adabelle stifles a giggle. "It's as though you two are best friends, although I believe you met for the first time the other day."

"I don't need years of friendship to know her type," Willow grumbles. She stands, ready to sock the truth out of Rose… or possibly burst into tears. Her jumbled emotions are still deciding.

Adabelle gives her a sympathetic smile and gestures toward the door. "Right this way, Mistress."

After twisting down a few hallways and past several rooms—all with doors closed, to Willow's disappointment—Adabelle pauses in front of a wooden door. She knocks gently, then turns the black knob to let Willow in.

Stepping inside, Willow finds herself a witness to the most intense glaring competition known to man. Hanas sits behind a dark wood desk with simple designs lining the top and bottom. He is leaning forward, fingers laced together, hiding his frown but not his piercingly cold glare. His eyes alone fling hundreds of parrying swords at Rose, longing to feel the victory course through him as she finally gives up her petty games.

Rose, on the other hand, sits back in an oak chair with crossed arms, her tousled ginger hair a stark contrast to the dark book-shelves standing straight against the walls behind her. She looks like she did put up a fight coming, her blouse partially untucked and jodhpur pants scuffed. Her snarl is so intense that it lifts her lip up to reveal razor sharp fangs. It's written all over her face that she would enjoy nothing less than sinking those fangs into Hanas, maybe jabbing a knife or two through him to see how *he* enjoys it.

The silent rage continues as Willow awkwardly slips farther into the room, looking between the two.

"So… guess she hasn't said much," Willow says eventually, joining Hanas' disapproving and fierce glare.

"We have only just begun," Hanas growls, although it sounds to Willow that the fight started long ago. "Care to inform us of the little mutinous ploy you pulled?"

"No," Rose says flatly.

"This is going to take a while," Willow observes. She folds her arms and paces toward Hanas' desk, wanting to sit on the ledge but feeling uneasy at the last second. "Maybe we should start somewhere specific. How about: where did you and your cronies take my dad?"

Rose doesn't blink. "Don't know. Don't care."

Willow's blood boils and she wonders how anyone keeps patience with this half-blood. She takes a threatening step forward. "You better start caring because you're not leaving here without giving answers!"

"Well, I guess you'll be wasting *a lot of* time with me instead of finding your dad, huh?"

"Listen, *toots*—" Willow says through her teeth.

"Let's pick a subject you *do* wish to speak on, then," Hanas interjects, resting his hands on the table.

Willow backs off, swallowing her rage.

"I recall you mentioning something about a reward from the Rogue? From what I gather, he promises you freedom from purebloods if you do as he asks."

"Something like that," Rose replies, still not taking her glare off Hanas.

"You do know the Rogue is a pureblood, right?" Willow scoffs.

Rose snaps her daggers at Willow. "Trying to sound high and mighty, *mortal?* Ha! You know *nothing!"*

"I assure you we will be well informed by the time we finish this discussion," Hanas warns her, his rage giving way to faux delight. "You have nowhere to go if you refuse us. Nowhere to run. Should your farce continue, I will be forced to send you to the Epiphany's where your fate may entail imprisonment, if not death. I am sure that neither of us want that."

"I beg to differ," Willow mutters under her breath.

Rose quirks a brow at Willow and adjusts her position haughtily, unsettling and irritating them both. "Death threats? Very original, my lord. Unfortunately for you, death would be sweet compared to a life of oppression under *your kind.* I won't be talking because I'll never give away the gift the Rogue has promised to hand to me—and to the rest of us half-bloods."

Willow slides a finger across the ridges of her Glock, wondering if killing Rose would really cost that much. "She won't give in, so I say we get rid of her. The Rogue can't do as much as he wants with no accomplice."

She smiles sweetly at Willow. "Oh, I'm not the accomplice."

Willow's glare deepens. "Liar!"

"She is more than likely telling the truth," Hanas says bitterly studying her. "Rose does not miss chances to gloat about position and strength when given it. However, you might as well be the accomplice, Rose, given your involvement."

She cocks her chin proudly, challengingly. It makes Willow want to cut her down all the more, but Hanas continues, his own resolve far from waning.

"So, as you say, death is not enough. Nor imprisonment. Then I propose this: if you refuse us the information we need again, then you can consider the deal good as done."

She eyes him. "Deal?"

He nods. "I know a certain neighboring pureblood who always enjoys receiving new half-bloods for his little army he builds. I imagine he would be more than pleased if I handed you to him." A sly smile spreads across his lips. "A half-blood with such ferocity and passion for fighting and killing humans—he would be beside himself."

Willow's brow goes up. He is referring to Devone Vitya, a pureblood infamous for his bloodthirsty habits and cruel treatment of anyone beside himself. "Wow, you play dirty."

Rose's expression melts off her face. "You wouldn't—" She shoots to her feet, outrage and horror distorting her features. "*You disgusting—*"

"*Sit. Down,*" Hanas commands. A horrible chill crawls across the room, a hint of his black, pit-like presence slinking through it.

Willow shivers and Rose drops back into her seat, looking murderous and bloodthirsty.

"This is why I *hate* your kind," Rose seethes.

"I would not send you off if you would simply comply to my rules and questions," he says evenly. "Now, it is clear to me that the Rogue is promising your freedom for something in return. What exactly does he want? What does the Rogue think he can gain by disrupting our society's functions?"

Rose laughs. "That's just like you monsters. As a pureblood, all you care about is what *you* gain from things. Have you ever thought that maybe some people do things because it's *right* or *fair?*"

Willow carefully sits on the edge of Hanas' desk. "So, you're saying the Rogue woke up one morning and decided he was a good man, and good men send hordes of half-bloods to massacre the towns of innocent humans?"

Rose shrugged a shoulder. "In order to create a revolution, people must fall."

Willow's nails dig into her arms. "You think that my Dad going missing and Rei-Com Dube being on the verge of death are nothing more than casualties?"

Rose looks her dead in the eyes and Willow suppresses an instinctual shiver. "Got a problem with that, *toots*?"

"You are *sooo* asking for it—"

"Ladies, please," Hanas interjects, giving Willow an understanding, yet warning look, then glaring Rose down. "You may think the Rogue is doing this from the kindness of his heart, but you must also remember he has murdered before. The Rogue obtained his name *before* he came here."

Willow nods her agreement, fighting the urge to put a bullet through Rose's skull.

Rose flicks a curl from her face. "Say whatever you want. I know what I was promised and I know who it came from."

Willow detects the lie and unease, watching her eyes shift to the left and her fingers rub a strand between them. She hides it well, but Hanas' words have stirred a question.

"Since you have obviously had a conversation with him," Hanas continues, irritation in his tone, "can you tell us where he is now?"

Rose shakes her head. "No one's seen him since he first showed up." Her tone is low, that question still picking her brain.

"So, his accomplice is doing all the work for him," Willow confirms.

Rose nods reluctantly.

"Then the Rogue is temporarily out of the picture," Hanas muses, leaning against his palm and tapping his cheek anxiously. "And you have no idea what direction he went in, be it general or otherwise?"

"I don't know," Rose spits, her anger flaring up again. Willow notes that it's likely due to her inability to resolve Hanas' logic.

The Rogue is lying. He has bigger plans than equality for half-bloods.

Rose refuses to make eye contact, reciting her words like they might offer comfort. "He was here and then he vanished. All I know is what I've been promised and what I need to do to make it happen." She tucks her hands under her armpits, feigning defiance. But Willow knows she's hiding twitching fingers.

Hanas' tapping pauses. "Do tell, Rose."

She smirks at Hanas. "I can't. We're given orders as they come."

"Then what are your current orders?" Willow tries.

"Attack the human town as a distraction and break into their Vampire Hunter headquarters to kidnap Desmond Hunter."

"So he's alive," Willow sighs in relief.

Rose gives Willow a hungry look. "You don't know that."

Willow's heart drops to her feet. *She's toying with you!* her mind yells in denial. *She has to be!*

"Why my Dad?" Willow manages to ask instead of spitting a string of insults and pummeling the hot-headed chick.

Rose shrugs. "Haven't gotten that far."

Willow feels Hanas' gaze on her back, but she can't meet it. Thoughts of how her Dad might be used against her, perhaps as a bargaining chip or to force her hand, swim in the tears brimming her eyes. *Not now!* she chides herself, rubbing them away under the pretense of a simple itch.

"Let's focus on the accomplice," Hanas says, taking his attention off her. "I'll ask you again, who is this accomplice?"

"I can't tell you," Rose says in a low tone.

The room drops a few degrees and seems to darken. Hanas' presence coils around the room and seizes Rose. She cries out in pain. Even with the presence not directly aimed at her, Willow struggles to breathe.

"If you don't want me to send you away..." he growls.

"Not even your stupid threats can pluck that answer from me!" Rose yells. "A fate worse than the one you threatened would become my reality if I did!"

The presence is sucked away by some invisible force. Willow masks her steadying breath with an annoyed sigh, then sneaks a worried glance at Hanas, not wanting to know what could be terrible enough to frighten a half-blood who doesn't even fear death.

The two stare each other down for several moments.

"I won't press," Hanas reluctantly relents. "It's become more than clear to me that the accomplice's identity must be discovered and not told. So, I will ask you this instead: do you know anything of this vial?" He slips the fancy glass tube from his frock's pocket.

Willow had forgotten about it, her mind full of swelling emotions she doesn't understand and thoughts of her dad she understands all too well... Even so, she doesn't forget to watch Rose's expression when the vial is revealed to her.

She arches a brow, confusion crowding her expression. "What does a vial have to do with the accomplice?"

"That's what we want to know," Willow says, unblinking as she studies Rose's mannerisms.

Rose gives a humorous half smile. "Never seen it before. I think you might be sniffing in the wrong area."

Hanas narrows his eyes at her and his presence begins to permeate the air again. "Are you certain?"

Rose's eyes go wide. "Yes, I swear! I'm telling the truth!"

"She is," Willow confirms.

Hanas looks to her, hiding bewilderment.

She glances back at him before saying, "I just... know." She isn't about to explain her methods of mannerism reading in front of Rose, and she feels it's a terrible idea to tell any vampire in general. *A trade secret,* she reminds herself.

Hanas pulls back his presence once more and tucks the vial away. "I will take your word for it," though he still looks skeptical. His attention goes back to Rose. "A final question: why did two of my half-bloods stay behind during the attack?"

Willow forgets to pretend like she knows this and turns on Hanas, eyes a flurry of questions. He doesn't look at her, perhaps as if to say, *"I will explain later."*

Rose huffs. "I guess you mean Thomas and Edwin." She flicks some hair from her face. "Edwin's a coward. Of course he won't fight. But Thomas wouldn't go because he's stupidly loyal to you." She snorts. "I wouldn't be surprised if he turns up dead, too, after tonight."

Another chilly wave of black maw grips Rose and Willow's hearts. "Explain," is all Hanas says.

Rose shifts in her chair, glancing between the two with shock and mockery. "You know, the whole finding Gavin dead thing? The Rogue killed him."

"We know that," Willow snaps, hating that 'you-infidels-should-know-this' tone of hers. "The Rogue killed him because he went after the accomplice."

Rose scoffs, but sweat beads her pale face. She is terribly aware of the mounting anger in Hanas. "You're cute. That's not why the Rogue killed him. Gavin died because he refused to help the Rogue." She turns careful, yet judging, eyes on Hanas. "Because he sided with you."

Willow's brain aches as an onslaught of new questions poor in.

Hanas doesn't move, his intense gaze locked on Rose. "And you say the Rogue has no goal."

She doesn't respond to him, so he asks the question hanging between him and Willow. "So, the Rogue has been after me all along?"

Rose swallows, her answer served with slow and delicate precision. "Like any leader, he will take down his enemies."

Willow stares at her incredulously. *Is she insinuating that we started this fight? He's the one who attacked us!*

Before she can voice her response, Hanas says in a dangerously low tone, "That will be all, Rose."

She needs no invitation. Rose stands and strides toward the door, expertly hiding her desire to run. In seconds, she's gone.

Willow faces Hanas, her expression one of confusion and worry. "Why would the Rogue consider us his enemies? I didn't know him until he tried to make a meal out of me!" Her own words make her suppress a shudder.

"I share this question as well," Hanas agrees, leaning back in his leather chair. "I only heard of the Rogue through word-of-mouth and the newspapers before this. I doubt questioning Rose on it will bring any answers to light, either. Truthfully, I do not think she knows as much as she thinks."

Willow presses her lips into a line, staring at the doors Rose disappeared through.

"Wait a moment…"

Willow looks back to him. "What?"

His expression is grim. "I believe I have our answer… Do you recall what the Rogue told you of his revolution?"

"Yeah? But what would Rose have to do with—" Her eyes widen. "The incentive!"

Hanas nods. "Correct. It sounds to me like this revolution of his will include the freedom of half-bloods. However, I do not understand how your father plays into this."

"I don't know," Willow admits. "But at least we have a start."

Hanas nods. "Indeed we do."

"Well," Willow sighs heavily. "The Rogue has ignited his revolution, now we just have to snuff it out."

CHAPTER
THIRTEEN

AFTER THE interrogation, Willow finds herself back to feeling one-hundred percent awkward and an additional fifty percent useless.

Hanas calls for a servant, intending to send the vial to some sort of deductive pureblood family for pursuit of its buyer. Rose may not have recognized the vial, but that doesn't mean its owner isn't the Rogue, and any information on his identity could be a key to his plans.

A small boy, with a messenger bag half the size of himself, appears moments later. He takes the vial with gloved hands and packages it with the delicacy of crown gems. Once he's left, Hanas announces he must go speak with Edwin in private, then address his half-bloods on the recent attack, come back and document it, inform the Vampiric Council on their soon-to-be lack of human blood, and Willow couldn't follow anything after that point.

"You've got your hands full, huh?" Willow clarifies.

Hanas smiles weakly. He looks tired already. "Now you see why I appreciate your assistance. My brain does not have the capacity to solve all these problems at once."

"Can I help?" Willow offers, although a tug inside her said she shouldn't help a vampire. "I mean, I can't just sit around.

There has to be something to do, some place to search for clues on my dad or the accomplice or the Rogue."

"I appreciate the offer, but it would be best for you to stay here when no one trustworthy is around to pro—" he paused and changed his word. "To aid you. The half-bloods are unpredictable, and may be even more so once I have a word with them." He caught Willow's fallen expression and amended, "But Edwin may have discovered something. I would not put it past him to have done some sleuthing while the others were away. I'll inform you if there is anything new."

Willow wasn't too hopeful, but she didn't let that show. "Yeah, alright."

Hanas reminded her to call on the servants if she needed them—he pointed out one of the entrances to their quarters—and then disappeared to be eaten alive by his duties. Willow was then left to the ringing silence of the mansion and her own discomforting thoughts.

Standing in the first-floor hall where Hanas had left her, Willow rubs her arm and gazes around at the open space. She eyes the small wooden door, slightly ajar, that leads down to the servants' quarters. For a heartbeat, she almost considers going down in search of company or maybe to assist in busy-body work, but she can't imagine Adabelle, with her "Mistress this, Mistress that" kind of talk, letting her help.

Willow folds her arms and puffs her cheeks into a big sigh. She stares down at her combat boots. *You never did get to work out last week.*

Getting in shape for an evident fight isn't such a bad idea, although part of Willow still hopes she'll never have to face the Rogue again. *Doesn't hurt to prepare for another half-blood attack,* Willow corrects. *But what can I use for exercise?* She glances around thoughtfully. *I could run laps around the manor... The stairs would be good for my legs... but what about weight lifting?*

She spots a vase. Willow can only imagine Hanas' reaction if she dropped it or set it down too hard. But her eye catches on something else: twine. A thick length of it was swirled around the vase's neck and tied off in a fancy bow. *If I could just find something heavy to tie up…*

"Mistress?"

Willow nearly jumps out of her suspenders. She turns, wondering when Adabelle had snuck up the servant stairs.

"Do your shoes have silencers on them or something?" Willow breathes.

"Please accept my deepest apologies, Mistress," Adabelle curtseys. "I do not know about silencers, but our shoes are padded so no one can hear us walking through the walls and corridors."

"You walk inside the walls?" Willow searches the ivory for cracks suggesting doors.

"Yes, Mistress." She studies Willow for a moment. "Are you lost?"

"No, just—" Willow chews her cheek. "You wouldn't happen to know of anything heavy to lift in this house? Like… I don't know, a weight?"

"To lift?" Adabelle asks, delicate features screwing up in confusion. She thinks about the question for a moment, despite her misunderstanding. "Well, if you need something heavy, there are always books."

"Perfect!" Willow says. "Weren't there some in Hanas' office?"

"Master Blackwell's study is locked when he is not inside, but there is a library."

Willow stares at her. "A library?"

Two halls and an entryway later, Adabelle pauses before two large wooden doors. She presses down on one of the thin handles and swings the door open, then gestures for Willow to go in first.

Stepping inside, Willow's first awed words are, "What does he even need all these for?"

The library spans the height of the two-story mansion. Black, railed stairs to her left and right lead to open balconies with isles upon isles of books. Polished oak tables line the middle of the ground floor and stop before the massive floor-to-ceiling window at the end. More rows of bookshelves stand to her left and right, presenting shadowed aisles of musty, ancient literature.

The stale air is spiced with old glue and yellowing pages, giving off the sensation of well-worn leather. Despite the age of the room's contents, the tables, shelves, and antique oil lamps are dust and grime free.

"Master Blackwell does not use all the books," Adabelle says, a small chuckle on her lips. "Just a few. They were left by the previous pureblood."

"Oh," is all Willow can say. She isn't really sure what else *to* say.

"Will this suffice, Mistress?"

Willow nods. "Yeah, thanks."

"If you need anything else, please call for me, Mistress." She curtsies and leaves Willow alone.

Willow paces slowly past the aisles, reading the stylistic writing on each shelf: Sciences, Strategies, Historic Literature, History. Her mind has wandered away from her work out, fascinated by all the information now present at her fingertips. She was never into reading, unless it was her gun magazines, but hoards of unknown knowledge was sitting in this room, growing old and—her adventurous side reminded her—never seen by human eyes.

You should be preparing for another fight! her brain reminds her from somewhere distant. *The accomplice or the half-bloods could attack at any time!* But even as Willow pulls the tomes from the shelf to make her makeshift dumbbell, she can't help but flip through the books. A few in particular catch her eye. One is maroon and tells of a Romanian pureblood who was hidden away several hundreds of years ago and was never found. A second goes into detail about war tactics purebloods once used. A third included the first half of vampiric history unknown to humans. Willow memorizes all the covers and decides to come back and read them later.

After plucking a few more thick books from the shelf and dropping them on the nearby table, Willow pulls the twine from the vase—having asked Adabelle's permission first—and begins to wrap up the books. In the process, a particularly fat black book thunks to the floor. Willow jumps at the echoing noise and glares down at it irritably. Her annoyance fades when she reaches down to pick it up and something flutters out.

Willow is hardly surprised—*Of course something would be tucked away in an old book*, she thinks—but her curiosity spurs on to excitement as she eagerly unfolds the parchment. She stares with wide eyes and takes a few slow breaths. Gazing back at her is a family: a brilliantly groomed father with satiny brunet hair, a luxurious mother with shimmering black waves, an amiable boy with an educated posture, and a second boy who Willow recognizes almost immediately. He is young, maybe twelve or thirteen, with neatly trimmed black hair, and a calm, yet slightly amused, shimmer in his eyes. Willow realizes with a start that this is Hanas.

"What's this doing in a book?" Willow murmurs to herself. She checks the cover. *The Hierarchy of Vampiric Nobility Through the Centuries.* She flips the book open to the page her thumb marks—the same page the photo fell from. Her expression crinkles all the more. The page is titled with *The Blackwell Family* and punctuated by a much older photograph of the same man and woman except each proudly holding a toddler in their arms. Under that are the printed words, *Vincent Blackwell (left) and his wife Cloris Blackwell (right) holding their children Anthes (left) and Hanas (right).*

So Hanas does *have a family somewhere,* Willow thinks, noting the lack of any information on deaths as she skims the thick paragraphs beside the photo. Her eyes alight on some concerning words: dangerous, powerful, untrustworthy. Her muscles tense as she slows to read a few lines.

> *The Blackwell family is widely considered dangerous and untrustworthy by many vampiric nobles. Their family is known for protecting sires by any means possible, which includes the use of powerful and extremely dangerous abilities. These abilities have been readily used against subjects deemed "a danger" to the sire family. Victims vanish from society, their remains never found, once a Blackwell has dealt with them. Due to this mysterious and unnerving power, it is said that not even the sires fully trust the Blackwells at times.*

Willow skims the paragraph a second time, thinking of the horror she may have just called an ally.

Her brain can't compute this. Not now. Not after trusting Hanas enough to live in his home.

She tucks the information away and instead turns to the notes stuck to the opposite page's side. One is a newspaper article with the carefully crafted headline of: BLACKWELL FAMILY TORN APART, CHILD MISSING. She knits her brow, trying to fit the pieces together. *Hanas lives without his family, there are no roads leading to his home, and what had he said before? "… I cannot retreat farther into my race's land if they overrun me!"*

Willow's skin turns clammy. *Was he kidnapped?*

The photograph and a paragraph underneath it provide her more information.

Willow stares at the black-and-white image of a half-burned mansion, then reads the text below it. The summary states that the home caught fire in the early evening, before many pure-bloods were awake. The mother had been seen at the train station minutes after the discovery of the burning mansion. The father was gone, and his car was missing as well. There were no traces of the eldest child, and the youngest was found unconscious, deep within their forested property. Despite all this, the Vampiric Council had said and done little to address the situation.

Not kidnapped, Willow concludes. *But why is he hiding?* Her attention flickers to the other articles stuck to the paper: "HANAS BLACKWELL NOT SEEN IN SOCIETY: Blackwell Supporters Demanding to Know His Whereabouts"; "END OF THE BLACKWELL LINE? Will the Sires Go Unprotected or Gain Freedom and Peace of Mind?"; "POLITICAL UPHEAVAL: Who Will Stand Beside the Sires?"

The headlines mean little to Willow, confusing her like a foreign language.

She turns the page hoping to find answers, but there are none. The next page is an entirely different family. Willow flips back, scanning the notes in frustration, then turning over the picture in her hand. She even peels back the corner of the glued articles, but underneath is just a long list of ancestry.

With a huff, Willow looks back to the photograph. Apparently, she has some investigating of her own to do.

She spends the afternoon conducting her investigation, forgetting almost completely about her exercise plans. She pulls books off the shelves and shakes them to see if anything will fall from between their pages. She flips through history and heritage books that somehow don't put her to sleep. Her only discovery is that certain letters look funny when you stare at them too long. She goes back to her pile, tying them up and curling her biceps and triceps while frowning at the Blackwell family page.

Her mind concocts many theories, none of which sound more legitimate than the last, until a knock sends her flying from her skin. She spins toward the double door entrance, her brain readjusting to the fact that she's in a library across the border and not in a "detective land" somewhere. She hides the photograph she'd been holding in her free hand behind her back.

"Adabelle informed me you would be here," Hanas says, striding into the room. "I have—" He pauses, staring at the pile of books she's lifting by a length of twine. "Have I... interrupted something important?"

Willow blinks, her voice tighter than she would like. "No."

He stares in bewilderment.

"Just... working out," Willow says after a moment, breaking into a sweat. *Have I been caught?* She sets down the book pile, closing *Vampiric Heritage Through the Centuries* as casually as possible.

"Working what out?" He asks curiously, glancing at the book beside her.

Willow swallows and is about to make up a half-baked excuse when she suddenly remembers that vampires don't exercise. She quickly changes her excuse to an explanation.

"Oh! Um, you know, like strengthening my muscles..." she says, then adds when his expression doesn't change. "To get stronger."

A light goes on in his mind. "Ah! Apologies. I had forgotten that humans required such actions to build their physique." He reverts back to the topic at hand. "I came to accompany you to Vamstadt if you are not terribly busy. Edwin has found something."

Willow's eyes grow wide. "What? Show me." As Hanas strides toward the door, Willow quickly stuffs *Vampiric Heritage Through the Centuries* under a book in her pile. She hurries after him, relieved that he didn't mention the book.

* * *

A thirty-minute drive and some speed walking deposits the two at Edwin's doorstep. In their haste and anxiousness, Hanas explained that he had managed to complete half of his work before Edwin informed him of an important discovery.

"He would not tell me what he found until I brought you," Hanas finishes saying as they take the front steps two at a time. "Which is probably best, so we can stay informed equally."

They stop at the door.

"Can't keep secrets or hold back information, can we?" Willow agrees. "Especially since our allies are narrowed down to just us." *Or is it just you?* a voice whispers, reminding her of her earlier discovery. *Dangerous. Powerful. Untrustworthy.*

Willow jumps when the front door flies open, no knock needed.

"Thank goodness! P-please come in!" Edwin waves them into his shadowy home.

Willow picks her way around the stacks of books, disorganized papers, and the new addition of chairs strewn around the room. She would have never guessed that the corner home could look messier than the last time she saw it.

Edwin gestures for them to sit on the already-cleared couches while he hurries to bring out his findings. He returns from behind a wall of stacked newspapers with an object that makes Willow's heart sink a little.

"Another vial?" She tries to not sound disheartened at the prospect of another empty glass tube.

"It's n-not the vial I... want to show you," Edwin says, letting it clink gently on the ink-spotted coffee table. "This-s-s is... what I w-want to show you." He holds up a different test tube, this one simple and resembling something a scientist might use. Only, this test tube isn't empty.

Willow leans forward on her elbows, staring at the smidge of deep red tainting the tube's bottom. "Is that... blood?"

Edwin shakes his head. "A drug."

Willow's eyes shoot up to his face, reading it for traces of a lie. "What?"

Hanas stands and Edwin offers him the vial with a shaky hand. "Do we know what sort of drug?" He holds it up in a sliver of light that leaks between the curtained windows.

"I had our c-chemist run… whatever tests he could. He, uh, thinks… the drug enhances."

Willow exchanges a confused expression with Hanas. "Enhances what?"

Edwin shakes his head.

Willow chews her cheek. "Maybe it's… a mood enhancer? Is that a thing?"

"I am not sure," Hanas says, handing the tube back to Edwin. "Whatever it is, I doubt it is legal. There are far and few drugs and medications that vampires need."

Willow leans back and slouches. "An illegal drug, huh? And one that enhances something, possibly moods or emotions or— what else can you even enhance with a drug?"

"Desire?" Edwin suggests.

Willow stares at the intricate vial on the coffee table. "Desire for what? Blood? Money?" Her eyes widen. "If it enhances their desire for blood, that would help explain the attack on Hidden Hill! Maybe they weren't just after my dad!"

"It is a possibility," Hanas agrees, stroking his chin. "Perhaps not money, but status? There is no vampiric currency. Position or class serves as such." He narrows his eyes, staring off. "Rose did mention feeling oppressed."

"Maybe it enhances many different things at once?" Willow says.

Hanas sits back down, gazing at the vial as though it holds all the world's secrets—right then, it may as well have.

Edwin follows suit, fidgeting as he watches the two with his calculating eyes.

Willow frowns at him. He knows more than them, has seen things they haven't—namely the accomplice—yet he sits there like a rich man dangling bread above the starved. It shaves away at her nerves.

"You know something," she says. "Many things, actually. So why can't you just tell us?"

Edwin purses his lips, which only irritates Willow all the more.

"I didn't come all the way from the mansion just to get more 'I don't knows' and shrugs! You're no better than Rose—!"

"Now just a moment," Hanas tries to cut in.

"Do you not understand the stakes?" Willow barrels on, leaning forward. "If we don't get this figured out, my dad will— we *all* will die!"

Hanas is about to say something but Edwin cuts in.

"I know the stakes, Willow."

She freezes, locked under Edwin's serious gaze. *He didn't stutter?*

"I know… what a b-bad outcome will… cost," he says a little less firmly. "I'm trying."

The way he lowers his head a little makes Willow feel awful. She sinks into the couch.

"Edwin is doing more than my other half-bloods," Hanas adds. "We are all frustrated and at the end of our nerves."

Willow sighs. "Must you always be the voice of reason?"

He cracks a small smile. "You have witnessed what happens when I am not. I will stay as such for your own safety."

"Sure." Willow smirks, but it falls away—his last word triggering a string of others. *Powerful. Dangerous. Untrustworthy.* She suddenly remembers the secret stuffed in her back pocket.

Not my secret. His. She glances to Hanas.

"I should finish my work." Hanas breaks the silence. "I will accompany you—"

"Actually, Lord B-Blackwell, if I… may… that is, c-could I, uh, hire… Willow for the evening?"

Willow cocks a brow. "Hire? Doing what?" she asks suspiciously, not entirely sure she's ready to be left alone with a half-blood in a sea of uncontrollable ones. Her mind flashes with images of the attack on Hidden Hill, and of broken and lifeless bodies.

"J-just for… information on the Rogue. I have, er, a few… theories." His eyes meet hers for a moment, a hint of desperation reflecting in them.

Something's up, Willow senses. *But maybe this will work in my favor. I could ask him about Hanas.*

Willow levels her eyes with his. "I may have a few questions, too."

Hanas's eyes dart between the two, confusion pushing one eyebrow up. "Well… alright then. I think you will be safe here, for the time being, and I will not be far if you need me."

Willow nods.

Hanas stands, still confused. "I will be back before sundown, then. Evening, Edwin."

"Good evening, Lord B-Blackwell."

With a last glance, Hanas leaves the corner home behind.

Willow feels like an invisible connection between them is stretching out. She fights the urge to follow him and go back to the somewhat safer mansion. Right now, she has more pressing matters, like a half-blood that may spill the beans.

"If-f-f, er, you would… Willow," Edwin says. "F-f-follow me."

Willow rises, feeling the comforting weight of her Glocks strapped to ether hip, and weaves through the maze of stacked and displaced items. Turning down a short hall, Edwin directs Willow into another cluttered room. All four windows are covered, making the centerpiece of tubes and vials faceted together glow above their tiny flames. All manner of chemistry books are spread around the brewing concoction, inky notes laid across the different pages. The rest of the room is nothing but shelves of useless objects crammed and tucked into every possible space.

Willow picks up a rusted derringer. She turns it over, noting the extra hole in the barrel and the lack of a trigger. "Quite the pack rat, aren't you?"

"I'll… use them eventually."

"Su-ure." Willow puts the derringer down and paces toward the table. "So is this thing how you discovered the drug is for enhancement?" She flicks a tube and a small *ding* follows.

"N-n-no, I... had our c-chemist... work on the drug. That is... my rep-replication of the drug," Edwin says, slipping up to it and examining the bubbling red liquid. "Or... its s-s-supposed to be."

Willow cocks a brow. "You're remaking the drug?"

Edwin sits on a stool, not seeming to mind that he's also squashed a pressed open book too. "I'm n-n-not having... much luck. B-but I... won't give up! I *can't*. You s-s-see, if I can re-re-create the drug and use it on... myself, then we w-w-will be... closer to knowing... what it really does."

"Logical," Willow says. "Except that you already know what the drug does."

Edwin says nothing, absentmindedly leafing through his notes.

Willow crosses her arms. "You wanted to tell me something. So tell me."

"I do. B-But you have... questions too." He pulls at his ivory collar and his sleeves. "You go... first. W-w-what do you want to know?"

"Chickening out? I don't think so, buddy." She pounds a fist on the table. "Tell me your theories on the Rogue!"

"Only if-f-f... you tell *me* w-why you don't... trust Lord B-Blackwell."

Willow is stunned for a moment. Her hand slips up her thigh, stopping just before her Glock. "How do you—"

"W-w-when you came with Lord B-Blackwell... previously, you were w-wary. N-n-now your... mannerisms show distrust."

Willow swallows. "I guess we're both smarter than we look."

Edwin smiles a little, and Willow wonders if it's for the first time.

"Fine. I'll go first." She pulls out the photograph. "I found this…" she begins, holding it up for Edwin to see. "It was tucked in some ancestry book."

Edwin's eyes cloud over as he nods in understanding.

"The book also had information about the Blackwell family. It said—"

"Untrustworthy… dangerous, p-powerful? You want… to know if-f-f you can trust Lord B-Blackwell."

Willow nods, lowering the photograph.

"That is up… to you," Edwin says. "That f-f-family holds… many ugly secrets. If-f-f you… uncovered the photo, then you m-m-must have… read the book too… and know that, c-currently, the B-Blackwells are no longer… thought to be a threat."

"Because they vanished?"

"They ran away," he corrects remorsefully. "Lady C-Cloriss—I don't know… what happened. She… went mad and fffled. Lord B-Blackwell, w-w-was the only one… found at the manor after it b-burned."

"But why is he here?" Willow glances toward the hall like Hanas might be standing there. "Why don't people trust him, and why is he considered powerful and dangerous?"

"The B-Blackwells guard the… the sss—" He takes a deep breath. "The royals… you know."

"Sires," Willow confirms.

Edwin nods. "Any threat to our leaders… would have b-been dealt with by… the B-Blackwells. Nnnow that they are gone, only the… vampiric military can p-protect the… the royals. There is po-po-litical upheaval… over who will take the B-Blackwells' place." He shifts uneasily. "The po-power… part I can't say in detail. I've sworn to ne-never tell, or I… will vanish too."

"Harsh," Willow remarks. "No offense, but who are you to the Blackwells, anyway? You're not a servant, otherwise you'd be working in Hanas' mansion, right?"

Edwin chuckles, but Willow can't tell if it's because he is sad or proud. "I'm-m-m actually Hanas' p-personal servant. Right… now, I am just, uh, acting as head over the half-bloods."

Willow pales a little. "Purebloods have personal servants? Like… a valet or something?"

"Yesss," Edwin says. "I have… known Lord B-Blackwell s-s-since he was… ninety."

Willow doesn't want to know how old that makes Edwin.

"About the p-powers, all I… can tell you is, the p-power is inherited and… whoever a B-Blackwell targets… will never be… seen again."

Willow rubs her temple. "So, to clarify, it's my choice to trust Hanas, he's dangerous because of some inherited power, he uses that power to protect the sire vampires, and his family abandoned him?"

Edwin nods.

Willow's head thrums with this new information. She almost wishes she'd never asked.

"Um, how… does that information… help you?" Edwin asks cautiously, sorting through his vial collection. "I thought you… wanted to f-f-find the Rogue and your…er, Mi-Mister Hunter."

Willow exhales. "Honestly, it really doesn't help with the Rogue, but I needed to know if I can trust Hanas before anything else happens. I trust him enough to not kill me on the spot, but I hardly know him. I'm still not sure about purebloods and vampires in general."

Edwin smiles a little, his lips twitching in a hidden past pain. "I… know that emotion well."

Willow taps an empty tube, eyeing him carefully. "You had something to share, too?"

"I, er… you s-s-see—" Edwin rearranges his inky notes haphazardly. "Do you… think the accomplice… is s-s-someone the Rogue p-pressured?"

Willow rubs the heel of her boot on the stool rung. "How so?"

Edwin shrugs, still rearranging things without any particular order. "If he... wanted s-s-something only the Rogue could give."

Willow has to calm her pounding heart. *Edwin said "he."* What's more, Willow was terribly aware of Edwin's alluding. *Something only the Rogue could give someone...* She turns back to the bubbling experiment, pretending to have missed the slip. "Like what?"

If it was possible for Edwin to look more nervous, he would have. "M-m-maybe." He pauses, staring at nothing in particular. "The chance to have a life again." His words come out barely louder than a whisper, his stutter gone once more.

Willow narrows her eyes at him. "You seem to know an awful lot about the accomplice."

Sadness clouds his red eyes, but he says nothing for several moments. Somehow, Willow gets the feeling he means her no harm, despite his unnerving revelation. She lets her muscles relax.

"So the Rogue is enticing the accomplice with something he can't resist? Something only he can give?"

Edwin flies back into his busybody work, this time rearranging the shelves. "S-s-sorry, I... wouldn't know anything... about that."

Willow folds her arms, giving his back a dry smirk. "Of course you wouldn't. But why give me info now? For that matter, why didn't you say anything to Hanas earlier?"

Edwin slowly turns, his index finger tapping the prong of a gear. Many painful emotions swirl through his eyes and twist his face. "B-because now I... know you'll see it through."

Willow cocks a brow. "Um, what—?" A loud *SLAM* followed by the rattling of a glass pane cuts her off.

Even footfalls bring an irritatingly familiar half-blood into the room. Rose stops in the doorway, glaring at Willow with one fist on her hip before shooting her dirty look to Edwin. "Lord

Blackwell wants you… and *her.* Apparently, he found more of those vials."

Willow is on her feet in seconds. "What? How?"

"More vials?" Edwin chimes in optimistically.

Rose snarls at Willow. "I'm not obligated to give you that information. I'm *not* a messenger boy."

Willow scoffs. "Could have fooled me."

"Where is Lord B-Blackwell," Edwin interrupts before the two can launch into a civil war.

"The abandoned shack just west of here." Rose smiles haughtily at Willow. "You can go there on your own. Good luck finding it."

"I'll lead you… there," Edwin tells Willow, tossing the old gear aside. "F-f-follow me."

The two hurry past Rose, Willow slamming a shoulder into her as they pass. Her mind and pulse chug ahead full steam, but she isn't excited like Edwin. Her gut sends her warnings, and her skin prickles. *Another clue already? Why are we finding so many all of a sudden?* Something isn't right, and Willow knows she's going to find out what very soon.

CHAPTER
FOURTEEN

HASTENING THROUGH the half-bloods in the streets, Willow catches more than one hungry and loathing glare. They come in frequent red flickers: a woman, still as a statue, with eyes following the two in hatred; a man, whittling with a crude-looking knife, watching them pass in murderous anticipation.

Willow is glad, but not relieved, when they leave Vamstadt behind. She checks over her shoulder for pursuers with violent intentions. *Were they like that when I came in?* she thinks. *Or did something happen while I was in Edwin's house?*

"They are hungry."

Willow jumps, snapping her attention back to Edwin. She nearly bumps her head on a low-hanging branch.

"The s-s-stares. They are hungry and... angry b-because Lord B-Blackwell rationed... their blood."

"What?" Willow says. "Why—" She suddenly recalls Rei-Com Ashe's order. "Less blood because the Batch won't be coming this winter."

Edwin nods reluctantly, peeking at Willow from his peripheral vision.

Willow focuses ahead, weaving through the sea of dying greenery. "But they weren't that upset earlier today. There must be something else..." She can't put her finger on it. "I don't like this," she whispers to herself.

By the time they reach their destination, Willow is winded. They slow their pace as pokey branches and withering undergrowth give way to a tilting shack. Hanas stands outside, deep in thought.

Willow approaches, glancing between him and the shack. "Rose said… you found more vials?" she asks between breaths.

"An alarming amount," Hanas replies grimly. He stares off in thought for a moment. "Come, I will show you."

Willow and Edwin follow him through a wooden door that had long turned into barely more than crumbling splinters. Inside, the floor is the happy home of many weeds, wild grasses, and fungus. Willow guesses that plant life is the only thing keeping the two-room shamble standing.

"How'd you find this place?" Willow asks, eyeing one wall jutting outward.

"Thomas tipped me off," Hanas says, waving her into the next room. "He could not say much, as usual, but this discovery nearly explains why."

At least one hundred vials litter the dirt, some still containing residue from their contents.

Willow squats, squinting at the trickles of red in the vials. "Someone drank these in a hurry–there's some left in them. Unless it tastes awful, so they didn't savor every drop."

"Either way, the culprit or drinker has not left us much to study," Hanas says reluctantly. "But this does bring some alarming theories to mind."

Willow picks up a shard of glass, turning it over for clues. "Yeah. You mentioned all these vials would explain why Thomas, and I'm assuming the others, won't talk."

Hanas crosses his arms. "I was thinking up until your arrival. There are too many vials here for any one person to drink. I imagine one vial would be plenty enough drug to enhance whatever this drug enhances."

Willow drops the glass, standing. "So maybe one person drank all of these over time?"

"Not, uh, likely," Edwin cuts in. "This-s-s charade w-w-with the Rogue... began two weeks ago, three at ma-maximum. That is only... twenty-one days or twenty-one vials if one is... drunk each day."

"So you think this validates that the half-bloods might be under the influence?" Willow clarifies.

Hanas nods. "There are one hundred vials here, I counted myself, and I had roughly three hundred half-bloods in the province—before the attack on Hidden Hill, that is."

"Then what's our current tally?"

"I was about to head a census when Thomas approached me, so I am not certain."

Willow shakes her head. "That still makes no sense. You had three hundred half-bloods before the attack, but only one-hundred were drugged? Why would the rest of the half-bloods not need the drug?"

Hanas thinks on this, stroking his chin, but comes up with no answers.

Willow turns back to the vials. "I don't like this. Something is *very* wrong."

"How so?" Hanas has to ask.

Willow rubs her arms, feeling the chill in the air tenfold. "I don't know, but doesn't this all seem a bit... odd to you?"

Hanas lifts a brow. "Mysterious purebloods and unnamed drugs are quite abnormal."

"Not that, I mean... first we find some empty vial as a clue, which I guess is normal, but then we suddenly find another, this one with part of the drug inside—just enough for us to make wild guesses about what it could be. Now, we find a whole treasure trove of these vials that partially confirms a theory we made up like, forty minutes ago?" She looks between Edwin, who is busily examining the vials, and Hanas. "Is that not really... strange?"

"I see what you are insinuating," Hanas says after a brief moment. "You think we are finding clues too easily, and practically having them handed to us."

Willow nods. "Plus, after leaving Vamstadt, either your half-bloods really are angry about rationing blood or they were upset over something else. They were all acting *really* bizarre."

Hanas pauses a moment, doubly intrigued. "Bizarre? How?"

"They were staring at me hungrily, but also, I dunno, like they were watching me." She shudders. "It was like they were stopping what they were doing just to watch me. I don't know why."

Hanas's expression knits together. His face asks the jumble of questions his lips won't produce—questions neither of them can answer.

"A trick, m-m-maybe?"

They both whirl on Edwin as he holds up a glass vial, one with red residue smeared along its mouth. "Lord B-Blackwell... this, er, liquid isn't the drug. It is b-blood."

Willow takes a step toward him. "What? Whose?"

"Never mind that," Hanas says tensely. "You said my half-bloods were keeping an eye on you. If Edwin is correct, then it may very well be that they were waiting for you to leave."

Willow's heart misses a beat. "Why?"

"I do not know. But if we have been tricked, then we need to get back to Vamstadt. *Immediately*."

* * *

Willow, Edwin, and Hanas dash back through the forest. A surge of adrenaline is the only thing allowing Willow to run again. With every thump of her boot, every snap of a twig, every gasp of breath, she feels a horrible reality dawning—a reality she isn't sure she wants to know.

The brush pulls away to reveal the aging tutor buildings of Vamstadt. The three of them halt at the wide cobblestone road leading into town. Hanas' shoulders tense, Edwin's posture slumps mournfully, and Willow's eyes grow wide as she scans the street. She can't believe what she's seeing.

"Where did they go?"

Doors are ajar, fresh cut wood sits unattended on the road-side, aprons lay thrown over carts of vegetables left to the cold. It is like a scene from a post-apocalyptic film.

Vamstadt is empty.

CHAPTER
FIFTEEN

FOR A moment, Willow feels stuck in her own reality; there is only her and the empty town. "I don't understand," she whispers to herself. Her whisper rings through the silence, snapping her from her daze.

She turns to Hanas and Edwin. "You don't think they went to attack Hidden Hill again, do you?"

"I do not personally believe so." He looks expectantly to Edwin who avoids his gaze entirely. A twinge of irritation flickers across his features before he continues. "By my logic, why would they wait until you were gone to attack Hidden Hill? It would seem more ideal to kill you off while in Vamstadt rather than waiting to deal with you in Hidden Hill."

"You've got a point," Willow mumbles. She isn't sure if the fact relieves her or worries her more.

"Er, you may... want to, ah, w-w-warn the other Hunters," Edwin suggests timidly.

Both Willow and Hanas turn knit brows and frowns on him.

"Why?" Willow asks suspiciously as Hanas says, "Care to inform us further?"

Edwin musses his hair uncomfortably. "If-f-f I could, uh, tell you m-m-more, then I... would." When neither Willow nor Hanas break their cold stares he adds in hastily, "You must b-b-believe me!"

Willow steps toward him. "Why should we? You've been no help! All you do is warn us about disasters as they happen! You obviously know a lot of things we don't, but you won't say *anything!*"

Edwin swallows and glances to Hanas for help.

"Willow is correct, Edwin," he says dispassionately. "The games need to end. My half-bloods are missing, completely out of my control. I am already in trouble with the Council. Let's not make this any worse."

"Lord B-Blackwell, you know I w-w-would never... I c-could never, er, in my w-w-wild—" He shakes his head. "Lord B-Blackwell, I'm not... playing games! If I c-could tell you—"

"*What* are you so frightened of?" Hanas snaps. "I have protected you before and I will do so again! I will go through whatever it *takes* to keep you in one piece, yet you still cower? Does the Blackwell name mean nothing to you, as well?" His tone turns to hurt on the last words.

Willow's eyes flicker between the two, only partially understanding the conversation. Hanas holds pride in his dangerous title, Willow assumes, but what's the deal with Hanas having protected Edwin in the past? Part of Willow wants to ask, but the overwhelmed side of her wins out.

"Hanas is right," Willow says. "You don't have a choice anymore. *Tell us what's going on.*"

Edwin purses his lips. It takes him several tries to form his next words. "To b-begin, Lord B-Blackwell, I have... complete faith in... you and, uh, the B-Blackwell name. And, Willow... I understand your... doubt, b-but I am giving you b-both all I... can!"

"It's not enough!" Willow practically shouts. "Look at the mess we're in! Just give us the stupid answers we need!"

"Enough," Hanas decides, rubbing between his eyes, but he doesn't sound convincing. "We should discuss this later. First, we *must* find those half-bloods before more harm is done.

Willow, do you suggest warning the Vampire Hunters? We do not know what my half-bloods are plotting."

Willow cocks a brow at him. "Do you really think the V.H. are going to listen to me? Or even let me back into Foxhound?" she scoffs.

"No. But, if you do, they cannot blame us if an attack comes and they are unprepared."

"Can't knock that logic," Willow grumbles, but all she can think about is Rei-Com Ashe's last words. Her blood boils, and she kicks at the cobblestone. "But I don't think we should warn them. We're not allies and if Rei-Com Ashe thinks she's so capable, then she can handle a half-blood attack on her own."

Edwin lifts a finger to object, but thinks better of it when Willow scowls at him.

Is she being unreasonable? Maybe. Is she angry and hurt? You bet. Does she worry about whether Rei-Com Ashe can *actually* protect the small town she calls home? Yes! But Rei-Com Ashe made her decision, so now Willow is making hers.

"Finding my dad and stopping the Rogue is our top priority," she tells them. "Rei-Com Ashe will have to pay the price if half-bloods attack."

Hanas nods. "I could not agree more." His tone hides a small pride that suggests he'd love to see Rei-Com Ashe taken down a peg. Willow doesn't blame him, because some awful part of her thinks the same. This whole fiasco is bigger than both their prejudices.

"So how are we going to track down these half-bloods? We couldn't stop them when they attacked Hidden Hill and couldn't even manage to find clues of the Rogue hiding in your province."

"Tracking down nearly two hundred half-bloods will be easier than just one," Hanas says, though he rubs his chin in thought. "We can begin by checking the parameters of Vamstadt. The ground is sodden from all this damp weather, so footprints should be left somewhere."

"Unless they covered their trail," Willow points out. "But we could check the ground to see if it's unnaturally uneven, pressed down, I mean, then we can tell if someone went that way."

Edwin clears his throat. "I c-can check the eastern s-s-side, er, if you... want."

Hanas shakes his head. "You have done enough, Edwin. You will stay with me where I can keep an eye on you. In fact, I believe it wise for us to stay together."

"I couldn't agree more," Willow sighs, glancing at the growing shadows that could hide any number of blood-thirsty half-bloods.

"We can start on the south side, since we are already here," Hanas advises.

"Then let's circle around to the east," Willow eyes Edwin, "since you were so keen to check there yourself."

Edwin looks away, frowning.

"Good plan," Hanas says with a suspicious, and slightly hurt, glance to his Head Half-blood.

Without much more conversation, they begin their tedious search. Willow crouches to examine the muddy and uneven soil, Hanas searches for snapped branches and trampled undergrowth, Edwin does a mix of the two. Every so often, Willow checks in his direction. It would be all too easy for him to find a clue and cover it up.

The shadows grow longer, deeper, darker as they search. Heavy clouds block out the last rays of light, and soon the moon also, as they move their search toward the east. Though she knows the Vampires can still see just fine, Willow is having a hard time seeing much of anything as the light grows dim. With the thickening cold and pressing silence, Willow becomes more and more certain that the half-bloods had simply vanished from where they stood. It was that, or they had someone very good at covering trails.

Willow tries to blow a little warmth into her hands, wishing she'd thought to ask for gloves. The vampiric clothing keeps the cold out almost flawlessly, but any bare skin is vulnerable to the oncoming chill of autumn.

"We have finished searching our area," Hanas informs her, his shoes softly crunching twigs as he approaches. "Did you happen across any clues?"

Willow stands, shaking her head as she turns to face him. "Nothing. Edwin hasn't been hiding any clues he's found?"

Hanas glances back toward the nervous half-blood. He stares off at nothing in particular, brows knit in irritation and frustration. "Nothing I have picked up on."

Willow huffs, rubbing her hands together. "Maybe you should send him back to your mansion. Lock him in a room until we can deal with him."

The idea seems to tempt Hanas. "No. I don't dare let him out of my sight, not even for a moment."

"He could be hindering us," Willow objects. "I don't trust him either. But we can't let him cover the half-blood's trail."

Hanas glances back to Edwin again, still in a daze, then says. "Let's check the north."

Willow throws up her arms, heading along the border of Vamstadt. "Fine. But I'm keeping an extra eye on him."

They continue their search until Willow's fingers begin to feel numb. She stuffs them in her coat pockets, brushing them against the fuzzy lining. "Nothing here!" She calls half-heartedly.

"Just a moment longer," Hanas says from where he examines the chipped root of a tree.

Willow rolls her eyes, trudging closer. "Hanas, we aren't going to find anything. Their tracks have been covered—" She freezes when she throws her gaze dramatically to her right.

"We do not know that for sure," Hanas says. "Not yet, anyway."

"Hanas…" Willow stares at a parting in the forest.

He looks up, catching the breathless tone of her voice. "Yes?"

She points, eyes wide. She can hardly believe it. They actually found a clue! "Deer path," she whispers. "Deer path!"

Hanas hurries over and Edwin follows. "Look what we have here." Hanas crouches, running his fingertips over the trodden soil. "Traveling single file, it seems. A wise move as width is easier to track."

Willow examines Edwin's expression from the corner of her eye, hoping to find some hint that this is the clue they need. But his knit brows, downturned mouth, and squinting eyes give Willow nothing.

Hanas stands. "Let's see where this leads, shall we?"

Willow nods, losing a bit of her excitement when Edwin doesn't react. That uneasy feeling returns. Something is amiss. But there is no other choice than to follow the path.

With Hanas in the lead and Edwin tailing uncertainly, they hastily follow the slim deer-path. Willow favors staying closer to Hanas' rear, her own tingling with the awareness of Edwin following behind.

The sky darkens all the more until night has risen anew. Willow is thankful when the clouds part to let the moon shine down. It washes their trail in silvery-blue light, but also casts deep shadows everywhere else. Only the snap of twigs underfoot, Willow's rhythmic breaths, and the rustle of clothing echoes in the night. Once again, the silence unnerves her, reminding her of the night Thomas and Gavin attacked, and of the Rogue and his sickly-sweet tone.

"Oof!" Willow runs into Hanas' back. Her fingers clamp down on the rough wool of his sleeve for support. "What did you stop for?" She peers around him and her eyebrows go up.

"The path… it just ends," he says, befuddled.

Willow steps around him, scanning the crossed branches, untrampled shrubbery, and lack of footprints altogether. "That's impossible! What did they do, fly away?"

Hanas turns his face up. "Highly unlikely."

Willow is too frustrated to explain her sarcasm. "Maybe they just... veered off somewhere. Or... oh! The trees!" She rushes up to a trunk, examining some torn off bark. "They could have climbed up and traveled that way. It's slower, but leaves next to no evidence."

Hanas contemplates this. "Not a terrible theory. But I find it hard to imagine half-bloods jumping through the trees like a band of uncivilized monkeys."

Willow scratches the tree, finding the base to be wet and the bark to have simply fallen off on its own. "Well, they attacked Hidden Hill that way. The vampires who captured me were in the trees. Besides, you can't get more uncivilized than attacking an entire town of people who did nothing to provoke you."

"One could debate that."

Willow turns around slowly. "Excuse me?"

Hanas glances up from where he crouches at the path's end. "I only mean that assailing a town is not the most uncivilized thing a vampire could do. You forget how greedy some pure-bloods can be, and most of society will not frown on them for it."

Willow folds her arms. "Greedy purebloods are why we're in this mess. How could I—" She stops, some odd sensation creeping at the edge of her senses.

"Willow?" Hanas slowly stands.

She stares into the tangle of shadows beyond the little deer path. Something dark and heavy is looming just beyond the thick of trees and shadow. Something like...

Willow's arms go slack. "A presence." Her eyes snap to Hanas'. "Do you feel that?"

He slowly stands, brow furrowed in concentration. "No. I feel nothing. Is it the Rogue, do you think?"

Willow shakes her head, staring back into the forest. "This is dark and heavy, not like the Rogue's freaky presence." Hand sliding over the grip of her Glock, Willow gives Hanas a look.

He nods and takes the lead, Willow warily in tow. She carefully pulls out her Glock, smooth and silent, as they creep through the growth.

Willow's heart threatens to pulse like that of a panicked rabbit, but she takes steadying breaths and calms the nerves warning her to run.

A dirt road, bathed in moonlight, peeks through the trunks and wispy shrubs. Willow's chest tightens when she spots a man, slightly taller than Hanas, standing beside what resembles a 1930 Model T Coupe. His back is toward them, his hands on hips as he toes at a tree leaning across the road and mumbles to himself.

Willow begins to raise her Glock as they step onto the road, but Hanas bursts out, "Councilor Albescu?"

The man jumps and turns. "Wha—Sir Blackwell?" He tilts back his embroidered broad brim hat. His eyes shift from Hanas, to Willow, and then to Edwin, who was standing uncomfortably in the brush. "What is this?" His gaze turns to linger on Willow.

She keeps her Glock lowered, but doesn't holster it. If this is a Councilor, one of several purebloods who governs all of the American Vampiric Society, Willow knows she should be more respectful. But, she has no reason to trust this man, and currently, nearly everyone seems to be an enemy.

"Simply checking on a matter, Councilor, nothing to be alarmed over," Hanas replies in a shockingly calm manner.

Willow has to try to not look impressed at his immediate and even response.

"With a human?" Councilor Albescu questions with a playful cock of his brow. "You haven't gotten into the practice of blood bonds, have you? It's very much out of fashion."

The new term is foreign to Willow's ears, and she suspects it connotes to a relationship of some kind because, to her surprise yet again, Hanas laughs.

"Definitely not, Councilor Albescu. I don't believe anyone has been tasteless enough to make a blood bond since the seventeen hundreds."

Councilor Albescu smiles. "Your blood might curdle if you heard what I just dealt with."

Willow frowns, somehow feeling like the butt of a joke. "Is anyone going to explain what's going on?" She looks between the two before settling her sour expression on Councilor Albescu. "No offense, but what's a Councilor doing all the way out here?"

His chestnut brow goes up. "I could ask you the same thing, young lady. A Vampire Hunter, of all humans, this far into a vampiric province? Curious."

Willow narrows her eyes. "How do you know I'm a Vampire Hunter? I could just be a regular human carrying a Glock."

Councilor Albescu chuckles. "I think we both know that most humans aren't so daring, my dear. Indeed, most *Vampire Hunters* aren't nearly as spunky as yourself." He grins, wrinkles creasing at the corners of his eyes. "I like you."

Willow isn't sure what to think of that or how to respond. Hanas saves her from having to come up with anything.

"We should return to the manor, Councilor Albescu. This conversation is one to be had in private."

Without much objection, Albescu invites everyone to pile into his car. Edwin politely declines and implores Hanas to allow him to return home where he will wait for instructions. Hanas doesn't debate too much, and Willow can hardly blame him. Edwin's turned at least two shades paler in the past few minutes. With instructions, as well as promises of severe punishment should Edwin disobey, Hanas allows him to return home. Willow adds her own threatening glare and does the universal sign for *"I'm watching you."*

After helping to move the obstruction from the road, Edwin lumbers his way back through the forest. Willow watches him intently as the car lurches into motion. Whatever chances they had at finding the half-bloods' whereabouts vanish with Edwin.

CHAPTER
SIXTEEN

WHEN THEY arrive at the mansion, it's nearing the late-night hours. Willow didn't realize how tired she was until she sat on the warm leather seats of Councilor Albescu's car. Her legs were all too glad not to support her weight and although the half-bloods' whereabouts were still unknown, Willow found herself just wanting sleep. She was sure something would turn up in the morning and she would have more energy then.

Willow jolts awake for the third time as the car halts beside Hanas' mansion. She chides herself. Sleeping among vampires is not a wise move, even if one of the vampires seems very chatty and kind.

"I do not think a pureblood has done something so controversial since the Epiphanys brought that dhampir home!" Councilor Albescu was saying as he climbed out of the front seat.

Hanas smiles genuinely. "I remember that. It was all anyone talked about for months. I never did get more than a glance at the boy, though."

They circle around the car toward an impatient Willow.

"He is rarely seen, even these days," Councilor Albescu says with an air of dismay. "Poor lad. He is a very interesting one when you do catch him. I see why the Epiphanys took him in. Oh! I am sorry, er, Ms. Willow was it?"

Willow frowns slightly. "Just Willow."

"I get to talking and forget about others on occasion. You should have spoken up so I could include you."

They walk toward the mansion's front door.

"It's fine. C'mon, let's get this talk over with."

"That should be my line," Hanas mumbles, remembering their upcoming discussion.

Inside, Adabelle leads them to a cozy sitting room. The low light, warm maroon walls, and plush sofas only make Willow feel extra groggy. She unceremoniously drops onto a couch while Hanas and Councilor Albescu take parlor chairs diagonal to each other.

"I will never cease to wonder how humans tire so quickly," Councilor Albescu says sympathetically. "Maybe you ought to have the servants bring her some wine."

"Some influence you are. I'm under age."

Albescu throws his hands up. "Oh, yes, I forgot."

"Under age?" Hanas asks.

"Humans have age limits for when they can consume alcohol," Councilor Albescu explains. "It is a matter of maturity."

Hanas nods as though some past encounters suddenly make perfect sense.

"I think some spiced tea or sugar may help," Adabelle offers with a small curtsey.

"Add in *a lot* of sugar," Willow tells her.

Adabelle bobs another curtsey and says she'll also prepare drinks for Hanas and Councilor Albescu. No sooner has she left than Hanas decides to get the talk over with. By the time they have finished discussing the latest events with the half-bloods, the Rogue, and the accomplice, Willow has downed two cups of heavily sugared tea and is forced to make at least one lavatory run. As she returns and flops back on the couch, Hanas is saying, "And that is where we are, currently."

Councilor Albescu has been silent the entire time, every so often raising incredulous eyebrows.

He sets his china tea cup on the coffee table. "A shortage of blood, and yet you have done me the courtesy of giving me some to drink. You are too kind, Hanas."

"I could never ask a Councilor, nor even a close friend, to drink animal blood mixed with wine," Hanas responds graciously.

"I imagine the shortage only made your half-bloods angrier and drove them all the more to leave," Councilor Albescu says grimly. "Is there not a way to make amends?"

"Not with Rei-Com Ashe," Willow grumbles. "She's as bull-headed as they come and would sooner fight one hundred vampires on her own before accepting aid from one."

Councilor Albescu cringes. "I do not blame her. I have seen firsthand some of the more awful things we have done to your kind. However, in this case, Hanas has done nothing wrong."

Willow shrugs. "Doesn't matter to her." She sits up, feeling the caffeine alert her senses. "Let's ask the bigger question, though. You're powerful, politically speaking, so can you help us?"

Councilor Albescu entwines his fingers. "No. I cannot—not without getting Hanas into more trouble than he is already in."

Willow frowns. "What do you mean?"

Hanas tenses, shifting uncomfortably. "I have not informed the Vampiric Council of what has transpired. They know the Rogue was seen in my province, but I have kept all other details from them."

Willow stifles a nervous chuckle. "Um… why?"

Councilor Albescu glances to Hanas who looks like he drank something bitter. Well, Willow supposed he actually had, but that was beside the point.

It takes a moment before Hanas says, "Do you remember when you asked about my parents while driving to Vamstadt?"

"If this is about all the 'your parents vanished and you inherited some mysterious and dangerous power' stuff, then I already heard about that."

Hanas's eyes widen in a silent question.

"I came across your cut out articles or whatever in that history book. Edwin explained most of what I didn't understand."

Hanas leans back in his chair. "I think I need to talk to Edwin about sharing family secrets," he says to no one in particular. "Well, since you know all that, I will skip those details. Essentially, ever since my mother went… well… a little crazy, the Vampiric Council was all too happy to finish the job of tearing the family apart. Any chance they get to blame me, they will take. The lower I sink in society, the less likely I will be to regain my role as a Blackwell."

Willow whistles. "That's intense."

Counselor Albescu added, "There is also the trouble that, lawfully speaking, Hanas *is* held responsible for everything that occurs in his province—regardless of it being within his power or not."

Willow folds her arms. "Sooo… if the Council finds out, he could get in trouble for endangering ties with the V.H. of Hidden Hill?"

"As well as any damages these missing half-bloods incur," Counselor Albescu confirms.

Willow bites her lip. "That's what you meant when you said you can't just run farther into vampire land." She slouches. "We really are alone in this."

"Not entirely," Albescu says slowly. "I may not be able to be of much help, but I can do some sleuthing of my own and see what I come up with. Maybe this Rogue character has some unsavory ties with higher ups. The Blood Moon festivities will be starting up soon, with October not too far off." He gives them a reassuring smile. "I will see what I can find. Until then, my lips are sealed on this matter."

"I greatly appreciate it, Councilor," Hanas says graciously.

Councilor Albescu waves a hand. "Think nothing of it. We are friends, after all. We can leave all those stuffy politics for later, hm?"

Willow slaps her thighs, startling Hanas and Councilor Albescu, then stands. "Well, if you guys are done with the important talk, I'm hitting the sack."

"We will be up for longer," Hanas informs her. "But we will not speak of anything vital without you."

Willow waves the comment away. She's so tired, so sluggish, so brain dead, that she hardly even cares. As she silently grumbles her way up to her annoyingly far bedroom, the events of the day bounce uselessly against the walls of her mind. Nothing seems to make sense and no one has any answers. There is some big piece missing and something still doesn't sit right with her.

Tossing her suspenders on the floor and face planting on her bed, the pieces in her mind begin to slow their rotation. As she drifts off to sleep, her mind focuses through the chaos on one piece. *Why had Edwin wanted to check the eastern border himself?* They hadn't found anything and Willow had kept a close eye on him during that time. *The east,* Willow thinks lethargically. *East... east... east.*

A dream of a memory floats through her mind. She is a little ten-year-old girl again. The mother she loves is gone, and with her are some of Willow's happiest memories: warm smiles, bedtimes tucks, making crafts and painting pictures.

A V.H. had been assigned to watch her, but she's snuck away from his watchful eyes.

She was told that her dad needed some time alone with her deceased mom. Little Willow doesn't want to separated, though. She will never see her mom's smile again, and she doesn't want to lose her dad's too.

A sound Willow has become all too familiar with echoes from the cracked door ahead. Through the slit, she can see her dad kneeling beside her mom's casket. His face is buried in his hands as he cries over his loss. Willow peeks into the room, new tears streaking her cheeks. She has never seen Mr. Hunter as upset as he's been for the past week. It scares her.

"It's a shame, isn't it?" a low voice says to Willow's left. She doesn't look. She knows who the voice belongs too. He is the head of the Vampire Hunter branch they are visiting, the ones who desperately tried to prevent her mom's death. "I can't imagine the pain he's going through."

A new voice, also to the left, responds callously, "Death is a fact of life. He will find a way to move forward."

"Maybe he will… but will his daughter?"

Little Willow's attention snaps toward the two speakers, one of which returns her gaze. Her heart gives a skip. She's been caught. But the Region Commander's soft gaze is only meant to point the second speaker in her direction.

Little Willow isn't sure what to think of the second man. He frightens her, somehow. It's not his tall stature or his strange clothes or the way death seems to be natural to him and unworthy of his attention. It's something little Willow, at the time, could not place, but now, in this moment. His honey-brown eyes meet hers—sharp like a predator and kindled with an intense anger that roars into an unquenchable fire.

Little Willow shrinks a little and his gaze snaps away. He strides toward another exit farther across the room, speaking only the curt words, "Excuse me."

Willow's dream lingers a moment, the pieces swirling around: East. Half-bloods. Anger. Death. *Devone Vitya.*

Her eyes fly open. She stares into the morning light. Her mind clicks the pieces together and she jolts up. *Edwin wanted to check the east because he probably knew that was where the half-bloods went! And East of here is the province of Devone Vitya…!*

"Oh no…" Willow whispers. The half-bloods are heading to the most violent and easily angered pureblood in America.

The Rogue's words slither through her mind. *"I'm going to start a revolution."*

Willow jumps out of bed and runs for Hanas' office.

CHAPTER
SEVENTEEN

RUNNING FULL speed down the hall, Willow slams into Hanas' office door and throws it open.

Hanas jumps at the *bang!* Of the door, his fountain pen leaving a long line across his work.

"I know where the half-bloods are!" Willow exclaims.

Hanas gives her wrinkled appearance a once over. "Did you sleep at all last night?"

"Yes! That's actually how I figured it out!"

Hanas cocks a brow. "By sleeping?" he confirms.

Willow hurries forward and presses her palms on his desk. "Listen. Edwin wanted to check the eastern side of Vamstadt, right? And he knows more than he's willing to tell us. Why else would he want to check the eastern side if it wasn't because that's where the half-bloods went?"

Hanas rests his elbows on the desk. "Yes, however, we checked the eastern side and there was nothing. The path we found was headed north."

"*Unless* that was a diversion. Maybe they headed north, then east."

Hanas nods in thought, rubbing his chin. "But why would they head east?"

Willow straightens with a triumphant smile. "One name: Devone Vitya."

Hanas frowns. "What about him?"

"C'mon, you know! He's the most violent, easily angered, bloodthirsty pureblood on the American continent!"

Hanas tilts his head in agreement.

"Remember what I told you the Rogue said? He wants a *revolution*. What better way to start one than to fire up the most irritable pureblood he can find?"

"Sir Vitya would not bend to any notions of revolution, I can promise you that. However…" he narrows his eyes in thought. "Do you recall the threat I made to Rose when she refused to talk?"

Willow folds her arms. "Yeah, you mentioned him then too."

Hanas nods. "I think it is more likely that the Rogue is trying to bolster an army of rebels. There are few better places to find those who would fight against oppression than those who sit in the oppressor's lap."

Willow's brow knits. "You mean… he's sent them over there to recruit?"

"It sounds disturbingly logical," Hanas agrees.

Willow chews her cheek in thought. "What do we do? We'll never make it to Vitya's province before them, and even if we did, what would we say to him? 'Hey, our half-bloods are out of control and stealing away your followers for a revolution! No hard feelings, right?'" Willow gasps. "Oh! Councilor Albescu can go to him! He'll *have* to listen to a Councilor."

"Councilor Albescu left early last night. He is eager to get a jump on the Rogue's intentions and stop this revolution before it begins." Hanas stares at his work remorsefully. "I think all we can do for now is wait and hope we can anticipate and prevent the Rogue or his accomplice's next move."

Willow shifts uneasily, her legs growing antsy. "We can't just do nothing! We have to do something in order to get ahead of the Rogue. We could… we could…" she looks around the room for ideas. "Maybe we could get Edwin to spill something!

If we tell him we know part of the plan, maybe he'll spill something else."

Hanas doesn't look thrilled at the prospect of facing Edwin, much less interrogating him. "I am not convinced he will speak."

"We have to do *something* about him," Willow objects. "He's hidden too much vital information for too long. He *let us* go on a wild goose chase *twice* and encouraged it the whole way!"

Hanas considers this, nodding slowly and uneasily. "I suppose something must be done. I will send for him."

"Good. I'm going to, uh…" she looks down at herself. "Fix myself up. I don't think I look very menacing right now."

Hanas cracks a smile. "You certainly startled *me*."

Willow rolls her eyes. "Ha-ha. Don't start without me. Call me when he gets here."

"Of course," Hanas says.

Willow turns to leave, her excitement deflating as she goes. She bolsters herself, though, with a promise that she'd get Edwin to spill something. No more games. No more lies. She *would* get an answer.

* * *

After returning to her room, Willow finds that Adabelle has left her a fresh pair of trousers, button-up shirt, and suspenders embroidered with roses and foliage. She changes, strapping her Glocks around her hips again, and decides to utilize the wash basin left for her as well. The water is still warm and vaguely scented with eucalyptus.

On her bedside table, Willow discovers a porcelain plate, with golden toast and several flavors of jam, alongside a healthy helping of warm oatmeal with a dainty cup of brown sugar. Willow eagerly downs all the food and drains the glass of orange juice. After missing dinner the night before, she considers asking Adabelle for seconds, but by now, Edwin is sure to be in

Hanas' office. No one has come to tell her of his arrival, but it shouldn't have taken long for him to come.

Willow strides from her room and follows the halls to their meeting place. Pausing in front of the door, she raises a fist and knocks.

No reply.

Willow tries again. *There's no way he didn't hear that… and he said he'd be in his office.*

No reply.

"Hanas? Are you in there?"

Silence.

She pushes down on the handle. "Ready or not, I'm coming in." The door swings open and her feet root her in place.

Hanas is on the floor in front of his desk, unconscious, and Edwin is kneeling over him with an almost empty vial in hand.

Their eyes lock, and horror and confusion passes between them.

Willow rips out her Glock but Edwin is faster. He's on his feet in seconds and throws her against the doorframe in his haste. Willow whirls into the hall, firing after him. The shot drills into the wall, inches from his shoulder. He turns down the stairs and vanishes.

"Edwin!" She runs after him, thundering down the stairs and hearing the slam of the front door. "Stop!"

She whisks past a startled servant as she bolts for the front door. "Hanas is unconscious—help him! Hurry!" she calls over her shoulder.

The black-blood needs no more information. He runs up the stairs in a streak.

Willow bursts into the cool morning air. Her ponytail slaps her shoulders as she locates Edwin. A blond head bobs between the trees to her right. *"Edwin!"* Her muscles pump with all the strength they have. She ducks the branches and vaults the shrubbery, never taking her eyes off Edwin's rippling ivory top, but his form grows smaller and smaller as he outruns Willow.

"Sto-o-o-p!" Willow screams. "Edwin, *sto-o-o-p!"* She pushes herself with all she has, but it's no use. She is human. She can never compare to his speed. Her anger and confusion blind her, obscuring the root that trips her. Willow is thrown onto the moist soil, her fresh clothes now covered in dirt and grass stains. The fall both heightens her anger and reminds her that she must calm down and think clearly.

She sits up, panting. Edwin has disappeared among the trees, not a trace of him left. She slams a fist on the dirt. *What even was that vial... was it what the half-bloods drank? And if Edwin has the vial, does that mean it was given to him or...?* She pauses. *Wait... he made Hanas drink that vial... oh no.*

Willow stands and runs back toward the mansion. If it was the enhancing drug, would Hanas go to Vitya's province too? If it wasn't, then could it be poison?

Willow skids to a halt inside the mansion with labored breaths, the cold air burning in her chest. She hardly notices the servants cluttering the halls and whispering among themselves. Willow begins to panic when she spots a few crying into their hands and others solemnly consoling them.

Her steps quicken and she soon pauses outside Hanas' office. At first, she is too afraid to turn the corner, then she steels herself and marches in. Yet again, an unsuspected scene awaits her.

Hanas is leaning against his desk, his head in his hands, as the servant she'd sent to help him lays at his feet... lifeless and still, with two punctures in his neck.

Willow knits her brow, holstering her Glock. "What is this—?"

"Just leave."

Willow blinks at him. "What—?"

"Leave!" A thick wave of his presence slams into her, making Willow's heart miss a beat. She jumps back, her concern growing. Adabelle approaches from behind and gently directs her from the room and down the hall. It isn't until they're nearly back at Willow's room that she speaks.

"I am sorry, Mistress. Master Blackwell is unstable right now... he needs time to himself."

Willow studies Adabelle's soft features, hoping to find some answers there. "What happened?" Her tone is almost a whisper.

Adabelle swallows before whispering, "Hanas lost control. When he woke up, a wave of thirst must have overtaken him... he killed Maurice on the spot."

Willow isn't sure what to think. Was it not the drug after all?

Adabelle slips the vial from her pocket, revealing three drops of the drug left. She presses the vial into Willow's palm. "We will take care of Master Blackwell. You must take this and try to discover what it is. At least for now, it is not safe to be around Master Blackwell. We have just lost our chemist, so deciphering this drug is out of our hands."

Willow grips the vial. "But I can't go back to Foxhound."

Adabelle smooths her embroidered apron. "I know you have been banished, and I am sure you harbor ill feelings as well, Mistress, but someone must discover what that drug is so we can acquire a cure. If we lose Master Blackwell to this drug as well, then countless lives will be lost in Hidden Hill."

Willow looks away, glaring at the grain in the wooden floors. "All the more so if Vitya attacks..."

Adabelle's brow flies up. "Lord Vitya...?"

Willow gives a short explanation of her thoughts on the half-bloods' whereabouts.

Adabelle presses her lips together. "If I may be so bold, Mistress, it sounds as though you have no choice but to warn your fellow hunters. Otherwise, many will be flattened under Lord Vitya's rage if what you say is true."

Rei-Com Ashe's decree of banishment comes to mind, her callous words and refusal to listen to Willow... especially when she was so hurt.

"Perhaps there is a friend you could visit...?" Adabelle suggests after a moment.

Martha pops into Willow's mind again. But Dr. Heartwood would be so busy at the hospital, and Mr. Heartwood would be working on endless reconstruction for the town—not to mention their home is small to begin with. Could she really impose?

She doesn't have a choice.

Willow sighs heavily and glances down at the vial in her hand. *Maybe the hospital can do some chemistry on this.* Willow looks up to Adabelle with a firm nod. "Alright. But send for me as soon as Hanas is ready to talk. We need to find Edwin and get answers before any more damage is done."

Adabelle curtseys. "Of course, Mistress." Once she rises again, her lips spread into a sad, yet confident, smile. "Your father would be proud of how strong you have become."

Willow's lips twitch into a smile, but it's gone in an instant. "Yeah, he will be when I find him."

She strides into her room and pauses when she finds her perfectly cleaned up uniform folded in a neat square on the edge of her bed. *Took them long enough to clean that,* Willow thinks. *Or maybe they kept it from me purposefully...* She snatches up the uniform and changes. She is startled as she exits the room, finding Adabelle just outsider her door with an embroidered cloth bag full of fresh vampiric clothes and the jacket Willow usually borrowed when going out.

She curtseys. "Mistress, I have brought fresh clothes for your time away. I assume Master Blackwell will be better in two days, but I packed four pairs just in case. I know you may not be fond of our clothing, but maintaining a clean appearance is important."

Willow smiles and takes the bag. "Guess I don't have a choice. But, just between you and me, I've kinda gotten used to the vampiric clothing. It's actually comfier than it looks." She shoots Adabelle a look. "But don't you *dare* tell Hanas I said that."

Adabelle giggles and curtseys. "Of course, Mistress."

"It's just Willow."

"Not to me, Mistress." She shows Willow to the front door and with a farewell, leaves her to trek back toward the border.

"So much has happened in so little time," Willow grumbles to herself. But, in the least, she could see some human faces again.

CHAPTER
EIGHTEEN

FOLLOWING THE path toward the border, Willow pauses when she sees Foxhound beginning to peek through the trees. Her blood still boils at Rei-Com Ashe's words, and she's positive she can't face her in a civil manner—not yet, anyway. She resolves to head west and cross the border closer to Hidden Hill. She will deal with warning Foxhound later.

Willow follows the border until Hidden Hill comes into sight. She pauses, leaning against a tree to watch the town. It is now riddled with construction equipment. In the cool afternoon air, the pounding of nails and the screech of saws drift toward her ears. It has only been a day, yet it feels like several since she last saw anything modern—since she last saw anything human.

Willow crosses the border, feeling uneasy and unsure of herself. She feels alienated after her banishment from home, alone now that her only ally is unstable and her dad missing in action. She feels increasingly awkward as she walks through town. She folds her arms, feeling naked and angry that the vampiric world is the less discomforting of the two. The streets are covered in miniature encampments for disaster relief, and at each corner lay swept up piles of debris, but Willow feels comfort in seeing living human faces working together amidst the destruction. No strange eye colors, no vampiric presences, no silent feet to sneak up on her. They're all physically aged and noisy.

Following the main street toward the hospital, Willow eyes the damages too. One vampiric attack has left the town in shambles, and it hadn't been a long-lasting attack either. Willow watches a woman with a blanket across her shoulders cradle the only family member she has left: a small baby. A cold shudder rattles Willow's spine as she thinks of the damage the Rogue's revolution could cause... for that matter, the damage even Devone Vitya could cause.

Willow forces the thoughts from her mind and focuses on what she'll say when she gets to Martha's house. She can't give out too much information, but the Heartwoods should know the danger Hidden Hill may be in. They're a second family to her, and she couldn't bear the thought of losing them.

Pausing on the doormat in front of their two-bedroom home, Willow takes a deep breath. She hopes someone is home— Martha should be. Willow presses the doorbell and waits.

A moment later, the frantic clicking of the lock sounds and the door flies open. Willow is tackled by Martha in a cry of joy.

"You're okay! Thank the heavens!"

Willow hugs her back tightly, breathing in the smell of gauze and sanitizer. "Of course I'm okay! What about you?"

Martha pulls away with a teary smile. "I have no room to talk. My house is intact and everyone is fine besides a bad scare. But you... I'm *so* sorry."

Willow swallows. "You heard?"

Martha glares, though not at Willow. "I heard Ashe banished you from the Vampire Hunters, and I heard your dad was proclaimed MIA."

Some pent-up emotions well inside Willow and spill over her cheeks. "He's alive. I know it."

Martha's lips press tight and she leads Willow inside. It's obvious she doesn't want to say that the chances of Mr. Hunter's survival are slim to none. Vampires don't take prisoners.

After sitting her on the couch, Martha puts a fuzzy blanket across Willow's shoulders and hands her a box of tissues. "Tell me everything."

Against Willow's plans, she does. Through her mostly controlled sobs, she recounts everything from her banishment up until Edwin used the mysterious vial on Hanas. Willow is embarrassed by her emotional outbreak, but she feels better after spilling out her troubles. She admits her annoying fear of vampires, her discomfort in both the human and vampiric worlds, the horror that she may never see her dad again. Through everything, Martha listens contently and only interjects to add her agreements and condolences.

"So here I am," Willow sniffs, plucking the fiftieth tissue from its box. "Somehow, I have to figure out this vial or... I don't even want to think about it."

Martha gives her a warm and tight hug. When she pulls away, she says, "Don't worry. We'll figure this out! And if you need anything—*anything* at all—come straight to me."

Willow smiles her thanks. "Sorry, I just sort of exploded on you."

"Think nothing of it. That's what friends are for!"

Willow slips the vial from her pocket and holds it up for Martha to see. "Do you think your mom can figure it out?"

Martha takes the vial carefully, eyeing the precious few drops left. "I can't promise anything. But I know she'll do her best!"

Willow and Martha spend the rest of the morning setting up an air mattress in Martha's room and catching up on what has transpired over the past twenty-four hours. Martha explains that the disaster relief group has been a huge help, but the hospital is flooded with the wounded. She says that Eric is alright, but his parents took such a scare from the attack that they want him to quit the V.H.

Willow sighs, annoyed, but she can understand their reasoning. "I'm glad he's alright, but we need Vampire Hunters now more than ever."

Martha nods. "Eric said the same thing."

Pulling on their jackets, they head for the hospital to give the vial to Dr. Heartwood.

"He's not wrong," Willow says as they head out the front door. A cool breeze stings her cheeks, warning of rain to come.

Martha eyes Willow's jacket thoughtfully. "Vampiric?" she asks, rubbing the sleeve of the material between her fingers.

"Yeah," Willow admits awkwardly. "I didn't have a coat on me the night of the attack, so I've been borrowing this one. You won't believe how warm these things can keep you."

Martha turns her attention to the streets ahead. The towering, bulky hospital is just a few blocks down. "What's Devone Vitya like?" she asks, worry turning her tone quiet. "You mentioned him earlier when talking about..." she glances around then whispers, "... the possibility of a new attack."

Willow chews her cheek for a moment. "In all honesty, I know very little about him. My knowledge of Devone Vitya is just gossip and hazy memories from when I was a kid." she pauses a moment, recalling the encounter, "I saw him, once, when my mom died. I remember his eyes were strange, like, even for a vampire. And when he looked at me, I was pretty scared... It was probably his presence I felt. All I know beyond that is that he's trouble. He loves war and power, and the tales I've heard coming from that end of the border are never good."

Martha purses her lips, her dark brows drawn close together. "I heard a story about a V.H. that was bitten by him. The pureblood didn't give him enough vampiric poison to even turn him into a black-blood. The V.H. convulsed before dying under his watch."

Willow had heard that story, and it'd made her blood boil every time. "I wish I had been there. I would have set him straight."

Or would she? Willow glowers at the pavement, remembering the slithering presence of the Rogue, his teeth sinking into her flesh, and how it had sent her nerves screaming. She shudders the thought away.

"We don't know for sure if the half-bloods went after him," Willow says after a minute. "But here's to hoping they didn't."

When they reach the hospital and meet up with Dr. Heartwood, she greets Willow with a tight hug. After nearly squeezing the life from Willow's lungs, Dr. Heartwood steps back with a stern gaze. "Next time you get into trouble, you call me, understand? If I didn't have so many patients, I would have marched across that border and brought you back!"

Willow blushes at the image of Dr. Heartwood at Hanas' door. "I'm sorry. I'm okay, though, I promise!"

Dr. Heartwood lifts a brow. "Mmhmm."

"I'm serious! Hanas bothered me a bit the first few days, but I guess he was just worried. That's beside the point—"

"I'll decide what's beside the point," Dr. Heartwood says, pointing to a chair in the corner of the private room. "I want to do a check-up on you while you're here."

Willow does as she says. Martha gives her a sympathetic look after sitting next to her.

"No changes in mood?" Dr. Heartwood asks, shining a light into both of Willow's eyes. "Unusual cravings? Heightened senses? Trouble breathing, eating, or sleeping?"

"No," Willow says.

Dr. Heartwood takes out her stethoscope, listening to her heart. "Really? Because you have bags under your eyes."

Willow has no doubt she does. "I went to bed pretty late once or twice, but I promise it's not because I couldn't fall sleep." Lately, sleep was becoming a privilege.

Dr. Heartwood instructs her to take deep breaths while listening to her lungs. Finally, she leans away. Her eyes dance with concern. "Healthy, as usual. Just make sure you get plenty of sleep, alright?"

"Catching up on sleep sounds like a good plan, especially since I'm here for a while," Willow admits, the thought only just occurring to her. Though she's worried about Hanas and this strange substance, sleep is something she has been lacking and something that proved useful over the last few hours.

Dr. Heartwood smiles kindly and pats her hand. "You sleep *all* you want. There's no rush for you to leave."

"Thanks. A place to be and sleep is what I need."

"So tell me," Dr. Heartwood says, glancing between her daughter and Willow. "What brings you back across the border? Or, more importantly, here? I know you didn't come because you *love* check-ups."

Willow pulls the vial from her pocket again. "Can you possibly do labs on this for me? Hanas and I are in a pickle—him more than me."

Dr. Heartwood takes the vial and squints at the contents. "Is this blood? Looks a bit watered down to me…"

"I think it's a drug. I need to know what it does ASAP."

Dr. Heartwood's eyes widen as she fixes her gaze on Willow. "You better not have been drugged!"

Willow shifts in her seat. "Not me, but Hanas." She gives the quick and simple details of Hanas' collapse.

Dr. Heartwood frowns in disapproval. "That vampire had better watch himself. I won't have him biting my girl."

Willow tries not to imagine Hanas' fangs sinking into her neck. She suppresses a shudder and presses that horrific image away.

"Well," Dr. Heartwood continues. "I like this Adabelle you told me about. If a vampire is unstable, then everyone is wise to stay away."

"I just hope we can fix whatever's wrong," Willow sighs. "If Hanas is out of commission and—uh—certain things happen, it *won't* be good."

Dr. Heartwood gives her the eye. "Certain things?"

Willow glances to Martha who shrugs. "Martha can give you the details later. Just don't spread them outside your family. And… be prepared for the worst."

"I don't like the sounds of that."

Knock, knock.

"Come in!" Dr. Heartwood calls.

The door opens, and a nurse pokes her head in. "I'm sorry to interrupt, Doctor, but we need you urgently."

Dr. Heartwood stands, giving Willow an understanding wink. "No rest for the weary, right? You girls take care. I probably won't be home again tonight." She holds up the vial. "I promise I'll get the labs on this as soon as possible."

"It means the world," Willow says.

With that, Dr. Heartwood hurries from the room, following the nurse. Willow and Martha stand to leave, but the whole way back to Martha's house, Willow can't help but wonder how much more sleep Dr. Heartwood will lose if Devone Vitya attacks.

* * *

Willow spends the rest of that day and the next resting and chatting with Martha. Sitting back, eating snacks, and laughing with her best friend feels strange and foreign. Hours before, she was knee-deep in never-ending troubles. Technically, she still is. But now she *really* can't do anything about it. The investigating has to be left to Dr. Heartwood, the healing left to Adabelle. All Willow can do is wait and hope for the best.

Martha asks about Hanas and what the world across the border is like. Willow recounts everything she can think of, including the uselessly large library and the sitting room filled with greenery. Martha is fascinated since much of the vampiric world lays unseen by civilian eyes—many parts are completely unknown to the human race as a whole. Willow feels a small sense of pride at having seen what most haven't, but the looming dread of what may come next snuffs it out.

The following Saturday, Willow decides that warning Rei-Com Ashe should come sooner than later. She knows her warning should have come sooner, but she struggles face Rei-Com

Ashe. Even now, it took Willow nearly the whole day to calm herself enough to face her.

Just go in, tell her, and leave, Willow reminds herself. As much as she wants to scream and fight with Rei-Com Ashe over her stupid decision, Willow knows that it is pointless. Having worn holes into the floor with her anxious pacing, Willow finally decides to leave for Foxhound that evening.

The sun is steadily setting, its warm, orange rays peering through gaps in the cloud cover. A cool breeze shifts her auburn locks and tells of new storms to come—more rain, more gloom. The fresh air feels good, though. Somehow, each breeze blows away another puffing plume of anger. Each step eases her urge to punch Rei-Com Ashe in her stubborn mouth—the mouth that banished her for siding with the only person who could help her find her dad; the mouth that tried to use her dad's words against her; the mouth that banished her from her only home and told her she could never come back. *But it's fine! Totally fine, not hurtful at all.* At least, that was what Willow tried to tell herself.

Soon enough, she turns the bend in the road where Foxhound sits, nestled in its clearing. Approaching the wired gate, Willow thinks to herself how ironic it is that Foxhound is set in a clearing, much like Hanas' mansion, as though they, too, have something to hide. But Willow's snark ebbs when she pauses just before the guard shack. Stepping on Foxhound property is disobeying a direct order.

Her resolve hardens at the thought of Rei-Com Ashe's words, at the unfairness of being banished from her own home, and at what would happen if Vitya attacked. He wouldn't leave Hidden Hill out of the fray. Yes, this is more serious than any ridiculous squabble of theirs.

Willow exhales heavily, breathing out whatever extra steam she can. With clenched fists, she marches up to the guard shack. The V.H. inside does a double take when he spots her.

"Pre-Initiate Hunter?"

Willow lifts her chin, trying to assume some sense of pride in light of her embarrassing banishment. "I need to speak with Rei-Com Ashe. It's important."

The guard sighs. "I'm sorry, Pre-Initiate, but you've been banished from these grounds. I can't let you in anymore."

Anger coils around Willow's heart. She slams both hands on the small ledge of the guard shack and hisses through her teeth. "We are on the verge of war. Get. Me. Rei-Com. Ashe."

The guard pales and calls for an escort. Within moments, Willow is brought inside, flanked by four men, and led to the munitions depot.

They stride inside, and Willow suppresses the urge to look around at the messy bins of ammo in nostalgia. The dull glint of metal, along with the lingering scent of gunpowder and gun cleaner, relaxes Willow's shoulders, reminding her of what was once her home.

No, Willow chides herself. *It still is. Rei-Com Ashe has no say in that.*

Eyes ahead, Willow finds herself holding her breath. Rei-Com Ashe only a few feet away, hunched on a worn stool as she aggressively flips through well-used maps and charts. She only ever does her office work in the munitions depot when she is upset or can't focus—sometimes both.

It becomes clear to Willow that Rei-Com Ashe is in a permanent bad mood when one of the men in her escort clears his throat uncomfortably to get her attention.

"Go home, Gregory," she grumbles. "I told you I won't change my mind on banishing Willow."

Willow frowns. "I already know that."

Rei-Com Ashe jumps and spins around, half-rising from her seat. "Willow! You scared the chestnuts out of me! What are ya' doing here?"

"I came to tell you something—"

Rei-Com Ashe sighs in exasperation, running a hand through her bushy black hair. "Willow, sweetie, even if you came to apologize, I can't go back on my word—"

"I didn't come here to apologize," Willow snaps. "I came here to warn you."

Rei-Com Ashe sits, wrinkling her nose in annoyance but also a little disappointment, Willow notes. "Oh. What's up, girl-stuff?"

"Some things have happened," Willow says, preferring to keep her information vague. "And now Devone Vitya might be coming to declare war on us."

Rei-Com Ashe's mouth drops open. "Willow Ashton Hunter, *what* have the two of you *done?"*

Willow glares, more annoyed that Rei-Com Ashe used her middle name than her unfair, accusatory tone. "It's not our fault! The Rogue and his accomplice planned this. At least *we're* trying to do something about it."

Rei-Com Ashe slaps the table of maps. "What do you think I'm slaving away here for?"

"Nothing! Because if I hadn't warned you, both you *and* Hidden Hill would be sitting ducks! Which, by the way, you would know on your own if you actually worked with us!"

Rei-Com Ashe stands, glaring. "I won't work with some bloodsucker who will stab me in the back later!"

The two glare each other down for several minutes. Willow's escort seems to melt under the heat as his eyes dart anxiously from mentor to apprentice.

Willow rolls her eyes. "Just double the patrols along the border and prepare yourself. There. I said what I needed. Later." She turns to storm out.

Rei-Com Ashe huffs, dropping back into her seat. "God bless America! What am I supposed to do? We only have a fraction of Hunters still in one piece after the last fiasco. And now I need enough manpower to fight off the most powerful pureblood this side of the U.S.?"

"Don't blame me," Willow grumbles, throwing a glare over her shoulder.

"I'm not." Rei-Com Ashe snaps. She runs her hands down her face. "Stupid vampires. We wouldn't be in this mess if that pureblood could handle his own flock," she mumbles to herself.

That made Willow's blood boil all the more. She and Hanas were doing everything they could to keep the half-bloods under control, but Rei-Com Ashe made it sound as though it was simple child's play.

She whirls around, hardly containing her furious shouts. "This isn't Hanas' fault! It's that stupid Rogue who's messing with us all! You don't even know *half* of what's going on. You just blame whoever you see fit and kick your feet up! And no thanks to you, but now I'm practically on my own because Hanas—" she stops abruptly. Hanas' accidental killing of his black-blood would only give Rei-Com Ashe more reason to not trust him. Willow really didn't need more enemies.

Rei-Com Ashe narrows her eyes. "What?"

"Nothing. Just keep an eye out, okay?" Willow turns in another attempt to leave but Rei-Com Ashe jumps up and crosses the room.

"Wait. Tell me what happened!" She grabs Willow's arm, turning her around to look her over with surprisingly genuine concern. "He didn't suck your blood did he?"

"No!" Willow yanks her arm from Rei-Com Ashe's grip. "Since when do you care, anyway?"

Rei-Com Ashe locks her with stern, serious eyes. "Willow…" She sighs heavily and looks away. "What I did was stupid. You know me, I get irrational sometimes. I do worry about ya. Especially with your father gone. I'm paying the price for the decision I made, but if that pureblood is hurting you—"

"He's not," Willow confirms, her own anger ebbing. "I'll see you later, okay?"

Rei-Com Ashe chews her lip as Willow finally leaves, a relieved escort in tow. Before she passed the next warehouse, she heard Rei-Com Ashe's voice call to her from behind. "If any-thing else happens… let me know! I wanna help however I can."

Willow pauses, glancing behind her in shock. In the waning evening light, she could see Rei-Com Ashe's uneasy smile. It communicated all Willow needed to hear. If Vitya did attack, she would have Rei-Com Ashe and the Vampire Hunters back. Now, she just had to hope that Hanas would be okay.

CHAPTER
NINETEEN

By the time Willow trudges through Martha's front door, the sun is no more than a few spare rays between the thick forest and its deep shadows that swallow Hidden Hill whole. She recounts to Martha her short talk with Rei-Com Ashe and mentions the slim string of hope she now has in her mentor again.

"Things are looking up, even if just a little," Martha says cheerily.

Willow appreciates her positivity in the midst of all the darkness, but she can still see the worry hidden in Martha's eyes. There is still the possibility of another attack, and right now, Hidden Hill is practically defenseless.

The click of a key signals someone's return. Willow and Martha turn on the couch to glance at the front door as Dr. Heartwood clambers and huffs her way inside.

"I didn't except you back so soon, mom!" Martha says in an air of surprise. "You looked really busy at work."

Dr. Heartwood kicks off her shoes and promptly deposits herself on the couch across from them. "Momma is ready for sleep!"

Willow smiles apathetically.

"Oh!" Dr. Heartwood pushes herself up, pulling the empty vial from the pocket of her scrubs. She leans forward to pass the vial and a square of folded paper to Willow. "I got this back. I made sure the examination was highest priority."

Willow unfolds the paper as Dr. Heartwood explains. "Whatever that is, it's unstable. The chemists told me that it appears to be some ill-created drug. They aren't sure if it did what was intended or not, but the side effects resulting from the concoction are brutal. To put it simply, the drug dries up specific blood cells and causes extreme anemia."

Willow glances up from the sheet of confusing terms with wide eyes. "Anemia? Then it's nothing permanent?"

Dr. Heartwood's lips spread in a thin line. "The result of this drug would be fatal for a human. I think your friend is very lucky to be a vampire."

Willow swallows, sharing in the happiness—for the first time—that vampires are so resilient. What would she do if Hanas had died? Willow doesn't want to think about that either. "That's a relief. I guess I just have to wait for him to recover before—"

Knock, knock!

All three jump, their eyes turning toward the door. Martha opens it a moment later, then steps aside, glancing nervously at Willow.

An Ensign Commander enters, standing rigidly, as is proper etiquette for his rank. His face, however, shows a hundred questions.

"Pre-Initiate Hunter, I have a letter for you," he says.

Willow stands, saluting. "Thank you, sir."

He hands her the letter and promptly sees himself out. Once he has left, Willow anxiously tears the ivory envelope open. Inside is the delicate handwriting of Adabelle.

> *Mistress Hunter,*
> *Master Blackwell summons you as his health has returned to a stable state. When you have obtained the information on the vial's contents, please return at once.*
> *I hope you rested well, Mistress Hunter.*
>
> *Sincerely, Adabelle*

"Sounds like I'm headed back," Willow says, stuffing the letter into her pocket.

Martha and Dr. Heartwood's eyebrows both go up in surprise.

"Now?" Martha asks.

Willow shakes her head, sitting back down. "I'll go back in the morning. I probably won't be getting much sleep once I get back, so I think one more night would be good. Not to mention crossing the border at night is dangerous." Plus, she didn't want to delve back into drama. She needs time to cool off after her encounter with Rei-Com Ashe.

"A wise decision," Dr. Heartwood agrees. "But if that boy isn't stable, you come back here, understand?"

Willow smiles in thanks. "I hate to say it, but he probably mostly recovered after draining that black-blood. He's probably still upset, though." At least that wouldn't put her in any danger... any immediate danger, that is.

Dr. Heartwood forces herself to her feet. "I'm off to bed, then. Make sure you get some rest before tomorrow. Sounds like you'll have a big day."

"Don't worry, I'll be out like a lamp again tonight, I'm sure," Willow says. "Thanks for your help, Mrs. Heartwood."

"Any time, sugar plum." She wobbles into her bedroom leaving Martha and Willow to talk until Mr. Heartwood drags himself indoors, too.

The following morning, Willow takes her time getting up, making pancakes with Martha, then gathering what little she'd brought with her. She changes into the vampiric clothing Adabelle packed for her, glad for the comfort and feeling that the trousers, embroidered suspenders, and soft cotton top will help her blend in when she arrives back across the border. If Vitya comes for a fight, bringing half-bloods with him, at least she could pretend to blend in or be a harmless follower of Hanas.

Pulling the dark coat on as much for warmth as to cover the Glocks holstered on either hip, Willow turns to the Heartwood family with a sincere smile. "Thanks for letting me stay."

Mr. Heartwood, a well-built man, smiles. "You're welcome anytime."

Dr. Heartwood nods. "You come back soon!" They give Willow tight hugs and Martha joins in too.

"You can do this, Willow," she whispers after letting go. "You'll find your dad, and he'll be perfectly fine!"

Willow swallows a lump of emotion rising in her throat. "Thanks."

"Now," Mr. Heartwood says, crossing his arms. "You go give that Rogue a kick in the pants!"

Somehow, his words pull Willow's lips into a smile. "I'll do my best."

She slings her sack of clothes over her shoulder, her cheeks flushing a bit as she feels like a hobo going on some wild adventure. "Stay safe, guys."

They all share in a promise, then Willow heads out the door and back across the border.

* * *

When Willow reaches the mansion, she heads straight for Hanas' office. Adabelle was waiting for her arrival and sluggishly leads the way. She looks like she hasn't slept well, nor eaten much. Willow suspects that she may have been crying based on the emotion in her tone. It irks Willow at first, as she wonders if maybe something happened to Hanas in the hours since the letter was sent. However, when Adabelle knocks on Hanas' office door, announcing Willow's arrival, and Hanas lets her enter, he looks to be his usual self.

Adabelle quietly offers to take Willow's sack after being dismissed and leaves Willow to an equally tired-looking Hanas.

Willow watches him for a moment. He sits in silence, staring at untouched work on his desk as though he had tried to distract himself but failed completely.

"You okay?" she asks, eventually.

"I am unsure how to face what has happened," he admits. "I am equally unsure how this came to be."

Willow wets her lips. "I took the vial to be tested in Hidden Hill. They said that it was like some faulty drug. The side effect is that it depletes certain blood cells and she said it would be fatal in any human."

Hanas nods slowly as though it makes perfect sense. "I have no doubts on that… but why do you suppose that…" He trails off, unable to finish his sentence.

Willow knows what he wants to say. She can see the hurt, anger, and confusion simmering in his chestnut eyes and creasing his dark brow. He wants to trust Edwin and has tried for as long as he could. But he couldn't anymore; they both couldn't.

"Have you ordered a search for him yet?"

"With what army?" Hanas counters, shaking his head. "I dare not ask my servants. They need time to grieve and are not skilled in scouring the forest." He pounds a fist on the desk. "Curse Edwin! And curse the Rogue and his accomplice! Everything is slipping… breaking away."

Willow isn't sure how to comfort him. They're practically in the same position, a loved one torn away and few allies to lean on. "At least we're in this together." Willow's lips form the words before she can stop them. Her cheeks flush and she turns away, pretending to examine the bookcase to her left nonchalantly.

Hanas looks up in surprise. His features soften a little as he says, "Yes… yes indeed."

Willow clears her throat awkwardly. "So what's our next move? Track Edwin down and make him talk?" She punches her other palm.

"Actually…"

Hanas slips a folded piece of paper from his pocket and holds it out to Willow. She unfolds it to find crisp and careful cursive. The body of the letter makes her eyes go wide, and then wider still when she reads the name etched at the bottom.

"I was thinking it is high time we take our fight to the Rogue... especially since he is offering it to us."

Willow scans the note again, her hands trembling in rage.

> *To Hanas Blackwell and Willow Hunter,*
>
> *I greet you from afar but soon I shall greet you up close. Your feeble attempts at stopping my revolution have come to my attention, and although they are as little of a consequence to me as a buzzing gnat, I cannot have such thoughts against my revolution floating among the young minds I am influencing. As such, I am afraid I must put an end to this foolery, particularly because, Willow my dear, you refused to back down after the unfortunate loss of your father—a feat, I might add, that was accomplished to weed out unnecessary resistance aid from any given human town. Sir Hanas, my boy, you must know you are also at fault for forcing poor Gavin into your pointless investigations—although they do amuse me.*
>
> *As such, I cordially invite Willow Hunter and Sir Hanas Blackwell to come to the small leaning shack. There, our differences will be settled for good. Prepare yourself. Of course, I know you are smarter than to face me alone. But know that Desmond Hunter, yes Willow Hunter, your precious father, is within my grasp. Should you refuse to show, I will be sending back his corpse to you. Let's keep him alive just a touch longer, shall we? I will see you at the shack tomorrow evening.*
>
> *The Rogue*

Any fear Willow holds of facing a pureblood, specifically the Rogue, is masked by emotion. She wads up the paper in her fists, cursing his very existence. "That haughty, egotistical blood-sucker!" She pitches it into the wastepaper basket. "I think you're right. We need to take him down!"

Hanas nods his agreement. "He has given us the courtesy to prepare and I suggest we do just that."

"Yeah, especially since this reeks of shade. I bet it's a trap."

"I agree. The only question is of what sort?"

Willow chews her cheek. "You don't think the whole disappearance of the half-bloods is a *complete* ruse, do you? He could get your half-bloods to surround us at the shack. It would be two against... what? Like two hundred?"

"Just about," Hanas says, staring across the room in thought. "However, it sounds to me like the Rogue wants a one on one. If he wished to slaughter us with my half-bloods, he could have done so long ago. No, I believe this will be a two on one and he will be perfectly prepared for whatever we bring to the fight."

A small spark flashes in Willow's mind. "What we bring... huh?"

Hanas lifts a brow. "Do you have something in mind?"

Willow grins, swishing back the sides of her jacket to reveal her Glocks. "The Rogue thinks we'll fight with the little resources he believes we have. I bet he wouldn't expect us to carry loads of specialty vampire slaying weapons."

Hanas rubs his chin. "Carmela Ashe would never allow such weapons off Foxhound grounds much less in the hands of a vampire across the border."

"I talked to her yesterday, and let's just say she's... more... willing, now."

A little sadistic smile pulls at the corner of Hanas' mouth. "Oh really? What did you do?"

Willow props a leg up on his desk, folding her arms. "I wish I could say I screamed at her, then tackled her to the floor with a few well-deserved punches, but... we just sorta argued."

Hanas stands. "Well, if she is feeling more cooperative, then will she lend us some men as well?"

Willow shakes her head. "After the attack on Hidden Hill our numbers are low. She needs every able-bodied man to protect the border, especially with the threat of Devone Vitya on the rise."

Hanas' brow crinkles momentarily in frustration. He circles his desk and heads to the door. "Then come. There is something I should show you if we plan to use weapons."

* * *

Willow follows Hanas around the corner and into his bedroom. Her brow goes up as she surveys the large room. It contains dual floor-to-ceiling windows in the far left corner and overlooks the back half of his province in all its forested greenery. Despite the grand scenery, Willow is more focused on the contents of the room.

She expected to find stuffy old books and artistically placed vases and trinkets worth more than her salary would ever pay. Instead, she finds a tall bookshelf to her left with organized groups of rolled parchment, pads of paper, ink bottles, quills, nibs, rulers, and other artistic tools Willow can't name. Most impressive to her is the massive map hanging above a practical, wooden desk covered in more art supplies. The map, which is about the size of a dinner table, shows both a home and a property. The lower left corner reads in flourished letters, *The Blackwell Province.*

Willow paces forward, studying its features and noting that it doesn't resemble this mansion at all.

Hanas, who is busy at the world's most immaculate vanity, glances over to her, then up at the map. "Do you like it?"

"Impressive," Willow says, not taking her eyes from the art-work. "But it doesn't really match the layout of this place. At least, not that I can tell."

He smiles. "That would be because it is not this mansion. You forget this place is not my true home."

Willow's eyes drop down to the desk below. "Oh. Wait... are you drawing this?" She leans forward to examine a half-inked map of yet another place she does not recognize.

Hanas turns away, a little bashful. "I enjoy drawing maps."

"Um. Whoa." Willow gazes at the maps a moment longer before pacing over to him. "You're *really* good. Is that your job or something?"

A small *click* sounds when Hanas turns a tiny key into a hid-den keyhole of the vanity. "No," he chuckles. "My profession is being a Blackwell, if you recall. In our society, one only uses their talents to rise in name. There is no position above me that I could take using such talent." He slides a few locks aside.

"Too bad you guys don't use currency. You could make a lot with those." Willow peers past him as a lid pops up. Her eyes stretch wide at the variety of throwing knives, parrying swords, and derringer pistols nestled within the ivory cloth of the secret compartment.

"Um, wow, you're well-armed!" Willow says. "What other surprises do you have? A pet goat, maybe?"

Hanas lifts a parrying knife that has a jade handle and a dev-ilishly sharp edge. He pinches the blade between his fingers, handing the weapon to Willow. "Have you ever used a parrying knife?"

Willow grips the handle, eyeing the glinting, silver blade and feeling the smooth of the jade against her palm. She grins. "No, but I'd love to use this wicked baby."

"I will show you the basics. I suspect the Rogue believes you will only use your vampire hunting weapons and I my vampiric ones. This may be a good way to catch him off guard."

Willow pictures herself driving the blade through the Rogue's side, delivering back tenfold the suffering he has inflicted on her and others. Her eyes glitter in fiery anticipation. "Teach me what you know, and I'll teach you what I know."

He smiles. "Then we best get to it."

CHAPTER
TWENTY

WILLOW AND Hanas spend the night in the yard, training and teaching each other tricks. Convincing Rei-Com Ashe to lend one or two extra Glocks was thankfully simple. Willow didn't have time for more arguments and neither did Hanas.

The two work diligently and patiently with each other, Willow struggling more than Hanas on the latter. She shows him how to reload the gun, basic aiming techniques, plus gun safety. Thankfully, some of it he was familiar with, having used a derringer before.

Willow found the flourishes and jabs for the parrying knife tricky and awkward at first, having been trained with a K-Bar rather than a fancy knife, but she begins to get the hang of it as midnight comes and goes.

When the sky turns from deep black to dark blue, Willow decides to call it a night—even though her night is completely lost. Sleep will be key to fighting off the Rogue, and Willow intended to sleep the day away. Before she trudged indoors, a little sore from forcing new moves into her muscle memory, Hanas mentions his battle plan.

"We now have the element of surprise," he tells Willow, picking up his frock from the patio chair he had draped it over. "I believe if you can aid me in getting in close to the Rogue, enough for my hand to meet his skin, then we can end this quickly."

Willow narrows her eyes, leaning against the doorframe leading into the greenhouse parlor. "What do you mean?"

"My vampiric power," he says, striding over. "Surely you know all purebloods have a power, something to enable us to control aspects of nature or, in some cases, influence the human mind."

"Yes…" Willow says slowly, not wanting to admit that she had forgotten. "So what's yours?"

He doesn't look at her. "I would rather you found out by seeing for yourself."

She blocks the doorway. "And I would rather you tell me now. Secrets get people killed."

"You know I have a power and I will tell you that the Rogue knows about it as well. So he will try to avoid my touch at all costs. That is no secret." He tries to shoulder past her, but Willow shifts in his way, arms folded.

"Hanas. Tell me."

He presses his lips together, eyeing her before finally saying. "I can kill anyone by touch."

Willow's eyes widen and she represses an urge to step away, becoming very conscious of his hands… and how many times he had touched her skin over the past several hours.

"I am completely in control of the ability," he reassures. "Your life was never in danger. But now you know why I hesitated to give you details beforehand."

Willow chuckles nervously, putting the pieces together. "Well, um… that makes this easier I guess."

"Only if I can reach him, and I must touch skin. The more contact I have, the easier the power is to conduct and expel. But the Rogue is aware of my ability, I am sure. Any criminal would be," he says bitterly.

"That's where the whole mistrust deal I read about comes from, right? You make people disappear, permanently."

Hanas smiles in a mix of pride and sadness. "Yes, you are correct. The power runs through my family and makes it easy to dispose of unwanted individuals threatening the Sire."

Willow shrugs. "That's another tool to utilize. I'll do what I can to get you an opening without the Rogue noticing."

Hanas nods his thanks as they head indoors. "Rest well. Tonight, we will end the Rogue for his troubles."

* * *

When Willow drifts from her heavy sleep, she finds the sun has already set. Her room is dark since the moon is covered by clouds. As she groggily sits up and ruffles her disheveled hair, a soft knock sounds at the door.

"Come in," Willow grunts.

Her bedroom door opens and a pair of red eyes against shadowed features make her jump. She is reminded of the Rogue for a moment before Hanas flips on the low lighting of her room. "It is nearly midnight. We should head out."

Willow is confused for a moment, then the memories of the Rogue's letter pour in like wine: dark and red with anger. Now that the moment has come, unease pulls faintly at Willow's gut. She wants to fight the Rogue, to end his games, but his immense strength, and the ease with which he pinned and sucked the blood from her, is unsettling. Then there was that slithering presence… Willow shivers.

"Nervous?" Hanas asks as Willow pulls frizzy strands back into her ponytail.

"A little," she admits.

"You are not alone," Hanas says, letting his gaze drift around the room. "I have never intentionally killed before. Even more to the point, I have never been forced to fight an enemy—but I am ready to stop the Rogue."

Willow isn't concerned about the death part, but facing and fighting what she previously failed to overcome is. "Just remember I don't have your crazy strength. I hate pointing out my weaknesses, especially to vampires, but my lack of strength is what nearly got me killed the first time around... and his presence," she adds on a little more quietly.

"It is only instinct," Hanas says, chestnut eyes sliding back to her. "Ignore it, and the trouble will be solved. I do not believe the Rogue will amplify his presence during the fight to cause you bodily and mental stress. It requires entirely too much concentration."

"You say that like it's easy," Willow grumbles, standing up and strapping her Glocks around her hips then slipping the sheathed parrying knife down her boot. "Thanks anyway. I'll just have to deal with whatever comes. That's what I'm trained for."

Hanas nods, although he doesn't completely understand. Moments later, the two have headed out the back of the mansion and into the dark forest.

* * *

The shack sits just the same as when they arrived the day before, except now with a looming dread and intense anticipation of who waits inside.

Pausing just a few paces from the shack, Willow steels herself. She is sweaty with nerves but calm in her thoughts; antsy for the end-all fight to start and finish, but prepared to fight no matter how long it takes.

Hanas glances around and so does Willow, but there is no sign of half-bloods, no sign of an ambush. At least, not yet. The two exchange ready looks before Willow readies her Glock and Hanas his parrying knife.

Together, they enter the shack.

From the next large room, a smooth, hauntingly familiar tone slips into their ears. "Oh wonderful! You have arrived, and with impeccably pristine timing."

Willow shudders as that cold, snake-like presence slithers toward her. Entering the next room, they find the Rogue standing by the aged and cracked remains of a window. He waits as though expecting to usher guests into a grand dining hall: a faux smile, slick and cold, spreads across his lips.

"We have come." Hanas' tone is steady, but underlined with unbounded anger. "Shall we begin your execution?"

The Rogue gives him a pitiful smile. "Let us settle this, mistaken one."

There is a loud *CRACK* and all four walls break in on themselves. The roof crumbles and smashes down on them, beams, shingles, and all. Willow drops to her knees, covering her head from the onslaught of splinters and thick, moldy beams. She hears Hanas yell beside her as he attempts to catch most of the weight on his shoulders. He throws off the snapping beams before they can crush her.

When Willow uncovers her head, there is a mass of deadly sharp wood and plant infested shingles strewn around them. She sucks in a breath, realizing she had nearly been crushed. She shoots a glare at the Rogue who stands unfazed on the sidelines, having somehow escaped the cave-in. She snarls when she finds an unpleasant ginger standing beside him, looking smug.

"So you *weren't* alone," Willow hisses, standing as Hanas rubs his shoulder. "Two can play foul games."

She fires two shots that force the Rogue and Rose to split. Willow bolts after Rose, images red with rage flashing through her mind of Rei-Com Dube's condition, of her dad's kidnapping, of the desolate condition her home and Hidden Hill were left in.

Rose pauses a few feet away, whirling to face Willow with bared fangs and a jagged dagger in hand. "Let's finish this, princess."

Willow feigns to take aim at Rose's vitals then changes in the last second to fire at her leg. Rose cries out in surprise but grits her teeth and rushes in with a blur of wicked metal. Willow leans back as the silver slashes open air, then fires a shot at Rose's shoulder. Miss. Rose flips away, nailing Willow in the chin with her boot. She staggers back, glad that she was already clenching her teeth.

Grunts and annoying, gentlemanly taunts remind Willow of the Rogue and Hanas's skirmish. She glances over, suddenly recalling their plan to get an opening on the Rogue. Hanas appears to be holding his own, slashing at the Rogue and maneuvering around in search for an opening, but Willow doesn't like how easily the Rogue blocks his movements, anticipating each strike and fending it off with little effort.

Movement turns Willow's attention back on her own fight. Rose darts for her, knife poised to stab her straight through the heart. Willow catches the blade with her Glock, knocking it away. In the same movement, she slips the parrying knife from her boot and slashes at an angle. The blade cuts across Rose's chest but the wound is shallow.

Rose jumps away and snarls, "Where did you get that?"

"Where do you think?" Willow shoots back, holstering her Glock and charging. She changes hands with the parrying knife and swings in arcs the way Hanas had taught her.

"Not left-handed," Rose notes, dodges each swing but retreating all the same. "No wonder you didn't cut deep. Oh, wait, I forgot—it's because you're weak."

Willow's parrying knife clangs with Rose's. Her blade is locked in one of its grooves. *Oh no...* Willow pales.

"Gotcha," Rose purrs. She rips Willow's knife from her grip. It flies through the air, hitting the dirt with a *shink.* Willow is thrown off balance, but her training kicks in. She catches herself and yanks her Glock from its holster, but Rose is faster. She slams a boot into Willow's chest and sends her sprawling. The air is forced from her lungs as a root jabs into her back.

The world goes black a moment, then Rose is on top of her, a wicked point racing toward her heart. Willow's eyes widen. She slaps the blade away and rolls, shoving Rose off her. Trading positions, she rips out her secondary Glock and aims it directly between Rose's eyes.

PABAM! She's pulled the trigger, but the shot misses as Willow cries out in pain. She's shoved back into the dirt, blood dripping from her forearm where Rose had cut her. Her fingers tremble as she attempts to aim again, but her second Glock is torn from her weakened grip.

Rose straddles Willow, pinning her to the ground with a knee on each hand. Willow grits her teeth against the pain and, feeling the mud beneath her, slips her good arm free from Rose's trap. Icy metal sears her cheek and tears blur Willow's vision. Rose lifts her knife, readying it for a second strike. Her teeth are bared, her eyes hungry, bloodthirsty. Willow struggles to twist away, but Rose grips her hair to hold her in place.

Without thinking, Willow manages to turn her head to the side. She clamps her teeth onto Rose's wrist, causing the half-blood to howl with pain and drop her knife. Hissing, she lunges for Willow's neck with her sinister fangs.

"Rose."

She pauses a mere inch from Willow's neck then sits up.

"We are done here," the Rogue says smoothly.

Willow follows Rose's gaze and her gut seizes.

The Rogue grips Hanas' shoulder and rips his parrying knife from deep within Hanas' chest. Hanas' eyes are wide. Pained chokes are tumbling from his mouth. His shirt and vest are wet with blood.

He crumples to the ground.

There is a scream, and it takes Willow a moment to realize it's her own. In a blur of rage, she throws Rose off her, rolls toward her Glock, snatches it up, and ends in a crouch with the nozzle aimed at the Rogue, but before she can fire, the ground buckles and pitches them all to the side. Willow is positive the impact on her shoulder will leave a bruise.

She staggers to her knees, clenching her teeth. The Rogue pushes himself up, a mix of annoyance and fear twisting his expression. Rose jolts up, snarling as she stares into the forest. "You...!" she spits.

A new presence ensnares Willow. It is powerful, overwhelming, terrifying... familiar. A tall figure steps from the darkness. His brown curls frame a strong jaw marred by red patches of skin. His honey-toned eyes are sharp like a predator, like an eagle locking on to its prey. His lips pull back in a sneer, revealing pearly white fangs.

"That... is quite... enough." He glances to each of them in turn then clicks his tongue when he spots Hanas' unmoving form. His eyes turn toward the Rogue. "I am disgusted by your acts. You are starting a war and did not invite me?" He shakes his head sadly.

Willow doesn't miss how carefully the Rogue stands as though any sudden movement may incur lawless wrath. "Sir Vitya, you have surprised me yet again."

His smirk twists into a scandalous grin. "I enjoy keeping others on their toes."

Unease prods Willow in her gut as she glances between the two. She feels like ripe fruit awaiting the inevitable fangs of hungry bats to suck her dry.

"You wish to join my efforts, then?" the Rogue inquires, straightening his now dirt-smeared top.

Rose begins to object, but the Rogue casts her a sharp look and she clenches her teeth.

"I do want to join in," Vitya confirms. "But not in the way you think."

The ground buckles and shakes vehemently. Willow lurches forward as dirt and debris jerk from under her and form a human-sized wave of penetrating spikes. Willow watches in a mix of horror and shock as the mass slams into the Rogue. His growl is cut off as the dirt overwhelms him. Rose gives a fierce cry, snatching up her knife and sprinting toward Vitya. He rips the ground right from under her legs with a simple glance in her direction. She slams into the mud and screams when the dirt fires needle-like splinters into her arms and legs.

The Rogue emerges from what Willow had hoped was his grave. He is bleeding badly and his fangs are bared in a seething rage. He slips a small knife from his sleeve and throws it. Vitya catches it between his fingers, turning a bored expression on the Rogue before flipping the blade around skillfully and whisking it back. It lodges into the Rogue's stomach with a *thwump*.

The Rogue doubles over, dropping to his knees. His voice is strained when he calls, "Go, Rose!"

Willow completely missed Rose's movements. She already has Hanas' limp form slung over her shoulders. Her eyes light with passion and concern as she gives the Rogue one last look then darts into the forest.

Grabbing her Glock, Willow jumps up. "*No!*"

But Rose has already vanished into the night. Willow huffs, fury rising. The stings from her cuts only adding to her rage. She whirls, Glock aimed at the Rogue, and growls through gritted teeth. "Bring. Him. Back."

The Rogue glances over his shoulder at her, gripping his sides in pain. "He is lost... my sweet," he manages.

Willow's rage spills over her cheeks. Somewhere, in the back of her mind, she is angry at herself for crying.

BANG! A bullet drills into the Rogue's shoulder. He grits his teeth, groaning.

Vitya nods to Willow in approval before turning his delightfully amused expression back to the Rogue. "You cannot bring Blackwell back, but you *will* tell me what you're planning. If you do, I may feel..." he muses over his emotions for a moment. "... inclined to let you go."

"*What?*" Willow shouts.

He ignores her. "I very much want a real fight with you. I want to see all your preparedness amount to nothing as I syphon the life from you *very slowly.*"

"You can't seriously—"

"Shut up!" Vitya snaps, shooting Willow a withering glare. "I do not *really* need you around so you will stay silent while I work, unless you wish to bleed out... which, I might add, you are currently doing a wonderful job of." He eyes her cuts hungrily.

Willow is about to spit an insult when the Rogue rasps. "There will be a war, Sir Vitya, a revolution. If you desire to face me, then do so in Hidden Hill when the moon rises again."

Willow pales.

Vitya's expression fills with perverse mirth. "That is what I like to hear." He slips his hands into the pockets of his maroon trench coat. "Get out of my sight. I will deal with you then."

Willow keeps her aim on the Rogue. "He's not going anywhere, except into his own grave."

Dirt surges upward and hardens around her hands and Glock. "What are you *doing*?" she yanks at the dirt, but it holds fast.

Vitya jerks his head toward the forest. The Rogue staggers to his feet, glowering at Vitya, but he says nothing as he limps away, not even when Willow screams and hurls insults at him. Eventually, he is gone, and Willow feels the overwhelming desire to put a few wind holes through Vitya.

"Let me go!" she screams. "That bloodsucker killed Hanas! He's going to have all of Hidden Hill murdered, *I won't let that bloodsucker die slowly*!"

Vitya rolls his eyes. "Will you shut up? Blackwell is not dead. Stakes and silver, you *are* an annoying one." He grumbles.

Willow pauses her fit. "What do you mean he's not dead? He was *stabbed* in his vitals! I'm not a moron, I know my vampire anatomy!"

"He purposefully missed by mere inches," Vitya says simply. "I expect he intends to leave Blackwell's death in the hands of his half-bloods—an awaited execution to end the man who oppressed them."

Willow tugs at the dirt. "Then *why* are we just *standing* here?"

"The Rogue will not let them kill Blackwell until after the bloodbath at Hidden Hill. We have time."

Willow gawks. "I can't believe you right now. Do you think this is a game?"

Vitya lets the dirt fall from her hands. "Everything is a game when you live as long as vampires do." He turns away. "Come. You have preparations to make if you desire to rescue Blackwell."

Willow considers shooting him in the back of his head, but after witnessing his power, how easily he subdued the Rogue, she knows she doesn't stand a chance. She locates and snatches up her secondary Glock then hurries after him, hoping he knows all the awful ways she is killing him in her mind.

"You're Devone Vitya, aren't you? What are you even doing here?"

"I am. And you will refer to me only by last name if you want to live. Also, in answer to your second question, I am picking a fight where it is due," he says, striding along as though he hadn't just impaled two vampires and made plans for a war.

"You're not picking a fight with Hanas, are you?" Willow growls. "His half-bloods were on your province stirring up trouble, weren't they?"

He smiles in reminiscence. "That was quite the surprise. I have Blackwell to thank for that. I was feeling a little bored, truthfully."

Willow knits her brow. "You're not... mad?"

"No. Although I am irritated that half my followers have left me for the Rogue. No matter, I will teach them what happens to deserters."

Willow isn't sure she likes the sound of that, but she also isn't sure she cares. "So, you're on our side?"

"For now."

"Noted." Willow distances herself from him. "Where are we going?"

"You are going back to where you belong. You can prepare for the fight or do whatever you must with your fellow humans." He gives her a sidelong glance. "You might also consider not bleeding."

Willow glowers at the drying blood all over her arms and legs. "Well, *sorry.*"

The remainder of the way back, Willow mulls over the events of the night, mostly trying to convince herself that Vitya is right. Hanas *can't* be dead. She knows he can't. *But what if he is? What if she has lost another ally... one of her* only *allies?*

Exhausted, limbs throbbing in a chorus of sharp stings, and emotionally at her end, Willow feels the tears well up. She focuses on not crying, she can't lose it in front of a pureblood—especially one so powerful—once she reaches the border and Vitya vows to meet her again at the next moon before vanishing into the night, Willow breaks down. She cries for several minutes, alone, before pulling herself back together with a few fortified sniffs. She feels better, even if just a little, but also feels vulnerable.

Willow marches up to the north gate, twinging as the deeper cuts protest. Seeing her bloodied state, the guard at the gate doesn't question letting her in. As bravely as possible, she marches into the munitions depot to find Rei-Com Ashe. She sits where she had before, looking no less stressed.

"Region Commander Ashe," she says through a cracked voice. "We have a situation."

CHAPTER
TWENTY-ONE

"SAINTS ABOVE!" Rei-Com Ashe gasps, which has to be one of her more serious exclamations. "Medic!" she yells. "Medic!" She yanks an emergency kit from the wall and fumbles to pull out some bandages and rubbing alcohol. "What in the blessed fifty states happened to you?"

Willow goes over everything this time, giving her all the details. She chokes a little when explaining how Hanas had been stabbed. Willow briefly wonders when Hanas started becoming this important to her.

"Bless the U.S.A., another attack on Hidden Hill is *just* what we need," she says sarcastically, pulling out her phone. "This is Region Commander Ashe requesting a code Scarlet evacuation. I repeat, this is Region Commander Ashe requesting a code Scarlet evacuation."

Seconds later, the blood chilling sirens wail from Hidden Hill.

Rei-Com Ashe drops her phone back into her pocket. "And to think Vitya rubbed his nose in this mess too," she seethes as the medics tend to Willow on a stretcher.

"Sounds like Vitya is going to help, but I think he might also make things worse," Willow agrees.

"You're not wrong," Rei-Com Ashe huffs, leaning against the wall. "I've never dealt with that bloodsucker in person, but everyone knows the stories he's famous for." She clicks her tongue. "Stupid Blackwell, goin' and gettin' stabbed."

Willow watches the medic wrap a bandage around a particularly deep gash along her bicep. Hanas had been holding his own, but only because the Rogue was letting him. He is skilled. Willow would have to remember that when she faced him and fired every last round into his vitals.

"Is that Rose chick the same bloodsucker my men mentioned? The one who seemed to orchestrate the attack on Hidden Hill?" Rei-Com Ashe asks after a moment.

Willow glowers and nods. Yet another vampire she plans to end brutally.

Rei-Com Ashe clicks her tongue and wrinkles her nose in disgust. "That bloodsucker won't be dying easy. I'm gonna make sure of that," she growls darkly.

"Not if I get to her first," Willow mutters.

Rei-Com Ashe smirks. "Just save a piece of her for me, 'kay?"

Willow smiles as the medics finish their work and leave her with instructions to rest and lay still to prevent her cuts from opening. She is positive they all know she won't be following those instructions.

"We've got roughly twenty-four hours before this throwdown," Rei-Com Ashe says, folding her arms. "You ready to prepare to kick some vampire butt?"

Willow stands, though she does try to do so gently. "I was ready when they first set foot in Hidden Hill. I'm ready to end this and get my dad and Hanas back."

Rei-Com Ashe grins. "Atta girl."

* * *

The rest of the night is spent evacuating Hidden Hill. From where Willow sits, in what used to be her living room, she can hear car horns and the occasional shout as civilians rush for safety. She rests on her couch, staring around at the mess and watching V.H. run by through the gaping holes in her home. She lets the sight fuel her tired, yet already-blazing, flame.

There isn't much to do except sit and think until the civilians evacuate. Rei-Com Ashe ordered that she find somewhere to rest until they need her for prepping Hidden Hill for the fight. After her recent encounter with Rose and the Rogue, Willow has no objections to that. Eventually, her eyes become heavy and she sleeps the rest of the night.

The following morning, Rei-Com Ashe comes to find Willow. The two set out in eight-wheeled, armored trucks. Willow helps direct the Trainees on putting up barricades and double-checking that all residents have been cleared. They lock down the hospital and set up metal, wired gates around it to protect the remaining staff and those too ill to flee. Willow sends a silent prayer that Dr. Heartwood will stay safe.

By evening, Hidden Hill is prepped for battle. Windows and doors have been boarded up or covered in thick metal sheets. Steel walls are mounted to the ground and crude metal poles crossing in an X are positioned to slow down charges and protect against flying projectiles. Most of the cars and other heavy objects have been removed, but vampires always seem to find something heavy they can squash their opponent with.

Willow now stands near the edge of town with her fellow Vampire Hunters. As evening draws in, the V.H. rush to their positions and anxiously wait. Only the higher ranks commune as silence envelopes the town.

Heavy rain clouds ink out the remaining rays of sunlight and wash the forest in deep shadows. The lights of Hidden Hill turn up to their brightest, illuminating their surroundings perfectly. It is eerie, unnatural. If Willow's cuts still weren't stinging, she might feel a hair-raising chill go up her arms.

"Looks like it's gonna rain," Rei-Com Ashe grumbles.

Willow glances to the sky above the treetops. A low rumble sounds in the distance and the sky flashes. "Maybe we'll get lucky and some vampires will be struck by lightning."

One of the commanding ensigns chuckles. "That would be a miracle."

Rei-Com Ashe strides over, shifting the strap of her P90. "Listen up! This is an end-all fight. Make sure you lure those half-bloods into the kill zones. I want the least amount of human deaths possible, understood?"

"Yes, ma'am!" Willow and the four other commanding ensigns say.

"Good. They should show up at any minute. You five need to be prepared for *anything* they might throw at you, figuratively and literally. The men are still uneasy after our last surprise and we're few in number. Let's teach these vampires who's boss!"

"Yes, ma'am!"

"Dismissed!"

The commanding ensigns split off to their respective areas of command. Willow tries not to think about how they're filling her dad and Rei-Com Dube's jobs. *We'll get things back to normal,* she promises herself.

"Oh, lovely," Rei-Com Ashe spits from the barricade beside Willow. "Look who showed up."

She turns and anger burns through her veins like lava. Vitya stalks down the street with a half-blood in his firm grasp— Edwin.

Willow storms a few steps forward and Rei-Com Ashe follows. "You disgusting, evil, traitorous, cowardly, bloodsucker!" She slaps Edwin clean across his ashamed face. She doesn't care that he flinches or that her slap only adds to the black eye he no doubt received from Vitya. "You better give me a *really* good reason to not kill you right now!"

"I c-came to tell you… everything," he says before Willow can decide she wants to slap him again.

"Little late, isn't it?" Willow snarls. "Hanas might be dead, thanks to you. Hidden Hill is about to turn into a bloodbath, and *now* you want to give us answers?"

Rei-Com Ashe huffs. "Ya better have some pretty substantial information, but either way, you're not coming out of this unscathed."

"This is something you will want to hear," Vitya assures with an amused smile.

Edwin wrings his hands, but he looks Willow directly in the eyes as he says, "My life is over as s-s-soon as I… tell you. The accomplice w-w-will know I have… given everything away. He will k-k-kill me unless you offer me… protection."

"Deal," Rei-Com Ashe says immediately. "You're officially under our custody anyhow, so spill it—*now*."

"You are, uh, right that this… drug we discovered en-en-hances the half-bloods. It en-enhances their… desires and ambitions. The drug is… created through the… Rogue's, uh, er, p-power. He is an alchemist… and uses his own b-blood to activate his p-power over whoever… drinks the b-blood in his con-concoctions."

"We already know it enhances, and I don't care about how it works," Willow snaps. "That's not helpful!"

Edwin raises his voice in determination. "The drug w-w-was never used… on the half-bloods. The drug you s-s-saw me… give to Lord B-Blackwell w-w-was an… an-antidote I… was trying to make." He stares pointedly at Willow.

She narrows her eyes. "What are you—"

BrOOOOOOoooooOOOOO!

The sirens sound off. A man crouched on the roof of a nearby home drops his binoculars and shouts, "Movement sighted across the border!"

Rei-Com Ashe readies her gun. "We talk later. I've got vampires to kill." She then shouts, "Everyone get ready!", then hurries behind a barricade with Vitya and Edwin in tow.

Willow pulls out her Glock and flips the safety off as she crouches and peers around the steel wall. All eyes are on the border as shadows shift and shapes begin to appear. Hundreds of glowing red eyes peer out from the darkness, multiplying and multiplying and multiplying until the border is a sea of red dots.

Willow whispers to Vitya standing behind her, "How many half-bloods did you lose?"

"Enough to make this entertaining," he purrs.

Rei-Com Ashe shakes her head. "That is *a lot* of blood-suckers."

Willow swallows nervously, but her muscles are aching for a fight. She is ready to end this. The half-bloods shift as someone steps forward. A slender, tall pureblood strides to the front of the line, surveying Hidden Hill like one might survey with pity. He seems to have mostly healed after Vitya's attacks, but Willow notices that he's struggling to stand up perfectly straight.

"That's him," Willow growls to Rei-Com Ashe. "That's the Rogue."

"Thin little whelp, ain't he?" Rei-Com Ashe sneers.

The Rogue's eyes scan the barricades until he spots Willow. "Willow Hunter!" he shouts. "I see you are still in admirable shape for fighting!"

Willow yells back, "Looking better than you! Now get your sorry butt down here so I can give you new air holes!"

The Rogue shakes his head. "It is not I who shall be facing you, my dear."

The crowd shifts again and a new figure emerges. Willow's eyes widen and her mouth drops, her Glock nearly slipping from her hands.

Hanas stands firmly beside the Rogue. "I hereby claim this town and all its inhabitants as my own. If you would, my half-bloods, go and teach these lowly humans who is *truly* in charge," he orders.

CHAPTER
TWENTY-TWO

THE WORLD becomes distant to Willow. Half-bloods charge toward Hidden Hill, their battle cries muffled by her shock. Rei-Com Ashe shouts something to the vampire hunters and gun nozzles flash to life. In response, throwing knives whisk toward the heads of V.H. in silver streaks. But to Willow, there is only her and Hanas.

None of it makes sense. Was Hanas lying to her? Was his anger toward the Rogue and Edwin just an act?

Someone grips Willow's arm and forces her back into reality. The *pata-pata* and *bang! bang!* of gunfire assaults her ears. Several groups of V.H. have jumped up from their hiding places on the roofs and turned Hidden Hill's main road into a kill zone. There is blood and shouting and chaos, and Willow struggles to process it all.

"Come." Vitya tugs at her arm, practically dragging her from the battle raging ahead. She stumbles a little before wrenching her arm from his grip and following him, Edwin, and Rei-Com Ashe around a corner.

"You better explain things fast, bloodsucker," Rei-Com Ashe snaps, pointing a finger in Edwin's face.

Willow finally reconnects with the situation. "Why is Hanas up there? What's going on?"

"I tried to explain, ah, b-b-before," Edwin says, frantically looking to each of them in turn. "The drug w-w-wasn't, er, given to the half-bloods. The Rogue... gave it to Lord B-Blackwell! He is... the one under the drug!"

Willow cocks a brow. "You're saying the drug is making him attack us?"

Edwin shakes his head. "Lord B-Blackwell is attacking, uh, of his own... accord. The... drug en-enhances the s-s-strongest desire of the... drinker. Lord B-Blackwell... desires to be in con-control. Ever s-s-since his... parents vanished, Lord B-Blackwell has... been under the con-control of the Vampiric Council."

Rei-Com Ashe grips her P90. "So the brat's got an inferiority complex?"

"No, it's complicated," Willow says, waving off Rei-Com Ashe's comment. "So he's mad that the Vampiric Council has him on a leash, but that doesn't explain why he would side with the Rogue in attacking us. He doesn't want problems with the Vampire Hunters, his 'no crossing the border' rule is proof of that!"

"That is w-w-where I need your... help, Willow." Edwin's brow knights in seriousness. "I gave you... hints. I sh-sh-should have b-been more up... upfront. The Rogue is using Lord B-Blackwell's... desire for con-control to m-m-manipulate him. The Rogue en-enticed Lord B-Blackwell by telling him that he c-could help... regain con-control from the Vampiric Council. B-B-But when Lord B-Blackwell learned about the Rogue's... revolution, he refused to... accept the help. The Rogue... attacked Lord B-Blackwell and f-f-forced him to take the en-enhancing drug. I'm... not sure how, b-but Lord B-Blackwell's mem-mem-ories of b-being drugged are... s-s-suppressed along with any mem-mem-ories gained while under the drug."

"I'm sure that is within the Rogue's range of capabilities for this enhancing power of his," Vitya says simply.

Rei-Com Ashe hefts her P90. "He's under an influence. We have no choice but to end him—"

"No!" Edwin shouts.

Willow and Rei-Com Ashe jump.

"P-please, you... you just... you c-can't!"

"Is there a way to pull him from the Rogue's control?" Willow asks. "I don't *want* to kill him." When Rei-Com Ashe raises her brow at her, Willow quickly adds, "He's kept the border quiet and peaceful for seven years! Sure, it was boring. But people weren't losing their lives, and the town wasn't being destroyed and... we just have to find a way to stop him *without* taking his life."

Edwin smiles and his shoulders droop in relief. "I, uh, think there is a w-w-way." He gestures to Willow. If you c-can get... through to Lord B-Blackwell, he will listen."

Willow's eyes widen. "Me? What? Why?"

"I am... one of Lord B-Blackwell's f-f-followers. I... can't disobey his com-com-mands. And..." he tugs at the wrinkled edges of his shirt. "He already... knows that I gave away information I sh-should not have. He w-w-will... kill me when he s-s-sees me." Edwin puts a cool hand on Willow's shoulder. "Lord B-Blackwell trusts you. You are... the only one who c-can fight against him if he attacks... and the only one he m-m-may listen to... right now."

Willow tries to take that in.

"What are you two, lovers?" Rei-Com Ashe asks unhelpfully.

"Let's make it a race," Vitya decides with a wicked grin. "Killing the Rogue will also lift the power from Blackwell. Let's see if I can kill the Rogue before you convince Blackwell to cease his attack."

A deafening *BOOM is heard,* followed by loud crunching and creaking sounds from around the corner. Seconds later, the remains of a car skid by, littering the pavement with glass and metal shrapnel.

"They found a car," Rei-Com Ashe sighs. "Pre-Initiate Willow, this is an order. Do what this... guy, says!"

"Edwin," Edwin corrects.

"Right. Do what this bloodsucker said and give it your best, but if you can't convince him... you know what you need to do."

Willow swallows. She wants to object, but she can't find the words.

"You... can con-convince him," Edwin says with an attempt at an encouraging smile.

Willow returns the gesture.

Vitya leans, peering casually around the corner. "Looks like our bats have flown from the cave. Good. I love a good hunt."

Willow pushes past him, whipping around the corner. Sure enough, the border is empty. All the blood-thirsty half-bloods are now swarming the streets and rooftops.

"I will go in search of the Rogue," Vitya continues. "I am guessing that wherever the Rogue is, Hanas is not. He promised me his death, after all, not Blackwell's."

"Then... I guess I'll wait until you find the Rogue, and then search wherever the Rogue isn't," Willow says uncertainly, pulling back from the corner.

He smirks at her and strides away before anyone can object to the plan.

Rei-Com Ashe makes a face at his back. "I better go babysit him. He'll flatten Hidden Hill if I don't." She glances to Edwin. "Go to Foxhound. Tell them Region Commander Ashe orders your safety and yes, I am annoyingly serious." Her gaze lands on Willow. "Stay safe, Pre-Initiate. Go deal with that pureblood and prove to me you can handle the initiate rank."

With that, she peeks around the corner then charges after Vitya. Edwin gives Willow a few last words of encouragement before hesitantly heading for Foxhound. Willow takes a deep breath, readies herself, then charges into the fray.

* * *

"Look out!" a commanding ensign calls.

Willow jumps, whirling around to find the underside of a car racing toward her. She ducks and rolls as it crunches the pavement where she once stood. A half-blood hisses, then charges seconds later. She whips up her Glock and fires into his vitals.

The half-blood's shoulder jolts back and he hits the pavement, exploding into a pile of ash. Willow gawks for a moment. Only really old half-bloods incinerate upon death, and most half-bloods never live that long.

A hand clamps on Willow's arm, spinning her around. "Pre-Initiate!" the commanding ensign shouts over an onslaught of gun fire and a cacophony of screams. "Focus!"

Willow glowers to herself. He is right. This is no time to be standing around gawking. She has to do whatever it takes to stop the Rogue and protect Hidden Hill. That begins with finding Hanas.

She ducks behind the barricade before peering out at the carnage ahead. She wants to look away from the bodies sprawled out unnaturally in pools of blood. She wants to shut out the blood-curdling screams of a V.H. whose arm is twisted as his life torn from his neck. She wants to block out the horrible memories of civilians being dragged into dark allies, or laying lifeless over smashed sills, and of children crying for their parents.

But she can't. She has no choice but to face it.

Willow cringes as a Vampire Hunter is thrown from a roof, his life ending with a *crack* on the pavement. She scans for Hanas among the half-bloods. He isn't there. She presses her back to the steel walls of a barricade, staring down the street where groups of Vampire Hunters assault half-bloods who have already passed the kill zone via alley or roof. One V.H. finds a knife lodged in his chest, but the rest of the group tears the half-blood apart with ammo.

Willow can feel her heartbeat thump faster as the group is rushed by four half-bloods. Two lift an already broken car and Willow darts toward them, firing at their legs and arms. The car crushes the half-bloods and Willow gasps, her eyes widening as pools of blood spill from underneath the tires.

The group quickly signals their thanks before rushing out of sight to deal with the next threat. Willow tears her eyes away, remembering to breathe. *They're the enemy,* she reminds herself, but somehow that isn't a comfort.

"Breach! Breach!"

Willow snaps around to see steel barricades being ripped from the ground as half-bloods overwhelm them.

"Fall back!" the commanding ensign yells.

The other Vampire Hunters retreat, landing whatever shots they can manage as they fall back.

Willow darts around the corner of a building. She glances first down the street behind the other Hunters, then to her left. The way is clear, except for a few stragglers. It won't stay that way for long, though. She darts to her left and takes a route skirting the main fight. She crosses the main street, not sparing a second glance as the commanding ensign chucks a flash grenade at the half-blood horde. The flash causes the half-bloods to howl in pain and rage.

Focus, Willow, focus! Find Hanas. Where would you be if you were him? Her eyes shoot in all directions, pausing only on men with black hair or dark colored jackets.

"Requesting back up!" a familiar voice shouts to her right. "Requesting back up!"

Willow skids to a halt, eyes widening as fifty half-bloods race down the streets, tearing into four broken up V.H. squads. She clenches her teeth and fires at the onslaught. Two drop, but they aren't dead.

"Retreat!" Darius shouts at the other groups. "*Retreat!*"

Willow falls into step with Darius and the fleeing vampire hunters. "What are you doing? Where's your commanding ensign?"

Darius fires two shots behind him. "We were split up by the hoard chasing us. I lost Josh too."

They duck behind a barricade and slow the half-bloods down with another onslaught of ammo. Willow gets in a few shots before pressing her back to the steel wall. "Have you seen Hanas?"

"Who?"

Willow jumps up, nailing a half-blood in the shoulder. He drops to the pavement. "Hanas Blackwell, the pureblood who was beside the Rogue."

Darius shakes his head, aiming his AR15 around the steel wall and taking out three half-bloods. "No, I haven't seen him or the Rogue."

Willow clicks her tongue. *Where is he?* She glances further down the street and pales. "Ambush from the rear!"

Darius casts a glance over his shoulder. "Oh no…"

"Split!" Willow shouts.

No one needs to be told twice. The four groups jump to their feet and dash for alleys on their respective sides. The half-bloods split off between the two again, fifty and thirty.

Willow thunders down the alley, the half-bloods vaulting off the walls overhead and dropping down on the Vampire Hunters. She keeps her eyes on the flashing shadows against the dark sky, each one dropping down in turn.

A half-blood lunges for Willow, red eyes blazing and fangs glistening, but she maneuvers away and punches it square in the jaw. She turns ahead again and vaults over a downed V.H.

She glances over her shoulder and her gut seizes.

"Run!" Darius screams, then he howls as the half-blood sinks its fangs into his neck.

Willow skids and darts back to him. "No!" she screams, struggling to shoulder past the other fleeing Hunters. She makes little progress, and is finally knocked back into someone. With a yelp, she lands on them and covers her face as half-bloods race over her, kicking and slamming their heels into her bandaged arms.

Willow tries to push herself up, but the person under her whispers harshly in her ear, "Don't move! Play dead!" Willow almost doesn't hear him because her focus is on the whooping and hollering above. *They think this is fun? I'll rip their voice boxes from their throats!* She moves to get up but a hand clamps on her arm.

"Willow! Still!"

She swallows at the familiar tone, holding herself still more from surprise than willful obedience. They wait until all the vampires have left, then give it another five minutes before moving.

"Safe!" the V.H. sighs in relief.

Willow rolls off him and props herself up. "Eric?"

He smiles weakly, hefting his MP7 up. Then his eyes lock on Darius laying a few feet away. "Darius!" He crawls closer, rolling him onto his back.

Willow bites her lip, checking his pulse. "He's weak," she says hoarsely.

"Darius!" Eric lightly slaps his cheek. "Darius, come on!" He tries a little harder, but Darius' response is little more than a soft groan.

"You have to get him to the medics," Willow says breathlessly. "Or the hospital."

Eric nods. "We both can."

"No."

Eric's eyes shoot up to hers.

"I have to go." She can't look at Darius's motionless form. "I have to find Hanas and stop all this."

Eric's brow furrows. "We both can, but after we get Darius to safety. Working together will be quicker."

"Finding Hanas is my mission, Eric." Willow says firmly. She gazes down the alley where a firefight has broken out. Vampire Hunters and half-bloods alike rush past covered in varying amounts of blood and festering wounds. "All this over greedy control," she whispers.

Eric gingerly sits Darius up, draping Darius's arm across his shoulders. "I'm guessing this Hanas dude is the accomplice you were looking for?"

Willow's lips quirk. "Yeah." How ironic that she was standing beside him, *working* with him the entire time.

No. She doesn't have time to think about that.

A heavy gust buffets Willow's hair, then a sheen of rain soaks her. A loud clash sounds—it could have either been thunder or a bomb.

"Do you even know where you're going?" Eric asks, trying for her companionship one last time.

FWOOM!

They both jump and face west. Something lurches above the roof tops in the distance, a monstrous mix of building and asphalt. "I do now."

Eric's brow shoots up. "What... was that?"

"Vitya," Willow grumbles. "If he's fighting the Rogue in the west, then that means..." she turns east.

The stadium style lights in the east flicker, then black out altogether. "Working in shadow, huh? Great."

Eric stares into the darkness as though it contains all his nightmares, and Willow doesn't doubt it does. Still, he says, "Stay safe, okay? Don't make me come and rescue you."

"No promises," she says. Without another word, she sets off down the alley to join the firefight, then it's into the blackness where a certain pureblood hides.

CHAPTER
TWENTY-THREE

IT TAKES Willow two hours to cross Hidden Hill. At nearly every turn, she has to help prevent a V.H. unit from being overrun. She had no idea until now how miserably outnumbered they were compared to the half-bloods.

Every street is littered with blood, the wounded, and the dead. Many buildings are beyond repair, their walls smashed through and their insides strewn across the streets as cruel weapons.

By the time Willow reaches the blacked-out section of Hidden Hill, most of the conflict is behind her, but that doesn't calm her pounding heart or her tingling nerves at all. The screams, howls, gunfire, and explosions are distant echoes now. Here, there is only the hush of rain spotting her uniform and streaking her boots and Glock.

She steps lightly and slowly, her eyes adjusting to the darkness of the shadows cast by the smashed homes. Her senses cry out that something is wrong. *So, so* wrong. Nothing stirs; no shadows of half-bloods or V.H. blood washes into the webbed cracks of windows or down the siding ripped from walls.

Willow fights to steady her ragged breath as she slinks from the alley into the open street. Entire chunks of walls have been torn from the front of homes, and splintered doors are awash with red and draped in uniforms. Her heart misses a beat. *No bodies.*

"No..." she whispers.

Willow's boot catches on something and she slowly looks down. Thunder rumbles and lightning cracks across the sky. The ground is littered with Vampire Hunter uniforms.

Someone cries out, sending chills down Willow's spine. Their ripe fear echoes from the next street. Willow bolts across the street and jumps over a collapsed wall. She stops dead at the other end.

These uniforms have bodies... pale and wet with eyes staring into Willow's soul yet not seeing anything at all. Then, at the center of it all, is a pureblood she once thought she could trust. But now his lips touch skin and his fangs sink deep into the flesh of a limp ensign... Josh Johnson.

Willow's hands tremble. A mixture of anger, hurt, and fear swell inside of her. As the pureblood's fangs slip from the teen's neck, he slowly looks up to Willow. His deep red eyes are covered in a milky film, evidence of the drug. But this isn't the drug alone. This is Hanas' desire. The drug only gives wings to it.

Willow raises her Glock. "Hanas... let Josh go."

He slowly lets Josh's form droop to the pavement and fixes her with an unnervingly calm gaze. "Another one? I admit to hoping the Vampire Hunters were running out of reinforcements."

Willow glares, wanting to send a bullet drilling through his very core, yet needing him to live. "I'm the last reinforcement you'll meet." Her voice betrays the hurt in her chest. "Unless you listen to me now and call off this attack."

Hanas stands, slow and careful, his eyes on the nozzle of her Glock. "And why should I heed the advice of a stranger?"

"You really don't remember me?" Willow barks out a harsh laugh. "We've been working together for the past week. We *fought the Rogue* together!"

Hanas narrows his eyes. "The Rogue is my ally..."

Willow swallows a round of nasty insults. "Oh really? What makes you think that bloodsucker is on your side?"

Hanas glowers. "Do *not* refer to the Rogue with such a de-rogatory term! But, if you must know, we struck a deal. I will give him Hidden Hill and all of you humans in exchange for control."

"Control of what?"

"*Everything,*" he snarls.

Willow's blood boils over. "You *greedy* little bloodsucker!" She runs toward Hanas, firing into his thigh. He collapses into a roll before she can reach him and slices his parrying knife across her ankle. Willow fires at his arm but it only grazes him, causing him to bleed red into his frock. He flashes his parrying knife but Willow catches it with her Glock, slapping it away and throwing Hanas off balance.

"So that's it?" she huffs. "You just want more control like every other filthy pureblood out there? I should have known you were no better than anyone else! In fact, I did know—yet I *still* worked with you!"

She swings her bad leg into a kick but Hanas catches it and throws her to the ground. He is on top of her in seconds, pinning down her arms. "I do not recall ever working with you. Do *not* pretend to know me! Furthermore, my ambitions are none of your business! I have reasons that you cannot possibly compre-hend!"

Willow squirms under his weight. "Like getting revenge on the Vampiric Council?"

He bares his fangs. "I do not intend to harm the Council. How *dare* you even suggest it!"

Willow pulls up her feet and slams them into Hanas' gut, changing their places. "Then maybe you've always wanted to lord over humanity and rule us like the pathetic pigs we are, huh?" she screams.

Hanas easily throws her off, slamming her into the pavement but this time pinning her arms and legs. "You know *nothing*, filthy human!" he snaps. "Nothing of societal pressures, of titles being pinned to you at birth, of being left to succumb to the disrespect of others merely because of some name!"

Realization sparks in Willow's brain. "It's not control you want... you want respect!"

Hanas blinks. "What?"

Willow feels a slight shift in his weight and her instincts take over. She lurches forward, slamming her head against Hanas before managing to twist from his grip. He tumbles backward but quickly regains his balance, jolting away from her swing.

"It's not control you want," Willow repeats, anger driving her every move. She puts away her Glock and slips the parrying knife from her boot. She rushes at him. "You want *respect,* you idiot!"

Hanas sidesteps and dodges each swing, then strikes back with his own knife. The metal blades clang together and slash with a *shing! Shick!* "Quiet! I want control! Control of everything!" But now he sounds uncertain.

Willow slices into his chest. "No you don't!" He cuts at her arm as she continues, "You want respect from your society because they call you untrustworthy!" Her knife rips open his vest. "You want respect from your half-bloods because they only see you as a power they can't overcome!"

"*No!*" Hanas shouts, the milky film in his eyes fading, then strengthening, then fading again. He twirls his blade around hers and tears it from her grip.

Willow jumps back, glowering as she snatches her Glock and aims. "Most of all, you want *respect* from the Vampiric Council!" she screams.

"*Just shut up!*" He throws his parrying knife.

Something slams into her stomach. Willow freezes. She looks down.

Metal protrudes from her abdomen.

Hanas stares, unable to move.

Willow gasps and collapses. Pain spikes in her brain, her hands shake, her eyes blink away the drops splattering down on her. She can't think of anything but the pain and her need of help—help that won't come. She writhes as though it might ease the pain but it doesn't.

She can see Hanas standing there, watching her. The milky film covering his eyes ebbs away and confusion fills his face. He blinks. "What was I...? Where is...?" He looks down at himself. His clothing is torn and bloodied and soaking wet. Her groans must catch his ears because his eyes trail up the pavement to where Willow lays. She loses sight of him as she rolls back and forth.

"Willow..." He stumbles to her side, his red eyes trailing over her cut and bloodied form then stopping on his own parrying knife protruding from her abdomen. He almost pulls it from her, but stops. Instead, he puts a hand to her cheek. "I am sorry, just..." His next words grow faint in Willow's ears. "Just wait, I will get—"

Something causes him to jump and Willow is vaguely aware of blurry flames rising into the sky in the distance.

Just before her vision fades, she reads the words on his lips. "What have I done?"

CHAPTER
TWENTY-FOUR

Beep… Beep… Beep…

The rhythmic noise slowly brings Willow into consciousness. Her heavy eyelids heave open to slits. She blinks several times before allowing her gaze to become hooded. Groggily, she surveys the room—ivory walls, a variety of medical machines, a grey door.

She lulls her head to the left and finds nothing of particular interest… until her eyes find a girl slumped in a chair. The book on her lap is entitled *Medical Experience for the Inexperienced*. A tired smile spreads across Willow's face as she croaks, "Martha!"

Martha stirs, her face scrunching as she sits up, stretching her arms above her head. She hunches over with a yawn, looking to the book on her lap and then to Willow's bed. Her eyes fly wide. "You're awake!" She jumps to her feet. "I'll go tell my mom!" She runs out the door before Willow can say another word.

Willow shifts and a snap of pain pinches her side. She grits her teeth and lifts the white blanket from across her chest. Her side has been carefully wrapped in fresh bandages. *Where did I get—*

The memories surge back into her mind. The attack. The Rogue's enhancing power. Hanas. A parrying knife with a deep blue hilt protruding from her abdomen.

The rest is a blur filled with indescribable amounts of pain and Hanas' surprised expression. Was Hanas still drugged? Was Hidden Hill safe? What about Vitya's fight with the Rogue?

Willow is forced from her thoughts as the door opens and Dr. Heartwood strolls in, smiling. "And how are you, Willow?"

"Forget that," Willow blurts out. "What's going on outside? Is the Rogue dead? What about Hanas? What are the casualties?"

Dr. Heartwood holds up her palm in a calming gesture as she walks closer. "Calm down, Willow. The fight is over. And from what I've been told, it's all thanks to you."

Willow presses her brows together. "What? I don't understand…"

Dr. Heartwood begins to check the machines. "I'm sure everyone will explain the details to you later. But, for now, relax and get well. Those wounds need time to heal."

"So… we won?"

Dr. Heartwood quirks a smile. She opens her mouth to say something, but a soft knock sounds and a nurse pokes her head in. "Dr. Heartwood, there is a visitor, um, strongly requesting to see Ms. Willow."

Dr. Heartwood glances to Willow. "Do you feel up to company? It's okay if you don't. They will understand that your recovery takes priority."

Willow shifts a little, but stings from wounds atop her old cuts cause her to stop. "I'll see anyone who can tell me what happened."

Dr. Heartwood nods reluctantly. "Alright, but no moving. If you need anything, pull that red cord to signal a nurse."

She nods to the nurse in the doorway who hurries off. There is an audible thumping of combat boots followed by a nurse insisting that the visitor walk and not run. Dr. Heartwood flashes Willow a warm smile before slipping out. "I'll leave you two alone."

The door swings open wide and Willow nearly leaps out of her bed. "Dad!"

Mr. Hunter beams, eyes beading with tears. "There's my heroic little Wills!" He rushes forward, squeezing between the machines and hugging Willow gently. He kisses her forehead. "You were so brave!" he chokes out.

Willow doesn't know what to say. All she can do it cry into Mr. Hunter's shirt. They stay that way for several minutes before letting go. Willow brushes away her tears, ignoring the stings along her arms.

"Tell me what happened," she says. "Where have you been? It sounded like the Rogue left you on the brink of death somewhere!"

Mr. Hunter rubs the back of his head. "I would say 'this may come as a surprise' but it sounds like you already knew Hanas was drugged and under the Rogue's power. So, in a way, I was still in the Rogue's clutches—just not directly, because..." He folds his arms and chuckles lightly. "Well, would you believe me if I said I was in Hanas' basement the entire time?"

Willow moans, slouching in her bed. "Please tell me you're joking."

He laughs and shakes his head. "'Fraid I'm not. And... I know this will make you mad, but I owe my life to one of the servants there. If it weren't for her, I'd be long dead from starvation, among other injuries." He eyes Willow. "Know a black-blood by the name of Adabelle?"

A smile breaks across Willow's face. "Yes! Wow. Maybe I should learn to bake so I can send her some cookies."

His brow shoots up. "Did I hear that right? Is my Wills actually saying nice things about a vampire—? Er, I mean, I'm proud of you!"

Willow rolls her eyes. "Yeah, stuff happened. That's all."

Mr. Hunter folds his arms. "I hope you'll fill me in later."

"Later," Willow agrees, then her smile wanes, and she studies her IV. "So... um, how is Hanas?"

Mr. Hunter shakes his head. "What can I say? He did what he could."

Willow chokes down a sob, tears threatening her eyes. But then her father bursts into laughter. "I'm just messing with you. He's fine. Little beat up, but he'll heal."

Tears run down her cheeks, although now they're from joy. She swats her dad in annoyance. "Don't joke like that!"

Mr. Hunter chuckles a little more before saying, "Sorry, you're right, you're right. I didn't think you'd actually get that worked up."

Willow looks away, her cheeks flushing as she blinks away her stupid tears. "I guess we started growing on each other. He's not too bad, except now everything is his fault."

Mr. Hunter sighs and runs a hand through his hair. "I would have never guessed him to be the accomplice. Well, I did start feeling that something wasn't right. He was acting a little strange… but his half-bloods got me before I could figure it out."

"I thought I could trust him," Willow whispers.

Mr. Hunter watches her a moment. "I think you still can. But it's up to you. Hanas didn't understand how to achieve what he *really* needed, and it sounds like you helped him realize what that achievement was and how to get it. I'll let the two of you talk that over, though, but only after you're feeling better."

Willow nods, unsure she can decipher her complex emotions at the moment anyway.

"So, I'm going to assume you found out that secret about Hanas' past, too?"

Willow nods. "I found out by accident, but I do know now. I guess the stress from the Council, mixed with all that societal junk, really hit him hard."

Mr. Hunter pulls up a chair. "Yes. Hanas has been through more than anyone should, and at a young age… well, for vampires." He folds his hands. "Hanas told me that you made him understand he wants respect and not control. You showed the true skills of a Vampire Hunter by pinpointing that. But there is something else he needs, too—something I think you both discovered you needed—particularly after Rei-Come Ashe's… less than wise decision."

Willow gives him a look. "If you say something corny like love, I will smack you again."

Mr. Hunter chuckles. "No, Wills. You both need an ally on common ground. Hanas has lost much and so have you, with your mom gone."

"I have Martha," Willow objects.

"But can Martha offer aid across the border? Can she fight by your side?"

Willow frowns. "So you're saying Martha is a bad friend?"

Mr. Hunter shakes his head. "I'm saying that you need allies across the border. You can't expect to keep friends among humans alone. Someday, you'll need Hanas' friendship desperately. It's part of the occupation."

Willow isn't sure she understands, but she decides to go along with it anyway. "Alright, fine. Maybe we do need to be allies… but he had better give me a pretty good apology. Maybe a steak dinner… I'd settle for some cash too—although I guess he doesn't really have money."

Mr. Hunter shakes his head. "That's my Wills." He stands up and pats her hand. "I was actually supposed to go check up on Rei-Com Dube, but I heard you were awake so I came here first."

"How is he, really?" Willow hates to admit that she almost forgot about him after losing her dad and being banished.

"Better, but he'll take a while longer to recover."

Willow nods, processing that. "And… our casualties?"

Mr. Hunter heaves a sigh. "Many. But we will recover."

CHAPTER
TWENTY-FIVE

A WEEK later, Dr. Heartwood pronounces Willow able to leave the hospital. She is prohibited from doing basically everything in her usual routine. No training, no working out, no doing anything strenuous that may reopen the cuts all over her body. She isn't even supposed to clean her Glocks, although Mr. Hunter lets that one slide. She doesn't really mind the relaxing part, even if it means she can't go out to the Rodeo Steak House to celebrate her promotion to Initiate. She needs the rest. But no matter how many card games she plays with Martha and Eric, no matter how many movies they laugh over, she just can't stop thinking about the Rogue.

According to Rei-Com Ashe, he vanished from the fight as soon as he started losing. Vitya chased him down but was irritated beyond reason at losing the slippery snake. It was anyone's guess where he might have gone.

As summer turns to autumn, Martha and Eric bring Willow the exciting news of their school semester being delayed. Apparently, the campus had been badly damaged during the fight, and like the rest of Hidden Hill, it needed repair. They were all off until further notice. That meant more time for Martha and Eric to spend with Willow, and none of them complained about that.

As the days pass, Willow finds herself continually looking to the border. Most of her rage toward Hanas has subsided, but she was still expecting an apology… or at least *something* at this point. But the border, now completely brown, yellow, and red with foliage, is quiet. Willow keeps telling herself that Hanas never came because he was busy dealing with his half-bloods or whatever else might have befallen him since the battle of Hidden Hill, but the thoughts do little to reassure her.

"What are you looking at?" Eric breaks her from her thoughts, following her gaze to the forested border. Eric and Martha had taken Willow on a walk to cure her cabin fever, and she couldn't help but pause near the north gate. "Do you see something?" He reaches for the Kimber Micro 9 he's become accustomed to carrying in case of danger.

Willow averts her gaze awkwardly. "No, nothing. Just thinking."

Eric relaxes. "Oh. What about?"

"Are you worried about Hanas?" Martha asks knowingly.

"No!" she says too quickly. "Just… I don't know."

Eric cracks a grin. "You're in *looove!*"

Willow kicks his shin. "Shut up! I am not! I haven't seen him since he went rogue on me. No pun intended."

Martha smiles softly. "I'm sure he'll come by when he gets the chance. I bet he's busy, especially since the Rogue is still on the loose." She shivers at that.

"Willow!" Mr. Hunter calls. He strides from around the corner along the fence line. "Come here for a minute!"

Willow cocks a brow. "Wonder what's up…"

"I guess we'll find out," Martha shrugs.

The three of them head for Mr. Hunter, pausing a few steps from the north gate. "Having fun? Not too cold, are you? You can always go to Martha's house to warm up."

Their home, like many others, is still being rebuilt. As a result, they are lodged at a mostly intact motel nearby.

"I'm fine," Willow says, wondering how she was ever annoyed at his constant checkups. "Come on, what's up now? Or did you seriously call me over just to ask if I was cold?"

Mr. Hunter grins. "A certain someone is here to see you." He jerks his head toward the border. Willow scans the sea of brown trunks and red and gold leaves, but sees no one. Then a form shifts from beside a tree and her eyes grow wide.

The north gate creaks open and Willow crosses through with little hesitation.

Hanas paces to the border's edge but doesn't move closer—respecting his own rule of not crossing the border yet again.

Willow pauses, suddenly not entirely sure of herself, but she steps away from her father and her friends to stand firm before him. "Took you long enough. Been busy?" She tries for an indifferent tone.

Hanas nods with uncertainty. "Rounding up my half-bloods, settling politics with Sir Vitya, and addressing the Vampiric Council has occupied all of my time."

Willow nods curtly. "I'm sure it does."

Hanas clears his throat. "I am certain you are furious over my being the accomplice. I cannot apologize enough. I assure you, though, I had no clue I was he the entire time we worked together."

Willow's tough act drops. "Yeah... I know it was the Rogue's power that held back the memories... and amplified what was already there," she says.

Hanas looks away. "That is entirely my fault. I *did* want control. There is no denying it. But I thank you for showing me reason."

Willow shrugs. "So long as you don't plan to rule the world again or whatever, I think we're fine."

Hanas blinks then a smile tugs at his lips. "I would greatly enjoy your continued companionship."

"Allies," Willow corrects. "Companionship is just... weird."

Hanas nods, but he clearly doesn't fully understand. "Yes, allies."

Willow paces along the border and Hanas follows at her side. "So is Edwin okay? I heard we protected him here until the fight was over, then sent him back across the border."

Hanas tugs the end of his sleeve. "He is well. It has taken some time to get close to him. For a while, he refused to speak with me out of fear. But in recent days, he has spoken and settled down."

Willow exhales. "That's a relief. Poor guy."

Hanas nods then drops his gaze. "I cannot apologize enough for what has happened. I'm sure your father has already told you that I had him locked in my basement."

"Better your basement than dead."

"That hardly makes my actions justifiable."

Willow folds her arms, half joking, half serious. "Then you had better gain my trust back. And, I warn you, it won't be easy."

"I will do what it takes," Hanas reassures her.

Willow smiles and rolls her eyes. "Lighten up." She shoves him. "We've got a Rogue to catch still, and feeling sorry for yourself isn't going to help us catch him."

Hanas considers this.

Willow heaves another sigh. "Listen, something's been on my mind since I left the hospital. I should apologize too, for being so biased against vampires and all. Maybe if I had learned to work together with you quicker, we would have figured this mess out sooner; if not me, then my dad definitely would have."

"We can only improve on ourselves at this point," Hanas says, then continues. "After some time, my memories from during the drug returned. The Rogue told me something I thought you ought to know, as well. He warned that he is coming after me and hinted that he may target others. I have no doubt that you may now be included in his future plans of suffering. Unfortunately, he never told me who would be his next target or why."

Willow kicks at the fallen leaves. "In other words... he's not done with us, and this is just the beginning."

Hanas nods gravely. "However, I do believe we have time before he strikes again. After all, he must heal his injuries and Sir Vitya more than hinted that he has many."

Willow twirls the strings on the end of her scarf. "Does my dad know?"

"Yes. I informed him as soon as the memories returned."

Willow stops and faces him. "Then we'll all be prepared."

"Indeed." He casts his gaze back the way they'd come. Mr. Hunter leans against the gate, watching. "I believe that is all the time we have, but before I leave, I wish to say another thing."

Willow tilts her head. "Oh?"

"You are always welcome across the border. I would like to regain any trust with you that I can."

Willow smiles. "Yeah, and then I can make sure you're keeping me up to date on anything involving the Rogue. Drug or no."

He smiles in amusement. "Of course. I must return to my own work, now."

"Hang in there," Willow says. "See you around."

Hanas inclines his head politely, then turns and disappears into the forest. Willow returns to Mr. Hunter, Martha, and Eric.

"Were you polite?" Mr. Hunter wants to know.

"Really?" Willow chuckles. "Yes. We're good now, I think."

"Whoa!" Eric exclaims. "You were so chill with that pureblood! I'm impressed."

Willow blinks, surprised with herself. A week before she would have been shivering from his *presence* and hating his very being. "Yeah, I guess I got used to it."

Martha smiles brightly. "Does that mean we have another friend to add to our group?"

Willow glances back to the border. "Yeah. I guess it does."

EPILOGUE

A YOUNG pureblooded man walks down the grand hallway of his chateau. His frown, though soft on his pale skin, is deep as he mutters under his breath in French, "What could those servants be doing? Such a ruckus."

He stops at a double-door where unfamiliar voices come from among small crashes and thumps. He grabs the handle, yanking the door open and speaking in lightly accented English, "What is going—"

He freezes. The floor is covered in blood and the bodies of several half-blood servants. Even worse, a vampire the pureblood knows all too well grins at him, holding Crystal by the hair. He presses a knife to her throat and a trickle of blood races down her slender neck.

"If you use your power, I shall kill her instantly."

"You," he hisses, but stays perfectly still. "How did you find this place?"

The Rogue looks momentarily offended. "You think I am unscrupulous enough to not discover your whereabouts? I am hurt."

The pureblood balls his fists. "Enough of these games. Let her go and leave us be!"

"Oh, I will," the Rogue assures, smiling in sincerity. "But not until you do a little something for me." He nods to a red-haired half-blood the pureblood has never seen. She saunters forward and hands him a piece of paper.

He takes it, eyeing the half-blood as she backs away. It shouldn't surprise him that she doesn't even bother to bow.

He scans the paper. A girl with auburn waves is staring back at him. He flicks his eyes back to the Rogue. "A photograph?"

The Rogue nods. "What say you? Will you help me with a small task involving the one you see before you?"

The pureblood looks to Crystal. She shakes her head ever so slightly.

"Hurry, hurry," the Rogue says. "I do not have all night. My hand may grow tired and slip across her throat..." He slides the knife across Crystal's skin, creating a red streak.

The pureblood's insides lurch. He hides his shaking hands by holding them behind his back. He wills his voice to be steady as his words spill out. "What would you have me do?"

ACKNOWLEDGMENTS

THIS BOOK would never have been completed without the encouragement and help of many people.

First, I want to thank the Lord for blessing me with wonderful stories, a passion in writing, and the caring friends and family He has surrounded me with.

Second, I want to say thank you to my mom and dad for supporting my dream of being an author. I wouldn't be here without all your help.

Third, I must thank my wonderful writing group, Realm Makers, for sharing their wisdom. Without the knowledge you all have graciously given, I would be hopelessly lost, and without all the fun, laughs, and friendship, I would be terribly lonely. You guys are the best!

And how could I possibly not mention my lovely and strengthening friends in The Neko Inklings? You all have been the bestest friends anyone could ask for! Your encouragement through thick and thin has been a blessing to me. Sending you guys all the hugs!

I also want to thank my fantastic editors. Without your time, dedication, and skill, my story wouldn't be where it is today. I appreciate all that you do!

Finally, this book wouldn't be nearly as good without all my wonderful beta readers! Thank you all for your time and constructive comments. You have helped me take this story to the next level.

ABOUT THE AUTHOR

MORIAH JANE strives to fill bookshelves with clean, high quality, and immersive stories. She writes fantasy, urban being her favorite, and loves writing for young adult and middle grade readers. She also enjoys drawing characters and wearing Victorian-eques clothing. Connect with her across social media!

CPSIA information can be obtained
at www.ICGtesting.com
Printed in the USA
LVHW042309310520
656995LV00002B/90

9 781087 817026